30.99

A Summer in Oakville

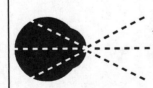

This Large Print Book carries the
Seal of Approval of N.A.V.H.

A SUMMER IN OAKVILLE

LISA J. LICKEL
AND SHELLIE NEUMEIER

THORNDIKE PRESS
A part of Gale, Cengage Learning

GALE
CENGAGE Learning·

Detroit • New York • San Francisco • New Haven, Conn • Waterville, Maine • London

GALE
CENGAGE Learning®

LIBRARY OF CONGRESS CATALOGING-IN-PUBLICATION DATA

Lickel, Lisa J., 1961.
  A summer in Oakville / by Lisa J. Lickel and Shellie Neumeier.
    pages ; cm. — (Thorndike Press large print clean reads)
  ISBN-13: 978-1-4104-5911-4 (hardcover)
  ISBN-10: 1-4104-5911-X (hardcover)
  1. Domestic fiction. 2. Large type books. I. Neumeier, Shellie. II. Title.
PS3612.I248S86 2013
813'.6—dc23   2013010844

Published in 2013 by arrangement with Black Lyon Publishing, LLC.

Printed in the United States of America
1 2 3 4 5 6 7 17 16 15 14 13

*For Susan, who loves family and home
as much as I.*
— Lisa J. Lickel

*To my husband who showers me
with love.*
— Shellie Neumeier

TESSA'S STORY

Psalm 84:3 "Even the sparrow finds a home and the swallow a nest for herself, where she may lay her young at your altars, O Lord of hosts, my King and my God."

CHAPTER ONE

Contessa Marie Hasmer Murphy closed her eyes and inhaled the scents of her summer kingdom. First hay cutting — sweet and fragrant alfalfa from Janssen's across the road — cress, and mint that she had just walked on. A cardinal's peculiar trilling keen and artesian water bubbling from the spring a yard in front of her rock throne seemed magnified in the leafy glen. Tessa wiggled against her backrest, the channeled bark of the century oak a solid comfort behind her.

Whiny mosquito! Tessa scrunched her brows and batted the insect from her ear. She sighed and sat up. Where's a good slave with a palm fan when you need one?

Who was she trying to kid? At age forty-eight all she'd been her whole life was a slave to her family, to Oakville. And unappreciated went her efforts to keep the family together. First, Robin. Married and moved so far away. Having grandbabies

Tessa couldn't hop in the Land Rover to visit. Skype was just not the same. Phil. Good riddance. He hadn't thanked her for anything in the past decade anyway. Lindsay . . . her baby girl coming home after earning her master's degree. But not home to mom. Home to grandma.

Tessa leaned over and plucked a small white lady slipper. Everything seemed to bloom earlier each spring. Even though she knew the flower, a member of the orchid family, had no fragrance, she brought it to her nose, always hoping something might have changed.

Something shimmied the leaves. A muffled step? Tessa stayed still, hoping to see a doe and maybe a fawn. When a large human hand thrust aside the leaves of her willow curtain, she stiffened. Her husband Phil had been gone three months and likely wasn't coming back. Her father was too weak to walk this far from the house.

"This is private property," she said.

"Excuse me, ma'am," a man's voice called. He entered her domain despite her warning. Tessa glanced around for a weapon, a stick, something. Crime was rare in rural Oakville, Wisconsin, but that didn't mean it was non-existent.

Hoping he was a hiker wandering off the

10

nearby popular Ice Age hiking trail that meandered through this glacier-gouged part of the state, she asked, "Can I help you? Are you lost?"

The stranger, a young man perhaps her daughter's age, straightened. "No, ma'am. I believe this is the Hasmer farm."

Tessa raised a regal brow. "The house is a quarter-mile east. Do you have an appointment?" As if her father was in shape to see anyone, anyway. "Are you looking for someone?" *My daughter, maybe?* Lindsay hadn't mentioned a beau. Such a handsome fella too, with lovely wavy hair and showing buff under his off-white polo. They'd certainly make a cute couple. Already tan, must work outdoors. Huh — or played a lot of golf. Like her husband.

"I'm just out for a walk. Sorry to disturb you."

He didn't look in the least like he was sorry as he scanned her special hideout. Hideout? A grown woman needed a place to hide? Tessa went on the defensive and rose from the comfy rock where she spent so many hours reading and dreaming and watching nature. "I'm Tessa Hasmer Murphy, and this is my father's farm." She stood in front of him and folded her arms. "Private property."

The young man's knowing little smile seemed to indicate introductions hadn't been necessary. She changed her mind from her first impression. Hopefully he wasn't here to see Lindsay. She tilted her head to look up at him. Did he . . . his deeply grooved mouth sent her back a couple decades, to college, and . . . but no. Why bring up old dead memories now?

"Sorry again. I didn't mean to disturb you." He turned and left the way he'd come before she could make her lips ask for his name.

Tessa slowly turned to survey her secret place. The ambiance had been ruined. No birds called. Janssen had started spreading manure on his field.

Still clutching the lady slipper, Tessa climbed out, ready to go back to her empty house in town. She walked across a field that hadn't been worked in ten years and was as tangled as her lonesome life.

CHAPTER TWO

Tessa punched the remote button that opened her garage door and parked her Land Rover in the middle of the space meant for three vehicles. The house she and Phil built was in a mature cul de sac across Oakville from her parents' farm. The land butted against the city limits and she knew there'd been rumors of annexation. No way would her parents give in to that kind of pressure.

She walked into her spotless echoing kitchen, studied the clock and decided to call her oldest daughter, Robin. California time meant she'd be phoning about the end of the baby's nap. Oh, well. Robin answered on the third ring. Tessa offered a quick "thank you Lord."

"Just checking in," Tessa said. "Is the baby over her cold yet?"

Tessa and Phil's daughter and corporate attorney son-in-law lived on the eastern edge of Los Angeles. Tessa had enjoyed visiting of course, but the weird palm trees and arid climate made her long for the wonderful undulating fields and woods.

Anna cooed in the background during their chat. "Maybe you and the girls could come and visit for a while," Tessa said.

"I'll talk to Jeff. Oops, gotta go. Dad's here."

"Okay! Okay, so you'll —" *Think about it,* Tessa said to the dial tone. Robin hadn't meant that Jeff, the girls' dad, was there. Phil the ratfink had jumped ship, abandoning his wife for a transfer to the new California office of Taylor Implements. Taylor's home office was in Oakville, where Phil had steadily climbed ranks to become regional sales manager. But no, that wasn't good enough for Phil.

Twenty-eight years they'd been married. Twenty-eight years of loving, fighting, raising their girls, maintaining the perfect family image, setting up housekeeping in their dream home, hosting Phil's company dinners and guests. Now he was turning her into the bad guy by showing up at Robin and Jeff's, probably telling them she didn't love them or she would have come.

Had Robin sounded a bit distracted lately? Their talks shorter? The doorbell played the

14

usually inspiring opening notes of *Ode to Joy.*

Tessa checked out the side window of the front door and debated. Curiosity and little bit of huffiness won out and she opened it to the young man she'd seen earlier on the farm.

"Okay, who are you and how did you find out where I live?" she asked. "Let me guess. You were in the neighborhood."

"Mrs. Murphy? I'm sorry to disturb you and your husband at home like this. My name is Brandon Calloway."

Calloway. Strange.

"I have to warn you that Oakville frowns on solicitations."

He laughed, showing straight, movie-star teeth. Whatever he was selling, he knew how to make it look good. Tessa buckled on her resolve.

"I'm not selling anything. Actually, I'm trying to buy."

What a scam artist. "I'm not interested," Tessa said.

"Wait!"

Why was she not closing the door?

"Please! I won't take much of your time," Brandon said. "Just, hear me out. Please."

"About what?"

Brandon reached in his pocket then

handed her a business card.

"C&D Developments?" Tessa's voice rose to a hysterical note of disbelief and anger she didn't bother to control. "You're kidding. What do you want with me? You want the rest of my yard for a strip mall? I doubt the city council would allow that even if it looked good next to Walgreen's. You're outta luck, buddy. Goodbye."

"Please."

Only a crazy nutso would go on listening to the guy with the familiar name. She should treat this visit like a sales phone call and hang up already. It had to have been his eyes. Or that cleft in his chin — so much like Josh's, her college boyfriend who said he'd wanted to marry her.

Wait a minute! Tessa looked for more clues while the man spoke his piece. She didn't even listen until the name "Joshua" fell from his mouth.

"Excuse me. Back up." Tessa hoped her knees would hold her. She grabbed the door knob and wrung her hands around it. "Joshua Calloway? You're related to a Josh Calloway? It's probably just a coincidence, but I used to know someone by that name."

Brandon's smile wasn't hesitant or fake this time. "My father. You're Tessa Hasmer, right? He knew you from his university days

16

at Marquette. He speaks of you often."

Tessa blinked at hot tears. "Are you sure he's the same man?" What a silly question. This boy wouldn't know about her former life and the heartaches.

Brandon laughed again. "He's the same, all right. There might be plenty of Calloways, but I bet the name 'Contessa Hasmer' is pretty unique."

Josh had teased her about it, calling her his royal girl. But this man . . . he was not Josh. But what would this man want from her? Tessa looked at the crumpled card in her hand. Two guesses what it was — and one didn't count.

No way was she inviting him in. She was alone after all, and not about to reveal that fact.

So why, five minutes later, was she scolding herself in the kitchen for offering that smooth-talker some iced tea? Tessa returned to the living room and set their tall glasses on coasters on the cherry wood glass-topped coffee table. Brandon stood near the mantel, looking at the framed photographs.

"I assume this is your family?" he asked.

"Yes. We — my — I have two daughters. Grown up. The oldest is married."

Brandon nodded, smiling the whole time. Probably one of those 'keep the conversation moving and stay positive things' they teach in business school.

"They look happy. You have grandchildren?"

Of course all grandmothers want to talk about their grandkids. Tessa was no exception. "Two. Both girls. The older one is three. The youngest is just eight months old. I'm hoping they'll come to visit soon."

Brandon sat and picked up his glass. "So they don't live around here."

Tessa knew she was being foolish. This had to be the classic setup, right? Lonely old lady invites the handsome stranger in. He plies her with compliments and a made-up story about being the son of an old friend. Her hand trembled and she set her glass down. She smoothed her hand against her slacks.

"I won't keep you much longer, Mrs. Murphy. To put it bluntly, my company . . . my father's company that I now run, plans to build in the area."

"Build what?"

"Oakville is growing. It needs a place to expand community services. Library, bigger police department. Even a senior living complex."

Tessa nodded cautiously. The nearest

nursing home was fifteen miles away and tiny.

"Wouldn't you like your parents to remain close to you?"

Tessa frowned. "They are."

"When they can no longer care for themselves?" Brandon pressed. "Look, I've seen your father. Don't you want what's best for him? The Hasmer farm —"

"My parents are not your business." Tessa stood and clenched her fists on either side. "My father isn't even seventy years-old. My mother is in great shape. I think this conversation is over."

Brandon Calloway followed her to the door. "With the well and septic going bad, it will be hard to sell for a home. Think about it."

"You — how do you know this?"

He looked at her with the gentle pity of his father on that last day they'd been together, when he told her he had a job in Houston all lined up.

"I take my work seriously," Brandon told her. "I've been staying in East Bend while I study the options for development."

Options. Josh had offered her options once. Tessa could finish her last two years of college down in Texas if she wanted after they were married. Or take care of him and their children.

She narrowed her eyes. "Let me guess. There's only one option that works."

"Look, I'm only trying to help your parents, do what's in the best interest of the community."

"And that involves forcing my parents from our land? Making us give up our heritage? Generations of my family ancestors are buried on that land. My brother, Otto, gave his life for that place. You may not care about things like being the fifth generation to own the same land, down there in Texas where your father lives."

"Texas?" Brandon shook his head. "No, we always lived in Chicago. It's where my mother grew up."

Tessa felt light-headed before a wave of anger crashed over her. "Your father never went to Texas?"

Now Brandon looked confused. "Well, just for a few months, he said. He met my mother and they got married and moved to Illinois."

Figured. Tessa nodded. "Tell him I said hello. And it's probably not nice to talk about me in front of your mother."

"My mother passed away six years ago. My senior year of high school."

Could this day get weirder? "I'm sorry."

Tessa pushed the door shut in an effort to end the conversation.

Brandon had the last words. "You can tell him hello yourself, though. He's coming this weekend."

Tessa leaned against the door with her eyes closed. Twenty-eight years since the last time she'd seen Josh Calloway. Twenty-eight years of keeping the biggest secret of her life. Why did she feel like a melted ice cube?

CHAPTER THREE

"Mom!" Tessa called the next morning as she pushed open the back door at the farm. "I'm here!"

LouAnn Hasmer, dust cloth in hand, peeked into the kitchen. Tessa stepped out of her shoes, leaving them on the mat at the back door. "Hi, what's up?"

"Nothing. Say, did a young man stop in yesterday? Talk to you or Dad?"

Tessa's mother, seventy-two and weathered, but with a figure Tessa envied and a snow white spiky 'do, chuckled. "What, we should hold him for your daughter?"

"So there was someone?"

Mom shook her head and turned away. "No one I haven't met before, darling."

Tessa followed, stepping over the cord to the vacuum cleaner. "Someone was walking on the farm."

"We don't post no trespassing signs, Tessa. Did he bother you? Threaten you? Should we call the sheriff?" Mom rubbed her cloth over the stair banisters in apparent nonchalance.

"No."

LouAnn stopped and winked. "You sound put out."

"Mom! I am not." Was she? "Here, let me help you with the vacuuming."

"You have your own house to take care of. Let me worry about mine. I have enough to do to get Lindsay's room ready."

A web of regret formed around Tessa's heart. She knew it was the right thing for her daughter to do, but it still hurt that Lindsay had chosen to move in with the folks instead of home with her.

"I don't want to be, like, the loser daughter who has to live with her mother," Lindsay had declared a few weeks earlier at her graduation ceremony. Three job interviews later and a roommate who got married and moved out left Tessa's daughter little choice. The part-time customer service job at Hinckley Springs hadn't covered the rent now that she had no one to share the apartment, and roommates were scarce over the summer months. "This is just temporary while I look for a real job," Lindsay had said. "Grandma thinks it's a great idea."

Tessa sighed, thinking about her empty

four-bedroom colonial. Phil had refused to give their youngest daughter money for expenses, and Lindsay, just as stubborn, declared she wouldn't take it anyway.

"Okay," Tessa said. "I guess I have enough dust to conquer in my own palace." She gave her mom a brief kiss and went to tell her dad goodbye.

On the way down the long driveway, Tessa met Lorrie the mail carrier just about to load her parents' mailbox. "Hey, Lorrie! How's it going?" Lorrie attended Community Church, the country congregation where they'd grown up as former neighbors.

"Not too bad. How's your dad these days?"

"About the same. He hates therapy, but he needs it to strengthen his left side after the last stroke."

"Stubborn old farmer." Lorrie laughed and waved on her way to the next mailbox.

Out of habit Tessa glanced through the stack of mail that she took back up to the house to drop off before going home. A letter marked *Third Notice* from the Town of Bakersfield stuck out. Torn between thinking she needed to stay out of her parents' business and concern for them, Tessa took the letters inside and risked asking her mother.

"Hi, I met Lorrie at the box and thought I'd save you a trip," Tessa called over the sound of the vacuum cleaner.

"Thanks! Put them there," LouAnn yelled back, pointing to the small desk in the corner of the living room.

Tessa set them down, glanced at her dad who seemed to be asleep, even though he had his eyes half open, and decided to wait until her mother finished the hall rug. When Mom started rewinding the cord, Tessa held up the letter. "What's this about? Third notice for what?"

Tessa's mother snatched the long envelope out of her hand. "Just junk."

"From the town treasurer? Is there something going on I should know about?"

Mom's lips zipped tight as a winter coat in January. "Thought I taught you better than to snoop in other people's private business."

"You and Dad aren't other people Mom. Is this about taxes? Didn't you pay them? I can —"

"No one can fix Hiriam Bakersfield," Tessa's mom said. She made shooing motions. "Go on now, git. I have work to do and so do you."

Tessa folded her arms. "If you need help,

I need to know. I'm not letting my daughter walk in here if you're in trouble."

With a quick peek at dad, Mom held her fingers to her lips and drew Tessa into the kitchen. "Oh, it's nothing. The well didn't pass the last test."

"That's why the bottled water," Tessa said.

"The septic system's a little outdated, too," Mom said.

"What? I didn't know that. You have to get those things fixed right away."

LouAnn stood up straight and proud and defiant. "I told you, we're trying. That stubborn old coot won't work with us over the taxes and a new mound system's going to cost a pretty penny."

"And the well. But why won't he help? It doesn't make any sense."

A choking cough and the creak of her dad's walker hushed them. "Not when . . . blasted idiot . . . town . . . wants . . . wants —"

"Otto, sit." LouAnn urged her husband and guided him to the kitchen table.

"Town wants what, Dad?"

Tessa's mother huffed. "Don't get him all worked up now."

Otto coughed. "Development."

"You're kidding," Tessa said. She rubbed her arms at the sudden shiver. "That young

26

man I talked to . . . he has something to do with this, doesn't he?"

"This is our farm, our land. No one can tell us what to do," Mom announced. "We don't even have to farm if we don't want. Back taxes, denying our septic permit. Huh!" She set her hands on Dad's shoulders. "And we're not moving. No matter what."

CHAPTER FOUR

"Lindsay, do you have any idea what you're getting yourself into?" Tessa could hardly wait to get home so she could telephone her daughter. When Lindsay's voice invited her to leave a message, Tessa urged her daughter to check in as soon as possible.

When Phil called that night, Tessa wanted to tell him about her parents and the farm troubles. When he first left around Easter time, he called three and four or times a day, telling her what he was doing, how the weather was, and what kind of houses or condos he was looking at. Gradually the calls dwindled to a nightly check-in. Lately they talked maybe once a week, and then only about the girls.

Phil's voice sounded different. Morose, Tessa decided, after their cautious greeting. She pictured him decked out in his golf uniform of knit polo shirt and plaid pants. He'd insisted on plaids like a terrier that wouldn't let go of a rat. Retro-chic seventies. Scary. Was he still trying to comb hair over his growing bald spot? Maybe he'd finally understood she was not coming. Maybe he wanted a divorce. Maybe he found someone new and Hollywood glamorous. He still had charm, Tessa admitted. He was plenty attractive at age fifty-two and a half. Tessa had caught plenty of ladies looking at his nice cheekbones and dimples. He'd be a good catch.

Did she care? She put him on speaker while she cleaned up her plate and the coffee pot.

"I should set up a local bank account," Phil said. "What do you think about that?"

"Sounds like you're making a new life for yourself." Tessa vigorously dried the plate.

"I hoped you'd help me pick out a house. Did you get the faxes? You didn't reply."

How many ways did he need to hear "no?" She stared at her dream kitchen with the shiny chrome appliances and black granite counter tops. "I live in the house we built together, Phillip. I don't want another one."

"We don't have to sell that one. We can rent it out."

Shivers made Tessa gag. "No. I'm not letting strangers in my house. For the last time, I'm not moving. My folks need me."

"We can hire help. Or bring them out and set them up in assisted living. You should see —"

"They would die if you made them leave Oakville and sent them to a home." She stabbed the button that ended the call. She stumbled to a kitchen chair and sank. They would, too. So would she.

Phillip Murphy, you make me so mad. I wanted to talk to you tonight about my folks. Not listen to you talk about putting them in a home. I should put your parents in a home. See how your family would like it.

One call she'd made earlier confirmed that her parents hadn't paid their taxes last year. The town was set to foreclose on the farm unless they paid up by the end of July. Her folks had ignored the last three years' worth of notices.

Tessa got out the checkbook. She'd have to transfer a little money to cover the full amount, but that wouldn't be any problem. She'd work out the new septic and well later. She booted up the computer and typed the password to their online banking account. And started to tremble when she stared at the balance. Where was all the money? Only two thousand dollars remained in their joint savings account.

Mom and Dad owed six. There'd been

30

fifteen thousand and some the last time she'd looked — oh, sometime last month. She'd been thinking of giving some to the girls and putting the rest in a long-term CD.

Tessa glared at the phone, anger and fear bubbling in unhappy competition in her stomach. Phil. And his new bank account. Was he trying to starve her out? She'd just see about that. She'd pay a visit to Jeannie Laird, their lawyer, in the morning.

Phil had no right to keep messing up her life long-distance.

Tessa parked in Oakville's municipal lot a little after nine AM the next morning and walked two blocks to Jeannie's office. She had a client until ten, Jeannie's assistant said. Could Tessa come back then?

Tessa had spent an hour working up a righteous steam and needed to vent. Could she keep it going another hour? Tessa nodded and walked out. The park. Big mistake. As soon as she saw the sign, Bakersfield Park, she almost blew. The green square with the gazebo, picnic tables and children's castle in the middle of Oakville had been donated by the Bakersfield family, of which her parents' town chairman, Hiriam, was one.

Turning around, she headed to the diner.

31

She'd definitely earned one of those caramel rolls, a big one with lots of butter cream frosting and a cup of hazelnut coffee. A tall one. With lots of creamer. Or maybe black if she was splurging on the roll.

She smacked against an immovable object. Oof. What? Who planted a statue — ?

"Excuse me, ma'am."

Tessa frowned. "I'm sorry." She looked up. And up. At five-foot-two-and-three-quarters, Tessa was used to looking up. When she got to the man's face, her antici-pated caramel roll turned to acid in her throat.

"Well, this is the happiest coincidence! I was planning to drop by your house after I had a cup of fortification."

Did I brush my teeth? Is my hair straight? Lipstick? "Josh Calloway!" Tessa squeaked.

Dark brown eyes, nearly black, with lashes no man should have, sucked her right back to their college days. He smiled with those eyes, took her hand and bowed over it. "Contessa Hasmer," he murmured, then pressed his warm lips to her knuckles.

"Murphy," she corrected absently. "I got married."

"I know," he said. He straightened and looked around as if he'd forgotten where he was. Perhaps he'd been planning to meet

32

someone. "Are you able to have a cup of coffee with me, for old times' sake?"

"I have an appointment at ten."

He led the way to the diner. "Forty-five minutes with you is a good start. We can have a leisurely lunch later."

What was the harm? She'd been headed for the diner anyway.

Tessa blinked when Josh looked at his Rolex and offered to escort her to her appointment.

"Oh! Thank you, but it's just a few doors down. Laird's."

"The law office?"

"Mm-hmm." Tessa didn't look at him while she set her crumpled napkin on her plate — the caramel roll had been worth the calories — and picked up her purse. How did he recognize the name of her lawyer? But more importantly, should she pay?

He reached over the table and placed his hands on hers. "My treat, of course."

She bit her lip. What was the protocol here? "Only if you let me pay next time." She smiled in his direction, feeling a flush that made her want to dab at her forehead. Then she thought of the mere three hundred dollars remaining in her checking account.

Ouch. Ratfink Phil. "Thank you, then," she told Josh. "I'd better get going. It was nice seeing you again."

"Where shall we have lunch? I know this great place on the north side —"

"I have to think about it. Excuse me. I don't want to be late." Tessa slid out in a rush and trotted the half block. What in the world had she been thinking? She was a married woman. She slowed down before pushing open Jeannie's front door. She was a married woman who had just enjoyed breakfast with another man and felt so befuddled she could hardly recall what they'd talked about. She'd made the worst mistake of her life the last time they'd been together, and she'd run right into Phil's arms. Now, here she was, picking up with him like nothing had happened.

Tessa shoved the door. "Jeannie! Help!"

Ten minutes later, Jeannie sat back in her chair behind her desk and folded her arms. "Hoo-boy. I never would have guessed Phil would treat you this way. Okay, girl, let's see what we can do to protect you. You'll be filing for legal separation?"

Tessa paused. The breath she took in hurt her lungs. She held it, letting the pain help her focus. "Sep-separation?"

Jeannie stared at her. "Aw, Tessa. You love

34

the guy."

Tessa stopped twisting her wedding rings and stared back. "Well, he's my husband." But, did she? Could she all of a sudden decide to hate him after almost three decades of living with him?

She tried to summon revulsion and couldn't. She'd picked up Phil's socks and cooked his dinner far too long. Even when he'd left, she'd assumed he would come back eventually, just like every other business trip. She shook her head. It wasn't that easy to about-face on her life.

Jeannie, half a head taller than Tessa, had celebrated her fortieth birthday last February. No one would guess her age, for her long straight black hair was the original color. Jeannie was an outdoor girl, enjoying the ski hill every chance she could, getting snowshoe parties together, even horse-back riding on the trails in the summer. Tessa wasn't quite as gung-ho as her single friend, but stumbled along. They had met through Tessa's biannual community fundraiser that picked up the gap left by United Way. Jeannie tossed her pen on the desk. "Do you think there might be someone else?"

Tessa widened her eyes and her breath caught. So soon? How could anyone have seen her and . . . oh, she meant Phil. Did

Phil have a girlfriend? Tessa took a cleansing gulp of air. "I don't know. When he called last night, something was different. He said something about setting up a bank account, like I told you." The anger came back. "Then he took all our money."

"You gonna be okay, financial-wise, while we work this out?"

"Yeah. It's just — my folks are in tax trouble and I want to help them."

Jeannie scrunched her eyebrows. "Really? That surprises me." But she wouldn't say any more. "Well, let's figure out what to do for you. What do you want to do?"

A half-hour later, Tessa left the office, hoping she'd done the right thing. Good ol' Phil was in for a surprise that night. And so was Tessa's mother.

Tessa's next act was to visit Hiriam Bakersfield and force him to tell her just what in the world he had against her parents, long-time upstanding Christian citizens, fourth-generation farmers who never hurt a fly. Well, not the ones who weren't bothering them first. Hiriam had no business taking advantage of her father like this, especially after the last stroke left him unable to work. Her folks had already sold off a hundred acres, and just had the last eighty and the house left. What more did he want? Blood?

Tessa drove to his home, where Gloria, his wife, refused to let her in. "He's not here."

"I have to talk to him about the farm. Gloria, surely you don't think what he's doing is right?"

"Town business is not my business. You have to talk to the clerk, get them on the agenda for the next board meeting."

"That's when?"

"Second Thursday of every month. Same as always. That's all I can say, Tessa. I'm sorry." She shut the door.

"But that's two weeks!" Clerk . . . who was the clerk? Tessa thought about knocking, but decided to visit the town hall. No one was there, but Tessa read the minutes posted on the public notice board. Yeah that's right. Dana London was the clerk; the girl who'd lived with her grandparents at their farm . . . the Weavers. A couple miles down the road. Dana had been in her brothers' class in high school, if she remembered right. Art had taken her to the prom. Tessa frowned. The same year Otto, Art's twin, was killed in the rollover tractor accident. Sad. Same year Josh Calloway about ruined her life. *Yech.*

She could call Dana later, after she convinced Mom and Dad to fight the board. And since her folks needed her, and her empty house was slurping her remaining resources, she knew what she had to do, failing septic or no. She'd transfer her Culligan bottled water account to the farm and do their laundry back in town.

Two hours later, Tessa drove her packed Land Rover into the circle drive in front of her childhood home.

"Mom! I'm home."

CHAPTER FIVE

"At least let me call," Tessa pleaded one more time. She sat at the kitchen table with her parents after supper. They'd worked out a plan of how to share the kitchen and the family room. Dad had smiled as Tessa and her mom talked about how much fun it would be to bake together. "Dana can advise you, get your case on the agenda for the next board meeting. There has to be something we can do. I can talk to Jeannie Laird for you."

Tessa's mom put her hand across her father's wrist. They shared a glance. "No," LouAnn said. "But I suppose we could make one more try at a variance. Your dad already called someone about the septic."

"I didn't notice anything wrong," Tessa said. "I walked around the yard and the septic field. There're no soft spots in the lawn or odor."

Mom got up and cleared their plates.

"Told you before. Isn't that bad." She grinned and got out a plastic dish washing tub. "We'll all just have to be careful until I can call for some bids. Three-minute showers . . ."

Tessa sighed over her spa tub at home. And shook her head at her silliness. She could hardly afford utility bills until she found out what Phil was up to. "I met someone today. Remember Josh Calloway?"

The sharp look her mother sent said it all. "I recall a certain young lady who spent her college time mooning over a young man by that name, until she came home the summer after her sophomore year and married Phillip Murphy."

Tessa dried the plate her mother handed her. "And never went back to finish college."

"You did a fine job with those girls," Mom said. "No higher calling than to be faithful with the lot you're given."

Tessa pursed her lips to keep worn-out regret from slipping out as a confession she'd never voiced to anyone. She met her mother's knowing glance. Had she known? All these years, had Tessa's secret not been as well-hidden as she thought?

Tessa grabbed the last pot, wiped it and put it away. "Thanks, Mom. I wanted to be a teacher, but I guess I would have had

40

trouble with leaving the girls in daycare. I don't regret my choice."

Mom flipped the light switch off as they went to sit with Tessa's dad. "I should hope not. Oh, by the way, I forgot to mention we had a call from your brother."

"Hey, how is Art doing? I guess I haven't talked to him much, since . . . well, since he and Andy visited us last Christmas anyway. I don't always know what to say about after Amy died." Tessa bit her lip, feeling guilty. Art was her baby brother. She should have more compassion. "And Andy? He's just finishing his junior year in high school. What's he going to do this summer?"

"That's why I'm cleaning out the other bedroom. We're hoping he'll stay with us this summer too."

A few days later, Tessa made her call to the clerk and got on the agenda for the next town board meeting to ask for leniency with the farm taxes. Dana had been an awkward girl, with big plastic glasses and second-hand clothes Tessa understood now that Dana's grandparents could hardly afford. Tessa hadn't come out to church as much after her girls grew up, or she might have gotten to know Dana better. She hadn't married; that much Tessa knew.

Tessa's phone rang. She puzzled at the

41

unfamiliar number with a 312 area code. Where was that? Probably a sales call. Should she answer? The ring stopped, and started again immediately. Tessa sighed. "Hello?"

"Tessa, it's Josh. Calloway."

Was her life an open book? Scary to think first the son so easily found her home address and now the father traced her private cell phone number.

"Are you all right?"

"Oh! Josh, yes, I'm sorry. I was surprised, that's all."

"Good surprised?"

She well remembered the slow sexy smile behind those words. "I'm not sure."

"Oh?"

Tessa shivered, as if his warm breath had tickled her ear.

"What can I do to change your mind?" he asked.

Tessa automatically rubbed her wedding ring, a habit to remind her to think first, speak later. Phillip! "I know I promised to take you out for lunch, Josh, but this really isn't a good time for me. My parents need me." *I have to focus.*

"I'm sorry to hear that." His suave tone changed to a stronger, more concerned one. "How can I help?"

What led Josh to offer help? Ratfink Phil ran away. Josh was here. What did that mean? Tessa pinched her nose and ordered herself to remain dry-eyed. Then she remembered who she was talking to. The founder of the company who was at the root of her parents' troubles. It didn't take much to turn Josh into the source of all of her problems, including being abandoned by her husband. She took a deep breath. "You can tell your son to stop trespassing, for one thing."

The silence on the other end made Tessa feel like apologizing.

"Tessa, your mother knows about everything. She gave Brandon permission to take pictures and soil samples. We only wanted to help."

There was that phrase again. "What if I went to your parents' home and told them they couldn't live there anymore? Believe me, Josh. You and your son are not helping." This time Tessa hung up.

Restless, she went to check Lindsay's bedroom again. Tessa had taken the tiny one across the hall and hoped Lindsay wouldn't have a tantrum when she found out that her mother was — what was it? In her space. Calming a tantrum sounded much easier than telling her about her father and the separation.

Mom had taken Dad in for his doctor's appointment. Tessa paced the wide boards of the covered front porch. She watered geraniums that were thriving in moist soil and healthy. She dumped and refilled the cat's water dish. When a little car turned down the driveway she almost groaned in relief at the welcome interruption.

"Lindsay!" Tessa went to welcome her daughter. "You're early. How was the trip?" Lindsay's car was packed to the roof. At least she had the biggest upstairs bedroom.

"That's why I didn't call you back, Mom," Lindsay told her, after their hug. She unlocked the trunk and handed over a large garbage bag of soft stuff. "So tell me what's up while I unpack."

Tessa followed her daughter upstairs, lugging boxes and bags until she thought she would drop. She thought her mother should be the one to share any real details about the farm, so she skipped over that topic, other than mentioning the failing septic and water that would force them to use bottled water. They'd do the laundry at the house in town. But Phil . . . how to tell Lindsay about her father? With care. Nothing had been decided for sure, of course. She'd just say he was on an extended trip or something that would make sense about why she was here.

Once they had finished unpacking the things Lindsay wanted in her room, they took a break. Lindsay splayed on the oak floor in a pool of sunshine, glass of lemonade in her hand.

"Okay, Mom. Spill."

Tessa sighed. "You know how Dad took that promotion, right?"

Lindsay jumped right in, gave her no chance to make something up. "Yeah, the one where you're planning to move to California to be by Robin."

"I told your father I wouldn't leave Oakville. I can't leave my parents."

Lindsay got up. She set a stack of T-shirts into an old dark dresser with sticky drawers. Its wheeled feet squeaked on the wide floorboards of the room. "So, I'm here now. I can take care of them."

"But for how long? There's so much work to do. It's not just the back taxes. It's a well and a new septic system."

Lindsay bowed her head so her long straight hair fell in a curtain that hid her expression.

"Look, I'm trying hard not to disrespect your father, but he's not making it easy. I told him when we got married that I never

45

wanted to live anywhere else."

"That's kind of unreasonable, Mom."

"You kids have no concept of home, of roots. The Hasmer farm has been in our family for generations. We have a cemetery on the land. What will happen if we sell? It's my heritage and yours, and I'm not going to abandon it to go traipsing halfway across the country just so your dad can call himself the national sales manager instead of regional sales manager."

"It means a lot to him."

Tessa frowned and tapped her foot. "You've been talking to him, haven't you?"

Lindsay looked up with a wide, innocent upraised smile. "Of course. He's my father."

"But . . . but aren't you upset that he refused to help you stay in your apartment while you interviewed and sent out more resumes?"

"I wouldn't have taken it anyway." Lindsay slammed the last drawer shut and shoved her suitcase under the double bed covered by a grandmother's flower garden-patterned quilt. "I'm twenty-four and I have to be responsible for myself."

"So you moved in with your grand-parents."

Lindsay flashed a grin on the way out the door. "At least I didn't have to go crawling back home to my mother. Come on, let's go grab a snack and talk."

"Wait, Linds. You might not have moved back to your mother. But I did."

"Excuse me?" Lindsay's eyebrows disappeared beneath her bangs. "What?"

"I took the little room across the hall. I moved out of the house."

CHAPTER SIX

Tessa's mom had been a bit flustered when she learned Lindsay had breezed in early, but mostly because she'd planned on serving leftovers for supper that night and hadn't been there to properly greet her granddaughter. The more Tessa watched the lovely young woman Lindsay had become interact with her grandparents, even playing a fierce battle of checkers with her grandfather, the more Tessa came to admire her verve and intelligence. How dare some company not realize what a great asset Lindsay would be to any business. She felt like calling all those nincompoops who'd had the audacity not to hire Lindsay and explain how sorry they would be about the wonderful opportunity they'd passed up.

Tessa shushed her phone before the ring got louder. She glanced at it and shoved it back in her pocket. She'd talk to Phil when she felt good and ready, and this wasn't the time.

Lindsay had thoughtfully brought all of her laundry home. She and Tessa were washing it at the house in town after a brief debate about going to the laundromat. That would raise questions from anyone who saw them, and she didn't feel like explaining about the septic system.

Tessa pulled a mass of towels from the washing machine. Should they take the time to use the dryer or haul the heavy mess back to the farm and hang them on the clothesline? Eyeing the white plastic clothes basket and thinking about her forty-eight-year-old back, Tessa groaned and began filling the basket. Using the gas dryer on a nice day was not eco-friendly.

"Are you okay? You didn't hurt yourself?"

Tessa straightened. "Just my pride. I should be more mindful of what God has given us and use his clothes dryer."

"Huh?"

"The clothesline." Tessa nodded outside. "It's a perfect drying day, as Mom used to say."

"We don't have one."

"The farm does. We can talk about weeding your grandma's vegetable garden."

"Thanks." Then Lindsay imitated Tessa's groan. "It's that time already, isn't it? At least I can watch the beans grow up close and personal instead of just helping snap. Well, I can carry the basket if you show me how to work a clothespin. How hard can it be?"

Tessa hugged her daughter and held in the moment of mixed laughter and tears.

On the way back to the farm, Tessa brought up the matter of Art's son coming after his high school let out.

"Right," Lindsay replied. "Andy's coming to stay. When? How long?"

"Not till after school's out in Madison. Another couple weeks. Grandma and Art hope the whole summer, as apparently Andy's been causing some problems."

"Hmm." Lindsay tapped the wheel. "I'm not babysitting a seventeen-year-old trouble-maker."

"I highly doubt your cousin will need your supervision, but maybe we can plan a few activities to keep him busy."

"I'll be looking for a job, sending out resumes and interviewing."

"I know." Tessa felt a spark of excitement, the kind that had been all too rare since her youngest daughter had left home. How had she managed to keep herself busy all this time? A few fundraisers to help the community, sure — but that was mostly asking others to do something. Here was another chance to help her brother who'd shunned Oakville for far too long. With any luck, Art might even decide to come home. Now wouldn't that be nice? Tessa drove up and stopped beside the garage. She got out, shielding her eyes. "Can you help me with the basket again?"

"Sure." Lindsay's cheery expression turned off like a thunderhead blocking the sun. "Someone could have warned me about the well and septic system problem. So what, it's a couple grand to fix?" She grabbed the clothes basket and heaved it toward the line that was strung between two T-poles not far from the kitchen door.

"Oh, Lindsay, it's —"

LouAnn, cloth bag of clothespins in hand, joined them. "Girls. I see you figured out how to work God's clothes dryer."

Tessa's mom had more peace on her face than Tessa had seen for weeks. She pegged her colorful terry towels in neat rows with precise efficiency.

Lindsay looked at a spring clothespin and the shirt she held up. "Um?"

"Now there's a sad case of neglect if I ever saw one," Mom said and shook her head,

51

laughing.

Tessa watched her mother show Lindsay how to hang a shirt on the line, feeling out of the loop. Lindsay and Robin had missed out on a lot of things by not growing up on the farm, true. And their neighborhood frowned on public displays of laundry hanging even in backyards. Tessa had not minded giving up that tradition, nor had she mourned washing dishes by hand since learning to rely on a dishwashing machine. Mom didn't seem as worried as Tessa would be if she had to change her whole life. But then it struck Tessa. *I am giving up everything I know.* Including a husband who had left her high and dry.

She tuned in to hear Lindsay ask something about plowing. Tessa watched her Mom's reaction. Dad had given up the big Taylor tractor after his second stroke. That's the one Otto rolled and died under, while Art watched helplessly, afraid to move it. Tessa shivered. She hadn't been able to go near the thing after, and was sure Dad's first strokes were from the stress of losing Otto. Thank goodness she'd just gotten married and had Phil to lean on. Mom happily drove around on the smaller Case tractor with the front bucket to plow snow in the winter. Tessa chuckled at Brandon and Josh Calloway's assessment of her parents needing assisted living. If Mom had taken better care of her skin, or had Botox treatments, they probably could have passed for sisters.

Movement from the kitchen door caught Tessa's attention. Her dad stood behind his walker, waving an old T-shirt. When he saw she was heading toward him, he turned and shuffled out of the house to the front porch. "Come sit with an old man."

She reached him in time to help him settle onto the porch swing.

"Nice day."

"It sure is." Tessa patted her dad's shoulder. "Can I get you some lemonade or something?"

He patted the swing with his good hand. "For both of us."

She kissed the top of his head and agreed to be right back.

Tessa went to pour tall glasses of lemonade for everyone. She returned and laughed as she watched Lindsay try to handle a half-dozen socks in one hand and talk around the clothespins in her mouth. The clothesline flapped away from her every time she tried to pin a new one. Lindsay was a smart girl. Robin, too.

She sat next to her father and pushed against the floor with her toe.

Dad patted her bare knee as they swung. "Good girl, that one." He pointed at Lindsay with his flyswatter.

"I sure hope she can find a decent job. She put in a lot of time and money earning that degree. I don't understand why her father wouldn't help her out until some firm comes to its senses and hires her."

Otto cleared his throat. "Has his reasons," he said with his harsh whisper of a voice, the rest of his sentence falling away.

"Who?" Tessa watched a bee bumble among the hanging red geraniums.

"Our Father."

Tessa looked up at the twinkle in her dad's eyes. He'd always been the most faith-filled person she knew, never harsh or judgmental, even when she announced she wasn't going back to college but marrying Phillip Murphy instead. Right away that summer. He'd never said an unkind word or given a cross-eyed look when four-and-a-half-pound Robin was born eight months after the wedding; just looked with pride and adoration at his first grandbaby.

Tessa heaved a sigh. Even then, nothing had been easy. She'd just turned twenty-one and felt like twelve holding on to a doll and playing house. Mom had waded in and gone to work.

"The beans are up already, Dad. They look great."

"Folks like beans. Farmer's market — help yer ma with . . . baking." He sipped the lemonade noisily. Tessa sat on her hands to keep from grabbing the glass and helping him. He was not ready for assisted living. "Sell lots of them. Gooseberry. Pies. Good year for apples."

"I'll do what I can to help. I'm glad I'm here."

"So am I."

Tessa heard her phone chirp again. " 'Scuse me." She didn't even look at the caller ID before picking up.

"Can we start over?" Josh's voice made her fingers numb. She scrambled to keep hold of her phone. "Don't hang up. Please. I just want to talk. Please."

Tessa took a deep breath and demanded that her knees stop quivering. "How can I hang up on a man who knows how to say please?"

His sigh breezed across the airwaves. "Thank you. I — this is pretty awkward."

"To say the least."

"Would you be willing to meet me? Somewhere. Just to catch up? No business, I promise. I just want to see you. It's been a long time. Nothing else. Promise."

So why shouldn't Tessa the independent have an innocent chat to catch up with a friend from college? She had swept her feelings for him under the run when she'd left him and married Phil. Maybe it was time to clear the air, talk about — things. Besides, Phil chatted all hours with his clients, without her. He must be having meetings all the time in California. There was nothing romantic or clandestine or even sneaky about meeting Josh Calloway in a public place just to talk. Romance, huh! Romance existed in fairy tales and nowhere else. At least, nowhere in her life. Phil had killed it a thousand times. "Sure, I can do that. Where and when?"

CHAPTER SEVEN

The Memorial Day weekend events had been cleaned up, evaluated and declared a financial success by Oakville's Main Street marketing group, of which Tessa currently served as Events chair. Memorial Day was also the kick off for the Saturday Farmer's Market, even though goods were scarce yet. They closed the two city blocks in front of Bakersfield Park Saturday mornings to give vendors more room. Later in the summer there would be music and the art fair.

In the beginning of June Lindsay sat at a table selling her grandmother's fresh-baked cinnamon rolls, offering free cups of lemonade and talking the ear off anyone who'd stay to listen about her job hunt. Networking, she called it.

Bob Ecklund, another member of the Bakersfield Town Board, and his wife Grace strolled in Tessa's direction. Bob's expression was cautiously neutral and Grace looked nervous. Tessa turned around. Rat-fink friends from high school. Acting like they knew all the answers. Bob ran a productive tool and die business on what used to be his uncle's farm. Sold the rest of the acreage and used the outbuildings. Why didn't he sell his place to the developers? Because he lives miles from Oakville out in the country. Face it, Mom and Dad's was perfect for a development project, butting right up against city limits. *So was Nelson's,* Tessa thought. Dana took the Hasmer side, even if it meant tension at the board meetings. *Oops . . .*

"Dana! Hi, there," Tessa said when the object of her thoughts stopped at the table. "Look at all the people."

Dana's cool little smile belied the sympathy Tessa had experienced since this farm nightmare had begun. "Your daughter talks a mean sales pitch," Dana said.

"She's loved to help her grandmother frost those rolls ever since she was a little girl."

Dana shifted. "Heard something about you and Phil. Sorry."

Jeannie Laird sauntered up to them, trying to bite into a big cinnamon roll without smearing her nose and chin with gooey caramel in the process. "These things ought to be illegal," she said with a sigh.

"Jeannie, hi," Tessa said, warmed at the appearance of her friend. "Do you know Dana London?"

"Sure, hello," Jeannie looked at her hand and laughed without offering it to Dana. "Sorry. Unless you want to get stuck to me for the day."

"Those certainly are amazing rolls your mom makes, Tessa," Dana said. "Well, nice seeing you. Excuse me."

Tessa smiled as Jeannie figured out a way to finish her roll by pinching off bites of it to pop in her mouth. Tessa had decided on the separation from Phil and would meet Jeannie on Monday.

Tessa felt his presence before she saw him. Josh at least knew better than to get too close to her in public, though he couldn't resist surreptitiously placing his hand on the small of her back and just as quickly removing it. Jeannie's eye went wide, and her face pinked while she swiped her lips with a napkin. "Hi, Josh," Tessa said. "Josh Calloway, this is my friend, Jeannie Laird."

Josh offered his hand. "Jeannie. Pleasure to meet you. Laird? That's your office?" He bobbed his head toward her windowed door across the street.

"Yes. I'm an attorney." Jeannie held her hand out in return, apparently unconcerned about being stuck to him for the day. Tessa narrowed her eyes, then scolded herself. They were all adults, and Tessa was the one who was least available. Besides, Josh was the enemy. Even if he was charming and a good listener. And had nice thick hair and kind eyes.

But could talk a rabbit out of its fur in the middle of winter. Careful, girl.

Another family joined their group. Lorrie the mail carrier tugged her teenaged son's shirt sleeve. "Hi, Tessa, all." She nodded as if she knew Josh Calloway. "When's your nephew coming? Hank's been moping around since school let out. No one to play with."

Stick-figured Hank cringed and turned redder than a hot pepper. "Mo-om! I'm sixteen. I do not play. I can drive a car."

"Well, you're driving me crazy with your sleeping in and moping around."

"I start work next week."

"Part-time."

Tessa stepped in. "Art's bringing Andy next week Friday. School goes later in Madison."

"And he's the same age as Hank?"

"Andy just finished his junior year."

Someone called Lorrie's name. She waved. "Good. Let's make sure the boys get together . . ." She walked off towing Hank, who hung his head as if he was on his way to the stocks.

Jeannie laughed. "Another good reason not to have kids."

"You're not married, Jeannie?"

Prickles of warning went up and down Tessa's arms at Josh's tone.

"Don't we have lunch reservations?" Tessa asked Josh. He put his hand on her shoulder and squeezed, then looked at her and made her feel as though there was no one else on the street.

Josh nodded at Jeannie. "It was nice meeting you, friend of Tessa."

Jeannie inclined her head. "Likewise. I'll see you Monday, Tessa, to talk about your case with Phil."

Tessa nodded, scared that she might have just alienated her best friend. And over what? As she walked with Josh to his silver Beemer for the drive down to Milwaukee, she decided that she'd ask Pastor Mike Suchar for some advice after church tomorrow. She needed a long appointment with somebody to remind her of all the reasons she broke up with Josh and married Phil nearly thirty years ago. Her life had not been water under the bridge. She was a mother and a grandmother, not to mention daughter, friend and aunt.

Josh took the buckle out of her hand and clicked it into place. "Ready?"

Right now, Tessa thought, in this moment, I am also a woman sorely in need of being treated like somebody special. Phil would never have taken her downtown to Watt's Tea Room for lunch, or stroll along the lakeshore, just to be with her.

"Yes, I'm ready."

Lindsay had insisted on going to the town board meeting on the second Thursday in June. She'd taken the sheaf of official papers her grandmother had been collecting.

Tessa stepped aside and let Lindsay tackle them. Experience is almost as good of a teacher as repetition. At least she could leave when a job turned up. *I have to face these people, my so-called friends, everyday.*

The day of the meeting, Tessa sat upstairs in the middle of her daughter's bare-walled bedroom, folding old clothes and packing them in boxes while she waited to hear the results of Lindsay's duel with Hiriam.

Oh, yes, and to think about whether or not to continue seeing Josh Calloway. He'd attempted nothing physical, other than take her hand or arm once in a while. Not even a kiss on the cheek. Tessa was the one with the problem. She was so lonely. She never thought she'd miss Phil singing quasi-baritone in the shower in the morning or messing with her dinner by opening the oven door several times and telling her to stir something. She certainly didn't think she'd miss wrestling over the blankets at night or arguing about what to watch on television. She hadn't even turned on a television since she'd moved out and barely paid attention to the shows her parents had on in the evenings.

Tessa found some peace out on the porch swing where she dreamed about Josh's deep voice and the tickle it sent from her ear to her stomach; remembering his college-days kisses. The trouble they'd caused.

Like a splash of cold water she heard the front door crash open downstairs and someone call out.

"Mom!"

"Up here, Linds. Your room."

Lindsay pounded up the stairs at Tessa's invitation. It took a good half-hour before the girl became coherent. Tessa watched Lindsay stomp around and wave her hands.

"Thousands in taxes? No one told me that part!" Lindsay raved. She had the Hasmer backbone, no doubt about it. "And how much more for a mound system? To dig

63

holes? Are they nuts?"

Lindsay stomped around some more. "And what else? Gram told me to talk to you. What else is going on? You're not at the farm while Dad's away so you can chauffeur them, I figured that one out myself when Gram came careening up the driveway yesterday like a bee for home after Gramps' appointment."

Tessa's throat tightened as she stared at Lindsay. Good old Phil had chickened out of telling her about the separation. Nice one.

"You are going to cover the tax bill, aren't you? You and Dad? You can't let them go into foreclosure. That's just not right! I should get a group together. Protest. I know Dad balked at giving me money, not that I would have taken it, but this — this is different. And I have no idea where they're going to come up with money for a septic . . ."

Tessa went to the window and looked out. "I was waiting for the right moment to tell you and your sister. Waiting until things were more final. I'm filing for legal separation."

"From Dad?" Lindsay squeaked. "Are you kidding? What for?"

Tessa folded her arms and faced her daughter. "He left me, Lindsay. I didn't do anything wrong. And he took all our money.

I certainly am not kidding. I wish I were, because that would mean I could help my parents instead of moving in with them."

Lindsay recovered quickly. "There's got to be something . . . Does Dad know about the farm? When was the last time you talked to him? It must be a mistake."

Tessa pursed her lips and squeezed her elbows to keep from blurting something about Phil that she'd regret. The situation was already messy. "This happened before you came."

Lindsay's face took on that patient look that meant something was fishy and she'd just have to straighten everybody out later when she had time.

"We've got our work cut out," Lindsay said. "If no one wants to sell."

"Of course not." Tessa folded another winter sweater and set it in a box. "And not to Josh Calloway."

"Josh? I thought it was Brandon."

Tessa winced. "How did you know that?"

Lindsay colored bright hyacinth pink straight into her hairline. "Linds?"

"We, ah, ran into each other. At the meeting."

"Ran into each other?" Memories of Josh's hard chest and strong hands flooded Tessa.

"Um, actually, my hand sort of ran into

65

Brandon's face."

Tessa saw stars as she stared at her daughter. "Oh, Lindsay."

"I know. You taught me better. I just — lost it, I guess. After all that's been happening since Easter. Losing Mark, graduation, not getting a job, and now this. I don't know." She plopped on the stripped twin bed and regarded Tessa with a teary look. "What's wrong with everything? With everyone? Really, chivalry is so dead. No one cares about anyone else anymore."

Tessa sat next to her and wrapped her arms around her shoulders. "Baby, sometimes I agree. People are always going to disappoint each other. But we have a better friend who will never let us down." Tessa blinked, wondering at the same time where that little nugget came from. It had been too long since she'd reminded herself of the maxim Dad had spouted. And one thing she promised herself was that, while she was with her parents, she'd go back to church every Sunday.

"You're so right, Mom. Jesus loves me, this I know." She hiccupped. "And forgives us, even when we can't forgive ourselves."

Tessa shivered and hoped it was true.

CHAPTER EIGHT

Tessa sat in church, not even bothering to pay attention to the service. The events of the last two weeks swirled like a maelstrom. Her nephew Andy arrived on a Friday, sullen but frightened underneath. Tessa had raised girls, but she recognized the underlying angst of teenaged rebellion mixed with the deep longing to be recognized, appreciated and loved. What had her geeky PhD brother Art been doing that left their relationship in tatters? Andy had promptly wrecked Dad's truck the next day, though wasn't badly hurt despite a face full of glass. Mom then convinced Pastor Suchar to make Andy clean the church. Some penance, especially since Mike Suchar's daughter Ella was the same age as Andy, adorable, and tended to hang out at church. The incident prompted Art to take a leave at work and come to Oakville the following week. With the farmhouse so crowded, she agreed he could stay at her empty one. At least she didn't have to go back there alone after church today. She shivered.

Tessa went home with her parents after church, changed clothes and headed out to garden to do some weeding and thinking, not necessarily in that order of importance. She shivered as she knelt in the dirt, despite the warmth of the day. Would the creeped-out feeling that someone had been in her house ever go away? The day Art moved in, he'd called to tease her about leaving dirty dishes in the sink, something she would never do. She'd met him there after she'd called the police. They had done a quick walk-through, but found nothing missing. She was so glad she was at the farm right now. What kind of burglar didn't take anything? Maybe she had left the toilet seat up after the last time she'd cleaned. Lunch at the diner afterward had helped calm her down — until she'd noticed that Brandon Calloway was there.

Seemed like Brandon and his father traded locations on a regular basis; when Brandon went back to Chicago, Josh was up here in Oakville. Brandon had tried to ingratiate himself to Mom and Dad, and even more to Lindsay. That threw warning flags all across her mother's intuition. But how could she talk to Lindsay without driving her toward Brandon instead of away from him? Young girls enjoyed flirting with danger. She should know.

The Fourth of July celebration committee met later in the week. Tessa was in charge of the children's parade this year. She grinned. Art could earn some of his rent by helping her. She also planned their own version of the wiener dog race that was so popular in the nearby community of Deutschberg. People came from all around the country to race their pet Dachshunds. It was hilarious when they did it for Octoberfest. Art could help with that, too.

That brother of hers. How could he think Mom and Dad were ready for the old folks' home? At least he'd be around for a few weeks and see otherwise.

Thinking of Art and the farm, Tessa decided to start on her dual-duty campaign before she did anything else. Save the farm. She took her gloves off, got out her cell phone and dialed Dana London. Save Art from a life of —

"Hello, Dana London."

"Dana, Tessa Hasmer. How are you? Good. So, Dana, I was remembering," Tessa said, "how you and Art used to go out in high school."

69

"Not really." Dana's tone was guarded. "Just that one time. Prom."

"But you two went out together on youth group trips."

"Sure, with a bunch of kids. What are you getting at, Tessa?" Tessa backed down. "Nothing. Nothing. Just that . . . well, you're not married. Art's not married."

"Thanks for pointing that out."

"And, I thought you'd like to know that Art is coming to stay in Oakville for the summer."

"Uh —"

"And since you used to be such good friends, and you know how hard it is for Art to be around since his wife passed away over a year ago, I was hoping you'd be a good sport and spend some time with him."

"Well —"

"Oh, good! Great! I knew I could count on you. Now, about the taxes on my parents' farm. What can we do to get an extension?"

"Tessa, I don't think you understand. We've given all the time that we can."

"But, we're working so hard."

"There are other influences at work here. Things you know nothing about."

What? Tessa's heart fluttered. What began as an innocent attempt to tap the town clerk for information turned into an ominous pronouncement. "Dana? What's going on?"

"Look, I'd rather you heard this from someone else, but there's been a report floating around that a water bottling company is making inquiries."

"Inquiries? About what? Lake Michigan water? I don't think anyone would drink that."

"No," Dana said softly.

"Then — where would they get the . . . oh." Tessa blinked slow and long, as if time had slowed. "But, who would have . . ." Another blink. "Brandon Calloway. He trespassed."

Tessa hung up. "Thank you," she said to the closed phone. What were those spirits in ancient legends called? The ones that sucked all the joy out of a person? Tessa held up her hands and stared at them, turning them back and forth. Why was she so cold in summer in Wisconsin? She got up slowly and went inside.

"Mom!"

Pastor Suchar's sermon on John 8:31-38 the last Sunday of June set Tessa to thinking about what was true in her life. Nothing much, these days.

Tessa couldn't keep her mind on the message. She had seen the way her youngest

71

daughter looked at Josh's son. Had Tessa looked that awestruck once upon a time? Maybe she still looked with that kind of wonder — that pathetic gratitude that a handsome man paid her attention. Made her feel things, want things no good girl should. Where was the faith Tessa'd been so sure about when she had talked to Lindsay after the board meeting? Or the marriage vows she'd taken?

The last truth Tessa had known had been shattered at the previous Friday fish fry. Josh had returned and asked to meet her at the restaurant. Discreet, but still earned her a frown from her mother when she said she was meeting a friend and wouldn't be home for supper.

Finding out that Phil was one of the investors in C&D should have broken her heart.

Tessa picked at her fuchsia nail polish. What feelings did she have left for her husband? Jeannie had sent the papers to him in California.

Ted Crawford had never been discreet, but did Phil's department VP have to tell everyone at Clancy's Restaurant about the new development proposal? Just because the Bakersfield Town Board had agreed to let C&D explore the options of development, particularly on her parents' farm,

72

didn't mean the plans were going through. Though Ted, who'd obviously enjoyed some belly-up to the bar time before his endless breaded lake perch and slaw dinner plate was plunked down before him, managed to cheerfully announce that Oakville was going to outshine the nearby city of East Bend one of these days. And with Phil Murphy's support, how could they lose?

Pastor Suchar announced the closing hymn. Tessa stood and gave lip-service only to *How Great Thou Art,* not wanting to offend God by having a melt-down right in the pew. Her heart had awakened, crying, all right. All weekend, as a matter of fact, after Josh took her home from the restaurant. At least he claimed he hadn't known about Phil's investment, having turned the daily operation of the business over to his son a couple of years earlier.

Well, that's where their money went. Maybe Phil thought he was helping. But helping whom? Them — as in the Phillip and Tessa Murphy family, or Phil Murphy, world's latest bachelor gift to California girls?

"Go in peace," the pastor said from the front, his arms spread wide.

Was that even possible?

Tessa followed her folks from the pew and

73

hoped she could make it to the car without having to talk to anyone. Definitely not her best friend Jeannie Laird, who'd decided to come to church this morning after a several-week absence.

"Morning, there, Tess. What a great sermon."

The same Jeannie who had been at Clancy's on Friday, too; what a coincidence. And who had witnessed her public humiliation over learning about Phil's endorsement of selling her family heritage to the highest bidder. Tessa wasn't sure who she was madder at: Jeannie for being there, or Josh for inviting Jeannie to join them. She'd told him later she thought they should stop seeing each other for a while. He'd agreed — way too quickly.

"Jeannie. Nice to see you — again. Glad you could make it." *Meow. Stop it!* Like they were fighting over the same high school boyfriend. *Nah, just my old college boyfriend. Whom I dumped.*

Jeannie's eyes flickered, but she kept her lawyer smile firmly clamped.

Tessa bit her lip and sighed. "I can't believe that just came out of my face." She shook her head and touched her friend's arm. "That was unbelievably rude and I beg your forgiveness."

Jeannie nodded. "We could probably use the punching bag at the Y instead, eh? Want to meet me for lunch later? Cedarburg?"

Tessa smiled at the thought of their favorite hangout in the antique former woolen mill. "Thanks. I can manage that."

"I heard about Andy's accident. I'm glad he's all right."

"Me, too."

"See you later."

Tessa flinched when another person touched her arm.

"Mom? You okay?"

"Oh, Linds. Yeah, honey. I'm just ready to take off. Could you tell Grams I'll be gone for —" Tessa looked up in time to see Brandon Calloway behind her daughter. Tessa narrowed her eyes, opened her mouth and decided against saying anything that could come back and haunt her later. She closed it again, turned heel and walked out. Everything was just too weird.

Strawberry Festival was winding down in Cedarburg, but there were still plenty of tourists roaming the streets, sampling strawberry shortcake, strawberry ice cream, strawberry drinks. Tessa and Jeannie waited in line for a table at the restaurant, The Creperie. Handmade crepes with the chef's signature cheese sauce was worth it.

"So, you're letting your brother stay at your house? Art is seriously staying in Oakville for the summer?" Jeannie asked after they'd finally been seated. "He's sure been through a lot."

Tessa flipped and smoothed her red cloth napkin over her knees. She blinked while studying the intricate stitching on the wall quilt hung near them. Jeannie gave her time to collect herself. "I feel so bad for him," she managed to say when she'd gotten some control. "Otto was my brother too, but he was Art's twin. I know the accident was forever ago, but still . . . and then losing his wife last year." Tessa's eyes swam again and she dabbed them with the napkin.

"He must have freaked when he got the call about Andy's accident."

"Oh, yeah. Drove here in record time. Strange."

"Why's that?"

"Well, Dana London was with him."

"They came together?"

"I don't know, really — Art said they'd met near the accident site. Apparently it's close to her place."

Jeannie nodded and sipped her cherry cider.

Their waitress set their plates in front of

them and asked if they needed anything else. A few minutes later, Tessa sat back with a sigh. "I'm so glad you suggested this. It's just what I needed."

"Things getting hot at home? You all still speaking to each other?"

Tessa laughed. "It's been pretty nice, actually. Andy's got some growing up to do, but I think he'll get headed in the right direction if the pastor and Dad have anything to say about it. Lindsay cooked up this scheme to help Mom and Dad pay off the tax bill, and she's got everyone helping."

"Oh?"

"She's selling crop shares from an organic salsa venture."

"Wow. Well, salsa's in these days."

"She even got a company that makes those juicers and peelers and steamer to give discounts to those who buy shares," Tessa said. She dragged a forkful of roast turkey crepe through the cheese sauce on her plate.

"That's incredible," Jeannie replied. "I never would have thought of that."

"She's got her father's gift of sales." Two seconds later Tessa realized how she sounded.

Jeannie didn't miss a beat. "So, heard from Phil lately?" Her casual tone set Tessa's suspicion-meter on high.

"Not since you and I talked last in your office. What did he say about the money?"

"I'm still waiting to hear from his attorney."

The excellent cheese sauce turned to sludge in Tessa's stomach. "You didn't tell me that."

"I was waiting for our next appointment," Jeannie said, "knowing how devastating public announcements can be, and all."

"Yeah, about that —"

"It'll blow over," Jeannie said firmly. "But, as your attorney, I also have to caution you about certain other activity that can lead to other actions that would adversely affect your present legal footprint."

Tessa threw her wadded napkin next to her plate. "See here. He left me. And took our money."

"Joint checking and savings accounts mean you both agree to allow the other partner free access to the accounts."

"But he moved out."

"He took a promotion, honey. And asked you to go with him. And you moved out, too."

"Whose side are you on?" Tessa jumped to her feet. At the silence and looks of the nearest patrons, she slowly sat. The waitress, a young thing with French-braided blonde hair and a concerned frown creasing her twenty-something forehead, strode toward them, check in hand. "Anything else I can do for you?"

Jeannie stared her down. She put the check back into her apron pocket. "We'd like a dessert crepe, please. The one that's on special. Divided. Thanks."

When she'd left, Jeannie pinned Tessa with one of her frank expressions. "You asked me to help you. I am trying hard, but you're not making it easy."

Tessa grabbed the napkin and wrung it.

"Don't give Phil any ammunition."

"That's your help?"

The waitress plunked down their plates of strawberry crepe topped with cream.

"Thank you," Jeannie told her. "I'll take the check." She tasted the crepe and made a happy face. "Heavenly. And yeah, girlfriend, that's the best advice you're going to get. On the house."

Tessa swirled some of the cream onto her spoon. She knew it was not right to spend time alone with Josh, even if he did make her feel like a princess. But, honestly, she felt more like a princess in a harem whenever they were out together. Josh enjoyed being around people of every age and gender and tended to touch or hug them;

even strangers. Although he asked to take her places, he often invited others to join them, like he had on Friday. Should she tell Jeannie she decided to break it off with Josh?

Tessa looked at Jeannie, who'd finished her dessert and was rooting in her handbag, probably for her wallet. Jeannie had acted interested in Josh. Would Jeannie jump in once Tessa was out? Tessa needed a reality check — and fast.

Thinking that Josh Calloway was anything more than a long-past relationship was a mistake. She might have forgiven him for the choices they'd made in college. Even though he'd been widowed a while, he didn't seem ready to settle down with one woman. She figured he'd only break her heart. Again. She wasn't about to let his son pull that same trick on her daughter.

Most importantly, if she asked him to leave her alone, her secret would stay safe.

CHAPTER NINE

On the first day of July Tessa wiped her forehead with the back of her right gloved hand. She surveyed the neat plots of onion sets along the string Lindsay and Mom had laid out. Lindsay on the tractor dragging the old plow behind her had been a sight. Tessa chuckled, thinking about it. Sure, the rows were a bit drunk, but the girl had got the job done and made her mother proud.

Who'd have thought salsa would be such a big hit? The idea of selling shares worked brilliantly. An impressive number had been sold; several of Tessa's friends had gone together on four of them.

Hopefully all their efforts would pay off. Mom and Dad had been a puzzle. For the hundredth time Tessa wished she had paid better attention to their situation. What kind of daughter lived so close and was so blind?

Josh had left town three days ago after Tessa had told him she shouldn't spend any more time with him. It was the right thing to do. So why was she annoyed that he so willingly agreed they not see each other? She had absolutely no business feeling put out by it.

But if she was attracted to another man besides her husband, had she really even loved Phil to begin with? The thought made their separation that much more poignant. How could she trust herself again? Maybe now was a good time to talk to the pastor, see if he had time for an appointment. She could use some more exercise anyway.

Tessa wasn't sure what to do if someone saw them. After being seen with Josh Calloway, how much more damage to her reputation could she stand? Not to mention ruining anyone else's. She called in the door to tell her folks where she was headed, then walked toward church not knowing if anyone would be around to let her in so she could sit in peace and pray. Her nephew Andy didn't start work for hours yet.

She arrived at the church and stood on the sidewalk in front of the doors. Pastor Suchar's small brown Chevy, rusting around the tire rims, was parked to the side. Should she knock? Tessa walked up to the front doors and pushed one side of the heavy paneled doors open. It swung without even a creak. Nice. Andy must be making himself useful. Tessa walked slowly down the center aisle, where she'd once walked to meet her groom. So much life had passed since.

She sat in the front pew, something she'd never done before, and folded her hands and closed her eyes.

"Dear Lord, how could I have done so much damage to everyone I love? Just little old me? I didn't go with my husband, like Ruth went with Naomi. I have sinful thoughts for a man other than my husband, although the, um, passion has turned more into hate, I guess, which is just as bad." She opened one eye. "Isn't it?" She closed her eye again. "My best friend would be a perfect catch for Josh, and I'm jealous. And I'm a bad daughter, not able to help my parents save the farm, which is selfish on my part, because I care most about my childhood playground."

Tessa put her hands over her face. "And I interfere with other people's lives."

"Sounds serious."

Tessa whirled at the sound of the voice behind her. "Pastor! I didn't hear you."

"I saw you come in, Tessa. You look like you need a spiritual hug."

A treacherous tear escaped her right eye. Tessa brushed at it. "Yeah. I guess." She flopped back against the pew. "I am so bad."

Pastor Suchar chuckled. "We all are. When you admit it, then you can move forward."

"I don't know if I can change."

"What do you want to change?"

Tessa shifted her shoulders. "I guess changing everything is too much."

"If you try it all at once. Is there something you want to talk about? I have time."

"Oh, thanks. I didn't want to interrupt you." His silence was both a challenge and a comfort. She continued to face forward so she didn't have to look at him. She sighed. "Well, you probably know that Phil left me."

Silence.

"And that I, that my — that I went to dinner a couple times with someone I used to know. Before Phil."

Silence.

"I didn't seek him out. In fact, I didn't even know he was around," Tessa said, needing to defend herself. She grimaced and closed her eyes. "But I still listened to him, and I made the choice to go with him when I knew it was wrong."

She felt as much as heard the sigh from the pastor.

"I know what it's like to be lonely, Tessa. All of us struggle with temptation. Even Christ. But it's how we deal with those

84

temptations that truly shows our inner character."

"I guess that makes my inner character Mata Hari."

He laughed again. "Don't be so hard on yourself. Every day is a new one as far as choices go. And the best part is God doesn't keep score when you're on his team."

"But how do you keep from doing the same stupid things every day?"

Pastor Suchar came around to sit next to her and twisted to face her. "Tessa, everyone is a sinner. That's why we need Christ every moment of every day. He is the one who changes our hearts when we ask him to. As we choose to spend more time with him and less time with the worries of this world, we are more likely to make more God-pleasing choices than people-pleasing choices."

Tessa sniffed. "I know that. In my heart I know that."

"I'm glad that you've come to church more often this summer."

Heat instantly dried her remaining tears. "It's been good." She smiled at the pastor. "We've had a tough time on the farm. But the problems seem to have drawn us closer as a family. Even Art's back and he hadn't set foot on the farm since Otto died."

"Art's twin."

Tessa nodded. "Right. Summer before their senior year the twins were baling. Otto was rushing it like always, and rolled the tractor."

"Tragic. Andy's accident must have been that much more frightening."

Shuddering, she said, "I think most parents care more about their children's lives than their own."

"I would have to agree."

"My daughter is about to make the biggest mistake of her life by getting involved with someone I have reason not to trust. Isn't it my duty to stop her? But how can I? She's a grown woman, she keeps reminding me."

"You have more than mother's intuition to go on about the trust issue?"

How much should she reveal? She looked at him. "Based on experience. I made a lot of bad choices and I don't want her to suffer like I did."

"Then I'm sure she'll understand. She loves you, I can tell."

"I'm so proud of her. You know what she's doing to try to help my parents." A river of helpless anger flooded across her soul again at the thought of Phil's betrayal. "While her own father is working against them, Lindsay is doing all she can to help."

"Tessa, I don't know all that's going on behind the scenes, but I do know there are more than one or even two sides to every story. I hope you'll listen to them all."

"I just want to start over, you know? Wake up tomorrow and not have anything to worry about."

"Don't we all." Pastor Suchar stood. "The one thing I know is that you are forgiven, Tessa. It's up to you to seek out those you've hurt and ask for their forgiveness, as Christ has forgiven you."

When Tessa got back to the house, she told her mom about the latest disaster. "The real reason behind the takeover is the investment in an artesian bottled water company, Mom. We can't allow that to happen."

"This is still our land, and we will decide how best to work it," LouAnn stated. "If growing water is what's best, then that's what we'll do. And we'll get to live here the rest of our days."

"But a factory." Tessa paced across the kitchen floor. "You're telling me you want to live next to a bottling plant?"

"We don't want that, Tessa, but we do want to have a say in what happens here. There doesn't have to be a big noisy factory right here. They can simply tap the water."

"How long have you known about this?"

"Since that young man mentioned the possibility. He took samples, you know."

"But that's my private place. You're going to let them ruin my glen?"

Mom raised both white brows. "I don't recall seeing your name on the deed. A grown woman ought not to have a play place any more. In fact, a grown woman with two grown daughters and grandchildren ought to be a role model and teacher to them."

"What are you saying?"

Mom stared back as fiercely as Tessa had ever seen. "You've got a good life, girl. You can't afford to throw any of it away. Think on that."

How does a forty-eight-year-old daughter respond to that?

"I've got a final Fourth of July Parade meeting in town. I'd better go or I'll be late."

The meeting broke up by four. Storm clouds were ready to let loose, matching Tessa's mood. She had battled Nancy Traynor over the Dachshund race and won. Nancy was from Deutschberg and didn't think Oakville should compete with them. Ha! Tessa narrowed her eyes and power-walked toward the park, sending children and small animals scurrying from her path. As if Deutschberg had a worry. Besides, the races were in totally different seasons.

It took Tessa three minutes to realize the source of the sharp stings on her neck and arms. Hail. The pavilion was a short run and Tessa took shelter in the ancient, open-sided building. She leaned her hip against the peeling balustrade and sent her "dare me" stare into the raging rainstorm.

"May I join you?"

Tessa swung around slowly to give herself time to rein in her frustration.

"I thought you were in Chicago, Josh."

"I was. I'm back."

She took a deep breath and stood. "I told you. I don't think we should see each other."

"I heard you."

Why did he have to use that rumbling low voice that made her heart flutter? In the intimate space of the pavilion, hidden by the rippling drape of rain, Tessa could easily pretend that the past decades had been a dream.

"Tessa, I know you wonder like I do what life would have been like if we'd gotten married, like I wanted."

Tessa kicked at a green acorn on the cement floor. Read her mind, did he? "We didn't, Josh. We both married other people."

"Julie was a good woman. I cared for her, loved her, but now she's gone."

Josh looked better than good in light blue jeans and a golden polo shirt. The hairs at his throat peppered light with dark. A few whites glowed at his temples, highlighting deep lines fanning from the corners of his dark eyes.

Get a grip, woman. "I'm sorry for your loss," Tessa said. "That doesn't change things. I'm still married."

"You're getting a divorce, aren't you?"

"I haven't gone that far. I'm not sure."

Josh took two more steps toward Tessa. She had no room to move away.

"A man who loves you and wants the best for you and your family knows how to make you certain of what you want."

Tessa shook her head to dislodge the hypnotic effect of his voice. She knew what was best for her and her family — not him. "A woman also wants to know she's the only woman in the world for the man who says he loves her."

Josh stopped. "Excuse me?"

"I've seen you look at Jeannie."

"Jeannie?" He lifted his chin slightly. "She's your best friend. I'm trying to be polite."

"Hmpf."

He laughed. He actually laughed. "You're jealous."

A streak of lightning raised the hair on Tessa's arms. She rubbed them and didn't jump when thunder followed closely. "I have no reason to be. I'm a married woman."

Josh closed the gap and gripped her elbows. "I wanted to marry you once."

Tessa needed to step away, but enervation stayed her. "Josh."

"Why did you leave me after graduation? I called and called." He dropped his touch and turned to pace. "I had it all planned. I had that job lined up. We would have been so happy."

"For a man who claims to know how to make me happy, you sure miss a lot." She took a deep breath. The rain began to lighten. "I'm not proud of the things we did in college. Once we . . . made choices we couldn't take back, I had a hard time forgiving myself. I was so ashamed. And afraid."

"Of what? There was nothing to be ashamed of. We were in love."

"I think maybe I thought I was in love more than I actually was."

Josh stopped near the rail and ran his finger through a puddle.

"But the most important issue back then was that I never wanted to live anywhere

91

but Oakville. I love it here. It's my family home and heritage. I told my husband the same thing." She moved past him toward the steps.

"Where's your sense of adventure."

Tessa faced him. "I travel. But how I feel about home has nothing to do with adventure, and everything to do with respect, with roots. I have roots and I see no reason to tear them out." She looked him directly in the eye. "Or drain and bottle them."

He nodded. "Ah. So it's out then."

"You could have just told me from the beginning."

"I never lied."

"So it's true? The company is really after the water? The glen is my favorite place on the farm. The one place I love." The pulse of a headache started. "A lie by omission is still a lie."

"I'll build you a pool anywhere you like. With a fountain even."

"How can you imagine I'd want a fake fountain?"

"Tessa, don't be ridiculous. Providing good water for people to drink is important."

"Water is one of those God-given freedoms. Make your profit on something else." She rubbed her temple. "If what you said about loving a person — you'd know that all I need is here in Oakville. And you're trying to ruin it for me. I'm not letting you take the most beautiful place I know away from me or my family." Tessa dashed past him, then turned. "And I'm not going to let your son do the same to my daughter. We deserve better."

Tessa flirted with the speed limit all the way back to the farm, skidding slightly on the rain-slicked curve. She slowed, shuddering at the thought of having a close encounter with one of the century oaks like Andy had earlier.

Another cloudburst soaked her as soon as she opened the car door. She shielded her eyes, getting that mother-sense that somehow her daughter was out in this weather. With him.

There! In the barn. Tessa stalked to the hail-lashed building and rushed through the gaping doorway. "Lindsay Murphy! What are you doing?"

CHAPTER TEN

Tessa tossed and fluffed the pillow all night, the humidity and stormy thoughts keeping her awake. Having alienated her friends and family, Tessa knew she had to get some perspective on her situation before she drove her entire life into the ground and took her daughter with her. All the pain of the years since college coalesced as Tessa saw Lindsay about to make the same mistake.

No good mother would let that happen. Lindsay might be a woman, but a mother's love — a mother's experience — outweighs the motives of young men's desires.

Once Lindsay knew the real reason behind the development, she understood the deceit of the son. Just like the father. And the son had admitted it, for sure.

The temptation of spending time with Josh Calloway had been wrong. Sinful. Knowing he wanted to take the glen forever spoiled the serenity she sought. Where else could she go to make her peace with God?

Jesus loves me, this I know . . .

Confess your sins and He is faithful and just to forgive us our sins . . .

The catechism verses she'd memorized as a child slipped out and nipped her heels at needed moments like this one.

Once daylight filtered through her shade, Tessa rose and stared out her bedroom window. She squinted at the figure striding across the field. Art. She thought she'd heard his voice last night, talking to Dad. Something important had happened to keep him overnight at the farm.

Some big sister she'd been. She used to be his shoulder, his sounding board after Otto died. She'd been glad to have him live with her and Phil after the wedding while she'd been pregnant and miserable. But ever since Amy died, it seemed like their cord had unraveled. Tessa felt nervous around Art, weirded out by Amy's heroic death in the Flight for Life helicopter crash. Tessa had liked her sister-in-law, loved her, sure. They all tiptoed around Art afterward, afraid of saying or doing anything that would remind him of her.

Tessa dressed quickly.

Now she knew what it felt like to be alone,

although to a much lesser degree than death. Art would be the first she'd ask to forgive her. He'd been able to move on, finally, figure out how to love again with Dana.

Phil hadn't even bothered to return her calls for the past weeks. She planned to ask Jeannie to file for divorce, since obviously she and Phil had nothing left to their marriage. She would seek his forgiveness and allow him to move on. But the thought of telling her parents made her shake worse than thinking her house had been broken into. She had failed and the divorce would shame them. Art would help her figure out what to say.

She knew that it was time she stopped trying to fight their battles for them, though, and work on taking back her life.

She quietly left the house and followed her brother across the field to their hideout. They'd be able to talk more freely out here, instead of at home where the walls seemed lined with ears.

She lifted aside trailing willow branches. "Art?"

Ten minutes later she watched Art toss a pebble into the spring. "One thing I've learned this summer," he said, "is that in order to grow, you have to forgive, accept yourself and your inability to be perfect. Sometimes you even have to take risks."

Forgiveness was what she was after. But risks? What did he mean by that? Before she could tell him she was sorry, he was patting her back.

"I think you need to go home."

Her mind roiling, Tessa walked away from her glen. Whatever she expected, it wasn't her cautious, philosophic brother telling her to take risks. Her life with Phil was over and she had to figure out how to pick up the pieces. After Josh's betrayal over the reason he'd been so nice, to get the artesian water rights, Tessa felt like a pawn with no purpose.

Home.

He should talk. Tessa took a deep breath of the early morning air, full of heavy dampness, tickling sweet alfalfa aroma and the promise of heat. All right already. She was going back to the empty house. Home is . . . where you hang your hat. Where your heart is.

Where was her heart?

So tattered she doubted the most skillful cardiologist could sew hers together again.

Back at the farmhouse, Mom didn't act

97

surprised by Tessa's announcement that she felt it was time to go back to her own house. Tessa's mom sat at the kitchen table, steaming mug in hand.

"You're always welcome here, you know, darling," Mom said, accompanied by a hug. "I do love you, and I am proud of you." She winked. "I'm not helping you pack, though."

Tessa had to blink hard at that, and laughed. "You're not getting rid of me completely. I'm just going back to reality. Maybe I'll go back to school, get my degree like I always wanted."

Mom toasted her with the mug. "Atta girl."

Tessa had gone for a walk in the park, then picked up some things she thought she'd need for the house. She went grocery shopping, and generally dawdled so that it was getting dark by the time she got home.

She unlocked her front door. The garage door had refused to budge for her, making her feel like a stranger visiting her own home. Art should have told her he changed the code, something she should have thought of after the burglar scare.

She set her laundry basket in the foyer and sniffed. Toast. Phil had always made toast. How long would it take for the smell to go away? She turned to close the front door and heard a creaking noise overhead.

"Who's there? Art? I'm home. I took your advice."

She set her keys on the rattan table. A film of dust covered the glass. Art was definitely going to have to clean before he left. "Art!"

Tessa picked up her basket and started up the steps. And stopped again. Someone was here. She could feel it. "He-hello?" She gripped the basket and debated whether to head up or down. Stuck in the middle of a decision again.

Tessa squared her shoulders. Not this time. She furrowed her brow, angry that everyone but her had control of her life. "I'm coming up. This is my house and no one's gonna make me afraid in my own house."

With all her might, Tessa stomped up the carpeted steps, furious. "If you're playing games with me, Art, you're going to regret it." She reached the top and started down the hall toward the master suite — her room. "If you're an intruder, believe me, it might still be early but I'm not having a great day, so . . ." Tessa reached her door and gave it a push. "So help me!"

At the sight of the person standing half-in, half-out of the bathroom, she let the basket drop to the floor and put her hands on her hips. Figured.

"Phillip Murphy, I could just wring your neck. You make me so mad!"

Then she cut loose with a pent-up window-rattling scream.

"Arthur Hasmer, you make me so mad!"

"Yeah, I get that a lot," Art's voice responded to Tessa's phone call.

"How long has this been going on?" She smacked herself on the forehead while she watched her husband pour himself some coffee and put another slice of bread in the toaster. "Since you moved in, right?"

"This, what?"

"Art!"

"I choose not to incriminate myself. However, I will stay away tonight so you two can talk."

Tessa heard the grin in his voice. Good thing he hung up before she could scream at him. She set the handset in the cradle on the kitchen desk with care before whirling to face her husband. So he wasn't an axe-murderer or burglar, but he might just as well have been the way he'd messed with her life.

"You didn't answer me," she said. "Why

didn't you return my calls?"

Phil swallowed before talking. "I left my charger at Robin's. My phone's dead." He took another bite.

There has got to be a rabbit hole some-where, Tessa thought. "Did you get fired?" He looked a little rough around the edges, not the usual dapper dresser she was used to. His hair was even touching his ears. She frowned. No sign of tan.

"No."

"Does Robin know where you are?"

"Yeah. She's the one who told me to go home. And Lindsay —"

"Lindsay?" Tessa's voice squeaked. "Everybody but me knew you were living here."

Phil shrugged.

Good thing he was on the other side of the table. "But you didn't get fired."

"No, I'm taking early retirement. I'm going to consult."

Tessa sighed. Now what? "Phil, you left me. I filed for a legal separation. And what made you think I'd go along with using all our money in some harem scarem scam like developing my parents' farm? What are we supposed to live on if the plan tanks? Which, by the way, is no longer about development, but about stealing our water."

Phil clasped his hands together and

rubbed his wedding ring in a rare sign of nerves. "Water? What are you talking about?" He frowned. "I kept in touch with people back home. Robin showed me the paperwork that Jeannie sent. She told me . . . told me that proving a point wasn't worth squat."

"That's what this was about? Proving a point? You reduced our marriage to a point value system. I'm honored." Tessa shook her head. "You also showed me the greatest disrespect for everything that I hold dear. I think you should leave."

"But I came back."

"Why?"

"I love you, Tessa. You're my wife."

Tessa turned to face Phil at this declaration. She crossed her arms and tapped her foot. "What do you want?"

"I want to go back to the way things were."

"You mean, when you were gone all the time."

He shook his head. "I'm retired. I can spend more time with you. I missed you."

"Doing what? I don't golf."

"Whatever you want. Um . . . shopping? I can do that."

She backed away from him and the hopeful little light in his eyes. He wasn't any different. He'd leave again with the next good wind. And he never cared about the same things she had.

"I hate shopping."

"So tell me then. I'll do anything."

She turned her back, all thoughts of asking his forgiveness too far up the path to catch. "Divorce me."

"Except that. Never."

"Why won't anybody listen to me?" Fury made the room spin in a kaleidoscope of colors and textures, spinning and making her dizzy. "All the time I try to help people. I try to do what's best, and I make a mess. I went to church yesterday and talked to Pastor Suchar. He said I should find the people I've hurt and ask their forgiveness. You know what? It's just not going to happen. You. Hurt. Me. I'm not the one who's supposed to be sorry about that. Not this time."

"Tessa, I never wanted to hurt you. I've never betrayed our marriage." He held out his hand, the left one with his gleaming wedding ring. "I understand now how lonely you must have been and I'm sorry."

"I don't care about that! I do care about how you never bothered to talk to me about one of the biggest decisions of our lives. You're trying to sell out my parents. You made me a laughing stock. How am I supposed to feel about that?"

"I can get the money back."

"How?"

"I'll go talk to the guy tomorrow."

Tessa went numb with shock that was magnified by a swish of lightning. "N-no. You can't do that."

CHAPTER ELEVEN

"You think I don't recognize the name, do you?" Phil asked. "That same one you went with in college?"

"How did you remember?"

"Like I could forget? At first I thought I was the luckiest guy in the world when you agreed to marry me, and so fast. You want to talk laughing stock? How about getting laughed at when your first child is born less than nine months after the wedding?" A flash of lightning from outside illuminated their argument. "Especially when she'd been going with another guy?"

Tessa swallowed and sank to the floor. Thunder rattled the window panes. "Phil, I —"

"The fact is and always will be that I love you. From the first time I met you when you were home from your first year at college and I was working in the sales department while you were doing that fund drive.

You were so cute, and knew everyone and were always doing something fun. I wanted so badly to be part of that."

He sat on the floor next to her. "You were still a teenager. I was only a few years older, but I thought I had time, that I could win you slowly. When your folks started talking about how their daughter was going with this rich, handsome businessman, I thought I'd lost you. But I kept calling, talking to you."

"I thought you were interested in my roommate."

"No." His gentle eyes turned hard. "I won you the first time and I'm not about to lose you to him again." He pushed himself upright and went for the door. "We'll just see about Mr. Bigstuff Josh Calloway."

Tessa watched him leave. *Okay, I came home. Now what?*

Follow him.

Really? Do I want to?

Of course I do. He's my husband, and he loves me enough to have possibly raised another man's child.

Re-energized, Tessa scrambled to her feet and ran out the door to see the rain-washed taillights of her Land Rover with Phil at the wheel. Where did he think he was going?

Great. Tessa pulled out her cell.

"Jeannie? Could you do me a favor?"

■ ■ ■ ■

When Jeannie Laird drove up the driveway, Tessa didn't even wait for her to come to a complete stop. She yanked on the door handle, winced at the two torn fingernails and buckled up. "I owe you an apology, and I plan to grovel for your forgiveness, but first we have to save, um . . ." Which man was likely to the worst of a tangle?

"Phil," Jeannie said, at the same time Tessa said, "Josh."

Tessa blinked away raindrops from her eyelashes and looked at her friend's profile. Jeannie glanced back before turning out of Tessa's subdivision onto the rural road heading toward the country. "Josh called me a while ago. He wants to hire me as his legal representative in his Wisconsin business ventures."

"I didn't know you did business law."

"A little of everything." Jeannie flushed and turned up the defogger.

"So . . ." Tessa prompted.

"He mentioned something about wanting to help his son buy the Nelson place and was going out to look at it now."

"Oh." That put a new wrinkle in things. Did Lindsay know about that? "Why would

Brandon want to buy the Nelson place?"

"Come on, Tess. Open your eyes. He loves her."

"Her? My Lindsay? But I told her to stay away from him. He's trouble."

"Not judging by the papers I helped him draw up."

"Papers?"

"Client privileges. I can't say any more, but I do know Brandon was going to meet his dad at the church before they went to the Nelson place."

Curiouser and curiouser. "But how would Phil —"

"Blame me! I told Phil I was the representative for the Calloways when he came to me last week —"

"See! I knew it! Everybody knew but me. Probably my own mother knew, too."

"So when I saw Phil screaming past my office a couple of minutes ago hot on the tail of Josh, who'd just left, I figured something was up."

Jeannie went through the four-way at County Road P with a flying stop. The church was in sight. And so were the men's cars. "And I'm the one who should apologize to you, Tessa," Jeannie said. "From the first time I saw Josh, I flirted with him, even though I knew he was your old boyfriend and hoped to maybe get back with you. I called Phil and told him that Josh was in town. I hoped he'd come back so I could make a move on Josh."

"Now Phil's story is making sense. And I don't think you need to go too far out of your way to attract Josh."

"Are you very mad at me?" Jeannie parked her car next to the Land Rover. Phil and Josh were just beyond the gravel on the grass under the big oaks, jabbing at each other's chests and shouting. Tessa glanced at the skidding steel blue clouds and hoped no one needed to tell a lie.

"Na. Deep down he's a decent guy. Just be careful."

"Careful I can do. Let's go save our guys."

Tessa winced as she watched her husband's fist connect with Josh's mouth.

"Phil! What do you think you're doing?"

Jeannie ran past to Josh's prone figure. "Josh! Are you all right?"

Phil stood there, a surprised look of pain on his face while he shook his hand. Rain had dampened everything like Tessa's mother used to do to the linens before setting up her ironing board.

Dana London came around the building on the sidewalk and stood there, shielding her eyes from the rain, a puzzled look on her face. "What's going on? Is Pastor Mike here? Should I call the police?"

Tessa shook her head, then watched her brother join their circus. She glanced at Dana in time to see her blanch, then flush peony pink.

Art came over. "What's going on?"

Tessa snorted. "Oh, just seeing who has the most testosterone."

"I came to see the pastor," Dana said.

"Me, too," Art replied, apparently mesmerized by Dana.

"Is he here?" Dana said.

"Let's go check." Art and Dana walked to the side door just as it flew open. Dana jumped out of the way as a teenaged boy hurtled out and disappeared into the dark.

"Who was that?" Jeannie asked Tessa.

"That troublemaker Andersen boy," Tessa said, squinting in the direction the boy had taken. Pastor Suchar drove in and sauntered over. Tessa sighed and turned back to her husband.

Phil seemed to collect himself and sent a glare at Josh. "Stay away from my wife!"

Tessa looked at her pastor, chagrined. "I'm so sorry. This is all my fault."

Pastor Suchar shook head. "I take it our discussion yesterday bore fruit?"

"More like fruit salad."

Pastor Suchar went to check on Josh, whose head rested quite comfortably in Jeannie's lap. The drizzle had stopped and Tessa shivered in her damp clothes. Mike Suchar spoke quietly to Phil before he slapped his shoulder and walked back to Tessa.

"Why don't you two use my office? I think you have some things to work out."

Tessa stared into Phil's mournful eyes.

"But, do you?" he asked.

"Oh, Phil, of course I do." Tessa shifted on the chair and picked up one of her husband's red-knuckled hands. "Does it hurt much?"

He squeezed back. "Not as much as my heart."

"I think I felt guilty, more than anything else." She braved a look at him, asking him to forgive her for the unspoken question all these years.

"You never needed to."

"Respect, then. I never felt I deserved your respect." Frustrated, Tessa dropped Phil's hand and bit her lip. "Or trust."

Phil's gentle touch on her jaw turned to face him. She studied the red mark on his cheek and the purpling bruise puffing up

111

his left eyebrow. "Do we have to talk about this now?"

"Yes."

"Robin — I was afraid. Ashamed of what I'd done. In college. With him." Tessa closed her eyes. "I can't — I can't believe it. All these years. I took advantage of you, of knowing how you felt about me."

"But you love me."

"Yes!" Tessa glanced away, toward a picture of an eagle on the office wall. "Yes, I do. The same as you — since we met." She laughed a little. "There's my sense of adventure. You were from someplace else, as exotic as could be."

"Ohio."

"Yes. Where they raise men properly." She studied him. "You would never — you wouldn't have treated me like — you wouldn't have asked me to do the thing Josh did to prove my feelings."

Phil gathered her close. Tessa set her damp cheek against his heartbeat. His chuckle made her sit upright and glare at him. "Maybe I would," Phil said. "You're a pretty tasty gal, you know. Mrs. Murphy." He nibbled at her lips.

Tessa swallowed and willed the heat of embarrassment to leave her face. "Phil! Not here. In church." When he laughed again, she let her stiff muscles relax, ready to finish her confession. "I still used you. I don't know if you can forgive me. For . . . you know . . . the baby. Robin."

"What about our daughter?" Phil's tone was even, barely a question. Tessa breathed in, slowly, gathering her courage to tell the truth out loud for the first time in twenty-eight years. "I wondered if I'd gotten pregnant. When . . . after . . . Josh." The diamond ring on her left finger cut into her palm. Tessa winced and separated her hands.

Phil folded his arms across his chest. Tessa waited. Then he unwound and leaned forward, bowing his forehead against his arms on the pastor's desk in front of them. "At first, I did too."

"Why did we wait so long to talk about this?"

"It was easier not to, I guess."

"What are we going to do?" Phil didn't answer. Tessa blew her nose. "Do you want to take a paternity test?"

Phil mumbled into his arms.

"What? What did you say?"

"I already did."

Tessa saw stars and realized she had to breathe. "Oh, no." She blew her nose some more. "I didn't know you'd always suspected. I am so sorry." She put her hand on his arm. "Please, look at me."

He'd been crying too. Tessa's heart threatened to splinter but she had to know. "What did the test say?"

Phil wiped his eyes. "I carried that envelope with the results around with me for years. Then I threw it away."

"But . . . but —"

Phil turned and took both her hands. "I never opened it. I didn't need to."

Tessa nodded. "Probably by then she looked enough like —"

"No." He shook his head. "I came to my senses. It didn't matter what the test said. I will always be Robin's father and nothing will change that."

How had she ever thought of Phillip as anything but wonderful? Tessa grabbed his wet shirt and kissed his bruised cheeks. God's loving forgiveness was way more powerful than anything else on earth to repair her heart and reestablish the husbandly adoration she'd simply misplaced for a while. "Thank you. Thank you, Lord, for loving me in ways I didn't understand."

Tessa adjusted the diaper over her shoulder as she jiggled her grandbaby gently. It wouldn't do to repeat her vows with drool dampening the front of her lavender dress.

Phil had helped her pick it out at Bayshore Mall last week. Baby Anna was every bit as precious as her big sister.

"Here, Mom. Let me take her." Robin took the toddler and passed her off to her husband Jeff.

Anna resembled Phil's plump-cheeked mother, much to Delores's delight. Delores and Rupert sat in the front pew on the right, as they had all those years ago. Tessa wondered if Delores's dress was the same one.

Tessa continued to check out the guests. The Calloways had come, and sat on the bride's side. Tessa glared at the back of Brandon's head and willed him to treat Lindsay right. Tessa forced herself to relax. He had proved himself to be a competent and kind young man.

Forgiving Josh had been hard, especially when he declared he didn't understand.

"Don't worry," Jeannie had said to her earlier, grinning and hanging onto his hand. "I'll explain it to him. And Happy Valentine's Day."

They would make a good couple.

Robin went to take her place next to her sister near the front. Art stood on the other side, looking so handsome in a gray suit and lavender tie. Andy had cleaned up pretty nicely too and looked only a little embarrassed. He sent a stiff-palmed wave toward the audience. Tessa squinted in the direction of the wave and caught the profile of the Suchar girl. Of course, Ella. Young love. How beautiful. Next to Ella sat Dana, who'd begged out of the wedding party, saying she'd rather watch. Art stared back at his bride of two months, smiling, proud, still a little loopy. Andy had to shove him out of the way when Pastor Mike and Phil took their places in front of the pews. The music started. *Amazing Grace* instead of a traditional wedding march.

Everyone stood.

"Ready?" Dad shuffled up next to Tessa, driving his walker, but looking just so proud in the gray tux and pearl tie pin. Someone had decorated the handles of his metal walker with white and lavender ribbons and white flowers. Lindsay, probably.

Tessa smiled and took his arm. "You betcha."

■ ■ ■ ■

LINDAY'S STORY

■ ■ ■ ■

1 John 2:15 "Do not love the world or anything in the world. If anyone loves the world, love for the Father is not in them."

CHAPTER ONE

Shoving the double doors wide, Lindsay Murphy brought the oppressive June air into the Bakersfield Town Board meeting. With the short-stack of notifications rolled into a tight cylinder, she ah-hem'ed as loudly as she could, calling all eyes to her. Pointing her magic wand of official documents at town chairman Hiriam Bakersfield, Lindsay leveled her best don't-mess-with-me glare on his watery eyes.

"What is the meaning of this?" Again she waved the notifications around like a fly-swatter near an old fruit plate.

Hiriam raised his palm in a slow and calm gesture. The speed of which irritated Lindsay more than the notices themselves.

"Ms. Murphy," he said in his throaty voice, probably worn scratchy by the cigar smoke she could smell. "You are out of turn."

"I don't care. If you are about to kick my

grandparents off their farm, I really don't think turns are something we should be arguing over."

Hiriam's face turned from pink to red to purple before he raised his other hand in a surrendered fashion. "Now see here, Ms. Murphy. We are doing the best we can to work through your grandparents' case."

"Are you insane?" She knew her voice had reached a level of whine that was neither persuasive nor adult. "You're doing nothing of the sort with this offer."

Hiriam's eyebrows rose to meet his bushy grey hairline. "There's no need to take that tone. We are working under the advice of our attorneys. With that faulty septic system and worn-out well, your grandparents won't be able to sell that farm anyway."

With an exasperated sigh, Lindsay crossed her arms over her chest and tipped her head to the side. "One question. Why my grand-parents' farm?"

This time Bob Ecklund leaned toward his table microphone and blasted the room with the clearing of his throat. When he inched back, he said, "Lindsay, hon, this is none of your business," Bob repeated the president's statement. "But in the interest of family, we'll just say that this move is in the best interest of all parties involved. The city gets to expand and we get our money back. In fact, it's an investment of sorts, when the new —"

"Mr. Ecklund," Hiram cut in. "It's an economic issue, not a personal one. C&D Development Company is working with the City of Oakville to make sure none of the rural appeal is lost."

Narrowing her eyes, she looked at each of the three men sitting at the conference table in their cushy padded chairs. "You mean to tell me, because my grandparents don't have a huge cattle or grain industry, you all have decided to sell them out? So what, you can get some big-wig developer in here? What are you hoping for? Another water park like the ones in the Dells?" When half the men blanched Lindsay wondered if she'd stumbled onto the real reason they had been pushing her grandparents off the land. She swallowed past the lump wedged inside her throat and shook her head.

"I won't let that happen. We'll get a lawyer. We'll pay the back taxes and you won't be able to — whatever. You can't have our farm. I'll chain myself to the silo if I have to." She shook the wad of papers she held in her hand letting the shuffling sound echo through the room before she spun on her heel and stomped toward the door.

In a quiet voice, not amplified by any microphone, Hiriam said, "Lindsay, your grandparents haven't paid their taxes in a long time. They owe thousands of dollars. And their septic and well are no longer up to code."

Lindsay stopped dead, but she did not turn back.

"Lindsay, if they don't pay, the town has the right to pursue other options including auctioning off the property. But the City of Oakville is just going to come in and declare eminent domain. Annex the whole thing."

Facing the board, Lindsay sighed. "Can't you grant them abatement or something?"

"No. We've been patient long enough. Your grandparents have ignored our communications for the three years. We can start legal action on July thirty-first," Bob added.

"If we pay the taxes, will you still take their farm?"

Each board member avoided her gaze as they looked toward one another.

Hiriam rubbed his chin and stared down his bulbous nose. "I'll make you a deal, Ms. Murphy. You get your grandparents to pay the money they owe then we'll talk."

Sucking in a ragged breath, Lindsay made her way toward the door. "I'll see what I can do." She shot the last bit over her shoulder as she laid her palm against the warm door.

Thousands of dollars. She turned to look back. "How many thousands of dollars are we talking about?"

No one answered. Dana London, the clerk, cleared her throat and pretended to study some papers. "Almost six. Thousand." She cleared her throat again. "Five thousand, four hundred, twenty-seven dollars and thirty-six cents. To be exact."

"Well, that's not that bad. We can pay that." Her heart lifted.

"We'll see." Hiriam sniffed.

With renewed determination, Lindsay pressed her hand against the silver release bar; the door swung wide knocking her off-balance. Pitching forward, Lindsay dropped her wand of notices and braced for the concrete impact she expected. Instead her palms hit silk threads woven throughout an ash-grey suit coat.

Warmth filled her face and prickled her skin as she sputtered an apology and stepped back. Her hands burned as if she'd grabbed a cookie sheet from the oven without her mitts. Feeling more than a little foolish, Lindsay bent down and scrambled to catch the papers the wind had begun to play with. When she glanced up, the sun glared behind the visitor's head and she couldn't make out who still held the door open for her. She sensed he was a stranger to Oakville. Perhaps it was the alligator shoes or the scent of masculine cologne — not something most guys around Oakville wore. Either way, if Lindsay guessed correctly, she'd say her visitor came from the city, not Milwaukee where the men still wore casual slacks with their sports coats, but the big city where suit coats were still the norm — Chicago.

When the guy crouched down to help her, she caught a glimpse of his clean-shaven face and his warm smile. And when she brought her gaze up to his eyes, the laughter she found there frightened the butterflies in her stomach.

"I've got this. Thank you." She reached for the last of the papers, which he held in his fingertips and when the paper didn't give right away, she sliced her finger against the edge of it. "Ow." Sliding her papers under her arm she stuffed her index finger into her mouth. Lindsay stood and tried to brush past him, but he seemed bent on keeping her captive as he continued to hold out the paper that had cut her. Sighing, she took it in her injured hand. Then she moved for the parking lot, leaving the sounds of

124

the council's latest soil content arguments fading at her back.

"Miss," a husky voice called — the stranger's voice no doubt.

Lindsay gritted her teeth and turned around. Why she had no idea. Should have stomped straight for her grandfather's truck. She would have too, if her mother's good manners hadn't made her hesitate.

"Brandon. Brandon Calloway." He'd covered the ground she'd walked in the time it took her to turn around. He stood in front of her offering his hand.

And for some odd reason that unsettled her more than his mocking smile. Lindsay tried to reorganize the mess of wrinkled papers and then smoothed the T-shirt she wore, a hopeless task. Standing in his well-dressed presence, she itched to revisit her closet. Why hadn't she worn the gauzy sleeveless number? It had been right there in her closet.

"And you are?" Brandon held out his hand and tipped his head.

A second wave of warmth fanned her cheeks as Lindsay wiped her free hand on her jeans. "Lindsay." She found it difficult to keep a straight thought in her mind with his hand squeezing hers. "I'm so sorry about all that. I'm not usually rude. I mean thank you. I appreciate your help with the door."

This time his smile turned up the edges of his mouth, every breath of mockery gone. "Not a problem," he said. "Trouble with the supervisory meeting?"

Chewing on her lower lip, Lindsay nodded. She'd forgotten about it for a second, but now the reprieve was gone. Six thousand dollars, only then would they start to talk.

Brandon's forehead furrowed as his smile disappeared. "Oh. Not good." His focus grew distracted as he scanned the parking lot. Lindsay sensed he wanted to add something, so she waited. When his gaze returned, he ran his fingers through his honey-colored waves. "I'd hoped for an easy crowd, but I guess I'll have to take what I can get.

"An easy crowd?"

"Yes, I'm scheduled to speak before the board at —" Brandon pulled back his sleeve, revealing a sleek silver watch — "eleven. And it's almost eleven now."

"Oh. Well, I won't keep you then. It was very nice to meet you. Brandon, right?"

He nodded and tipped his head to the side. "I'm new around here and I'd love to get to know the place a bit better. Do you give tours?"

For the third time that morning heat

spread through Lindsay's cheeks and fanned out until it prickled the back of her neck. "Sure. I guess. I'm not great at that sort of thing, but I can show you around, if you'd like." Mesmerized by his gaze, she giggled like a silly school girl. She tried to cover the noise with a dainty cough, but it sounded ridiculous even to her ears. And it only served to widen his grin.

"Wonderful. Can you meet me here around noon? I'll even spring for lunch."

A date? With him? Lindsay's mind began to spin. It had been so long, since — She reached for her braid, pulling it over her shoulder and toying with its end. She couldn't go. Not on a date with a guy like this. A city-man just like Mark, her ex-what, boyfriend slash almost fiancé? Neon danger signs flashed through her mind, but when he picked up a stray paper that had freed itself from her arms, his hand brushed against hers with an electric shock. *Run.* No good would come of this. But when she opened her mouth to speak, it seemed to have a mind of its own. "Sure."

"Great." Then he glanced at his watch again. "I better go. Don't want to keep the board waiting. I hear they're pretty eager to learn about our company."

As he spoke, Lindsay forced her breathing

to slow and focused on asking normal get-to-know-you type questions. Not the tank top she wanted to change into. Or the way the sun made his eyes shine. "What do you do?"

"I run Calloway and Dunn Developers — C&D Development Company? And I'm here to discuss the investment opportunities we envision for the new property that is being made available."

Lindsay blinked as her heart thumped against her chest like a wrecking ball. "You're from the development company?"

"Mm-hmm." He nodded.

Snake!

She raised her hand and slapped his face. Spinning on her heels, she ran back to her truck.

CHAPTER TWO

"Insane!" Lindsay blasted the air conditioning, but in Grandpa Otto's old truck, that wasn't high enough by any standards, since it was some add-in Al, the local mechanic, put in a year ago. "Verifiably nuts." She slapped the dashboard twice for good measure, regretting the action as she pulled back her stinging palm. "What was I thinking?" What had she been thinking? Easy. She'd been thinking about Mark. *No. I'm not going there.*

Lindsay pressed the gas pedal down, zipping along the deserted country road. "Well, now what, Miss smarty-pants?" she asked herself. One glance in the mirror told her a public place was out of the question, so she turned down Bunker Hill Road and headed to home. Not the apartment she shared with her best friend, that one had been packed up and cleared out shortly after Cindy had gotten engaged. Even now, she wondered if she'd made the right decision to give up city life. Well, she hadn't given up as much as she'd been shoved out. No money, no job and no prospects made her homeless, daddy-dependent or farm-bound. Since the first two simply wouldn't do, she'd chosen to return to her grandparents' farm. Besides, they needed a little help from time to time. But now Bakersfield threatened to take the farm too. She wondered if there was any choice to make at all.

She parked by the chicken coop, long since empty of any feathered creatures, and rested her head against the steering wheel.

Dear God, show me what you want. I left Mark because I thought that was your will. I left Chicago because I thought that was your will. Now, the village may make us all leave. Tell me that's not your will. Please. Tell Brandon to take his development company and —

"Lindsay, darling? Get out of that infernal beast and come have some lemonade." Grandma LouAnn may be older than life itself, but she spoke with the strength that comes from living many years. "Kids these days. Doesn't she know she'll die of heat stroke in there? Especially with the air turned off. Goodness, mercy me." Grandma mumbled all the way back to the screen door, which banged against its frame when her heels disappeared.

Lindsay couldn't help but smile as a warm peace filled her. God loved her Gram more than she ever could. What was she worried about? He'd take care of her. Of all of them. She just needed a little patience — and faith.

So she pulled her purse from the passenger seat and slid out the door, following Gram inside. The kitchen smelled of poppy-seed bread and lemons. Despite the summer's heat and lack of air, the room stayed cool in the shadow of an ancient oak tree. The very tree Lindsay had broken her arm under when she got the fool idea to climb to the top. No one told her it was harder going down than up. At least without falling.

Gram set a lemon-scented glass in front of her along with a platter of raisin oatmeal cookies. Lindsay took a bite and let the coarse texture remind her of pig-tails and butterfly chases.

"Goodness, girl you look a million miles away."

The scritch of chair legs on the worn linoleum opened Lindsay's eyes and brought to mind all those good manners, her mother, Tessa Hasmer Murphy, had tried so hard to instill in her. "Thank you,

131

Gram. I'm sorry. That was rude of me. Seems to be a new habit these days. Would you like a cookie?" She raised the plate to Gram who sat across the table and cradled her chin in the palm of her hand.

"No, doll. I want to know what that infernal man told you."

Lindsay smiled at the use of her Gram's favorite word. A new word won the right to be overused each week, this week infernal had beaten all the others. "Hiriam? He said you have to pay your taxes or they're going to foreclose and auction off the property. The city wants to annex. You could have told me that."

Gram hrmpf'd and fell back against the chair rest. "I'm not paying that man a dime so he can stay in cahoots with those criminals in the city. We've lived here all our lives. He owes us for being such good citizens."

"But Gram, they are property taxes. You have to pay."

"Or what? They'll have my family property over my dead body. Soon as I heard about that development project, I put my foot down. I am not giving anybody the deed to my land. It's been paid for, squared and all."

Lindsay spent the next hour explaining Hiriam's demands, but she spared Gram the wretched tale of Brandon Calloway.

132

That would remain Lindsay's embarrassing secret. The last thing Lindsay needed was for Gram to tell her mother. What a nightmare that would be. Lindsay rolled her eyes at the thought.

"Now don't you get all uppity with me, young lady. I have every right to refuse to pay. This is a free country and all."

Pat, pat, pat went Lindsay's hand on Gram's rough hand. "Yes, you do. And they have every right to take the property if you make that choice."

"But the taxes shot through the barn loft last year. It isn't right, I tell you. And they had the gall to suggest we go right into the new assisted living they wanted to build. Ha! Over my dead body."

"Gram, it's no use fighting over that now. We need to figure out what we're going to do about this. Do you and Gramps have the funds to pay the bill in full?"

Gram dropped her eyes and wrung her napkin. "No. Just enough to put in a new septic system and well. Grandpa's already called the people."

"Didn't you sell off a chunk of land last year? Could you do that again?"

Gram shook her head as a drop fell from her cheek to her lap. "No. We've sold all but the glen, the back meadow, and the buildings." Regaining a bit of the Gram-spitfire Lindsay was used to, Gram sniffed and dismissed her with a wave of her hand. "This is nothing for you to be concerned with. Nothing at all. I've gone over all of this with your mother. Hiriam will just have to wait."

"There's nothing?" Lindsay could taste panic as it rose bitterly in her throat.

The simple shake of Gram's head was all the response she needed. In short order, anger replaced the panic she felt. It's that developer's fault. If he hadn't come in promising big returns for some investment, Hiriam wouldn't be so fired up to take Gram and Gramp's property. They were probably offered the moon and more. Foolish man. If Hiriam had half the business sense he thought he had, he would recognize bait and switch when he saw it. Why would anyone travel to nowheresville for one waterpark when the waterpark capitol of the world was a couple hours west of them? It would make more sense to capitalize on what God gave their village naturally. Like the rolling landscape carved by glaciers or the caverns etched from limestone. Now those would attract even the most frugal Illinois tourist, but no. Hiriam had to have his waterpark, or so she guessed. And assisted living? That was nuts. She couldn't fathom what Brandon Calloway wanted. Her pulse quickened when the question called his image to mind.

With a shake of her head, Lindsay shook free from the ghostly image. "Gram, Hiriam isn't about to wait. He gave us less than six weeks to pay this bill."

Gram's hand flew to her chest as her mouth formed an O.

"Six weeks?" Gramps wobbled in using his walker for support. Each word slurred in his mouth as if he spoke through a dozen marbles — a reminder of the stroke's power.

Lindsay rose and ushered Gramps into her chair. "Yes, sir." When he sat down hard, his shoulders slumped forward more than usual.

There has to be a fix. How hard could it be? She was a college graduate for crying out loud. From the University of Illinois School of Business. Besides, the farm had been in Gram's family for more generations than Lindsay knew could count. That development company could not have it. Period.

"What should we do, Lindsay?" For the first time in Lindsay's twenty-four years, her grandmother looked shaken. Dare she say, scared?

Lindsay scratched her forehead. "I'm not

sure." When she looked up, she met her Gramp's pale face. That pricked Lindsay. "Mom knows, right? Why doesn't she just pay? Where is she?" When Gram averted her eyes, Lindsay caught the drift. "You couldn't tell her everything because my dad left. Thought it would be too much for her?"

"No. She knows. Your mom's the one who made your appointment with the board this morning. She said she had something to take care of back at the house."

Relief flooded Lindsay, making her want to sag into the chair beside Gramps, but she leaned against his backrest instead, trying to infuse strength into his drawn face. "Well, there you go. Mom and Dad have the funds to clear the bill. I'll text Mom and let her know the board refused to budge. The bill'll be paid by tomorrow." Lindsay whipped out her cell and started punching buttons as she spoke. But when Gram reached up to take her hand, Gram's face stopped Lindsay cold. Fear had been replaced by something else. Something more sinister, like sorrow.

"What? Did I miss something?" Lindsay asked.

"I think you need to talk to your mother, dear."

"Right. That's what I'm doing." Lindsay

bent her head once more.

"No. I mean you need to talk to her in person."

The lump that seized her belly grew as Lindsay swung her gaze from Gram to Gramps and back again.

"Pardon?"

"You two have a lot to talk about — the kind you have to do face to face."

"Well then. When was she getting back?"

Gram craned her neck to look at the clock above the cabinets — the old-school-lunchroom clock. It had been a gift from Uncle Art when he was a boy, Gram had told her. And since Uncle Art never came to visit, it was Gram's way of having a bit of him around all the time. "I think she said she'd be packing a few things up at her place until four."

"Fine. I'll head over now."

"Lindsay, you may not like what you hear. And your mom has had such a rough spell."

"Don't worry, Gram. I'll play nice."

CHAPTER THREE

"Mom!" Lindsay's voice carried through the near-empty living room and echoed off the 80s vintage kitchen cabinets. "Mom, are you here?"

"Yes, hon. I'm in your old room. Come on up."

When she was a little girl, going to the farm had been an adventure. Now she realized the City of Oakville had slowly encroached until the house and old barn and decrepit silo were mere minutes from civilization. Lindsay took the stairs two at a time until she reached the landing. When she rounded the corner to her room, she hesitated. Her mom had her Strawberry Shortcake knickknacks and N'Sync posters packed away, but she still sat in the middle of an old pile of jeans and T-shirts. "You kept these?" Lindsay nudged the pile with her toe and forced a smile on her face.

Tessa's face tightened as she stretched and

rose to her feet. "Something wrong? Is it Dad — I mean Grampa?"

Lindsay reached for her mother's hands and pulled her over to the bare mattress. When she perched on the edge, her mother followed suit, waiting. "Mom." Lindsay glanced around.

"Spit it out, Linds."

"Hiriam won't budge. Gram and Gramps have six weeks before he takes action." Lindsay didn't like the way her mother sucked in her breath and dropped her hands. "I told Gram you'd cover the tax bill and she just said I had to talk to you. Not text, but talk. What's going on?"

Tessa walked over to the window, the one overlooking what used to be a wild meadow filled with toads to catch and bird nests to peer into. The meadow had been plowed under when Lindsay started graduate school. A Walgreens stood in its place.

"Mom?"

"I wasn't going to tell you or your sister until everything was more final."

"What? What was more final? Now you're scaring me."

"Your Dad and I are separated."

"I know. You already told me he's in California and you don't want to move. You'll figure it out, though. You guys always do." Lindsay blew the strands of hair from her eyes as she patted her mother's shoulder.

"No. Not this time."

A tightness seized her heart and squeezed. "What? Why? Because he moved to California?"

"That and more. So much more."

Lindsay leaned her head against her mom's shoulder and hugged her. "I'm so sorry Mom." Tessa sighed beneath her embrace.

Like a slow-motion sports replay, Lindsay backed up and dropped her arms to her sides.

"Your dad emptied our accounts. I can barely pay for my groceries, let alone my parents' bills." Tears sparkled in her eyes. "I'm not much help to anyone these days."

"Oh Mom. That's not true."

Tess flung her arms wide and gave an exasperated sigh. "It is true. The farm is in trouble because I can't pay that tax bill. And with Andy arriving tomorrow, I'm not sure how we're going to handle it all. How do we feed five people off my parents' social security? How did it ever get this bad?" She had wandered back to the pile of jeans, which she kicked across the floor.

Lindsay sidestepped a pair of flying Levis.

"Feel better?"

The faintest smile curled at the ends of her mouth. "A bit."

"Good. Get it all out now, 'cause we've got our work cut out for us. And has anyone talked to Uncle Art yet?"

"Work? What work? And no, I don't know if Art knows anything. I'm sure he'd rather let the place go."

"Really? That's what you think? Is that what you want, too?" Lindsay asked as she picked up the scattered clothes.

"Absolutely not. And certainly not to Josh Calloway."

Pausing in mid-stride, Lindsay tipped her head. "Who's Josh? I thought his name was Brandon."

"Oh there's that one, too. Come here. I guess it's about time I told you a part of my past I thought had been long since buried."

Hours later as the sun began its descent, Lindsay rode with her mother back to the farm in her Land Rover filled with boxes of memories. Without a resolution in hand, both rode in silence. But it wasn't her mother's college involvement with Brandon's father that bothered her as much as their financial situation. The former died years ago, but the latter? Lindsay wondered what if anything could be done to save the farm she loved. If not where would she go? Back to Chicago? To Mark? No, she couldn't go back to Mark. Not the way she all but begged him to get married, which he refused. She shook her head. No good could come from this.

The arrival of Lindsay's cousin Andy alighted with no small amount of tension. Lindsay remembered moments with her mother where her teen brain wouldn't listen and couldn't speak her mom's language, but Andy and Uncle Art seemed to have those problems in spades, especially when Dana London, an old high school friend who happened to be the town clerk, arrived. By the time they left Andy retreated to the quiet safety of his room.

Lindsay decided to do the same. She yanked a load of darks from the dryer and wandered back to what used to be her mother's room. But as Lindsay headed to her room, she sensed an epiphany of sorts. So she dropped the basket and took a detour across the hall.

Lindsay rapped twice on her cousin's door before she called out. "Andy? I hope it's not too late, but I have a quick question to ask." Okay, so it's not such a quick question. Then again, he is a seventeen year-old boy.

It may be very quick. "Andy?" Her knuckles grew sore. Why wasn't he answering? What if he had decided to run? What if he pried open the paint-stuck window and ditched them? Or what if he did something drastic? "Andy!"

Hesitating one moment more, Lindsay tested the doorknob before she shoved the door wide and searched the interior. Andy yelped as the door made contact with a sickening thud.

"Watch it!" Andy cried as he pulled the ear buds free. Anger flashed in his eyes, making her question the wisdom of what she was about to do.

Lindsay backed up a step. "I'm so sorry. I knocked, but you didn't answer, so I thought — oh, it doesn't matter what I thought. I'm sorry." She took another step into the hallway, but stopped when she noticed the wadded tissue near Andy's knees. "Are you okay?"

Andy shrugged, so Lindsay took liberty. She stepped inside and shut the door behind her. Once upon a long time ago, she and Andy wouldn't have given each other more than a cursory greeting. He had visited during the holidays at least once or twice, but he was so much younger than she. It was her fault they weren't closer. She should have taken more time to connect. That would change here and now.

"Wanna talk?"

Without raising his head, he shook his head.

"Mind if I ask your opinion on something?"

Again a shake with a sniff.

Lindsay sat in front of him, cross-legged on the floor. "The way I see it, you're as much a part of this issue as I am, so I want to know what you think about losing the farm."

That did it. Andy's head tilted up as he locked eyes with her.

"Did your dad tell you Gram and Gramps might lose the farm if they don't pay back taxes?"

His eyes opened wide.

Lindsay tucked a stray band of hair behind her ear. "It's a bit of a mess, but it boils down to our needing to raise a whole lot of money."

"Don't they have savings or something?"

"They do, but they don't want to use it. At least not all of it on this." When his face clouded with what looked like confusion, she smiled. "They're stubborn."

"Yah. I can imagine." For a moment Andy stared across the room and sighed.

"Your dad?"

"Mm-hmm. Way stubborn."

"Just him?" Lindsay waited, wondering if she had pressed too far until he met her gaze with a hint of a smile in his eyes.

"So what's it to me?" he asked.

"This land is our heritage. Shoot, your relatives are buried here; it's been in the family for generations."

"So. It's not like I'm going to farm it."

Lindsay snickered as she pictured him decked out in overalls, carrying a pitchfork in his hand. "No, I suppose not. Frankly, I don't want to either. As soon as I find a decent job I'm out of here."

"So why do you care?"

"Because Gram does. Gramps loves this place, too. I think it would kill him to leave."

Again, Andy seemed to drift off for a bit. Lindsay pulled at a stray piece of fuzz, letting Andy think in peace.

"Yah." It was the only sound he made except for his breathing.

"Yah, what?" Lindsay asked.

"Yah I'll help. For Gram and Gramps that is and for as long as I'm here. What do you need me to do? You're not gonna make me sell cookies or something are you?"

Lindsay took a deep breath. "That's the thing. I don't know what we're going to do.

145

I can't find a job to save my life and there doesn't seem to be any other source we can draw from, at least not before the July deadline Hiriam gave us."

Whistling low, Andy frowned. "That soon? That stinks."

Lindsay could only nod.

"Why don't you grow something? Sell it at the market."

He doesn't farm. At all. "We couldn't take it to market until August at the earliest."

"Not if you sell shares. I have a friend of mine back home who buys shares in some farm on the outskirts of Madison. Her folks pay a mint for the produce every year, 'cause it's organic. Can't you do that?"

Lindsay leaned back on her hands and chewed her lower lip. Shares? If she sold shares, they wouldn't have to harvest everything to make the money they needed. And Gram had mentioned Gramps hadn't farmed for a decade. The ground had to be good enough for organic growing, didn't it? A little research should answer that question.

"Gram said they only own the meadow, the cemetery, the glen and the pond. The rest they sold over the last few years. Do you think we could make enough with just the meadow?"

"Sure. I mean Crystal's folks pay five hundred bucks a year. It shouldn't take many shares to pay for whatever they owe. How much do you need to raise?" Andy leaned forward and intensified his look.

"About six grand."

He whistled. "Dude. Easy. That's twelve shares. How big is the meadow?"

"Don't know exactly. About fifteen — maybe twenty acres."

"I bet that's plenty. It's just rows of stuff."

Lindsay rocked back and forth as she stewed over the idea. "Let me look a few things up tomorrow. If we did this, would you be willing to help me?"

Andy picked up the ear buds that lay in his lap and plugged one into his right ear. "I'm not farming if that's what you're asking. I guess I could help you sell the shares or something." Then he plugged in the left and dismissed her with the bop of his head to an unheard tune.

"Right. Something." She grinned to herself as she stepped into the hall and thought about the prospects. A wider grin filled her face when she considered the damage this would do to Hiriam Bakersfield and Brandon Calloway's new friendship. This might just work. But when she leaned over her

147

laundry basket, another thought struck her. *I have no idea how to farm a thing.*

CHAPTER FOUR

Sunday, a day of rest, was something Lindsay needed after Andy's truck accident the day after he'd arrived. As Lindsay rolled her bulletin into a tight cylinder, she knew better. A nap held no appeal. What she longed to do was lock herself away in the corner of the county library to find out about farming and organic certification and share selling. Now here she sat beside her mother, listening to Pastor Suchar drone on about something or the other. No matter how hard Lindsay tried, she couldn't follow the man's sermon. Not that it was his fault. Normally she loved his sermons. Just not today.

Once the dishes had been cleared from lunch, Lindsay took to the backyard and wandered toward the meadow. When she reached its center, she squatted down and dug into the dark soil and let it sift through her fingers. Dark dirt was good for farming, wasn't it? She hoped it was.

"Making mud pies?" a deep voice asked.

Startled, Lindsay jumped up, but lost her footing and landed firmly on her backside in the grass. When Brandon Calloway sauntered into view, Lindsay's heart drummed against her chest as her lunch curdled in her belly. "What are you doing here?"

He offered his hand, which she flicked away.

"Missed your sweet disposition." Then he took a step back as she rose to her feet. "You're not going to slap me again are you?"

She narrowed her eyes, though she couldn't keep a smile from tugging at the corners of her mouth. "No, but I ought to shoot you for trespassing."

His eyes made a quick scan, looking for a weapon she assumed. Keep him on his toes.

"You wouldn't do that. Would you?" His eyes widened and he kept the space between them.

"Haven't decided." She crossed her arms over her chest and squared her shoulders. Smiling, Lindsay wondered if she could intimidate someone who towered a good foot over her. "What are you doing here?"

"Taking a stroll," he said with a note of question at the end.

"Take one on the sidewalks of Oakville."

"But the scenery isn't nearly as breathtaking." A lopsided grin told her any chance of intimidation had passed. The intensity of his stare sent goose flesh across her arms and heat to her face.

Lindsay released a dramatic sigh. "Are you always this annoying?"

Closing the gap between them, his eyes darkened with a guarded emotion. "Are you always this infuriating?"

"Yes." She stood her ground although the closer he got, the more she wanted to run. Doubting she'd make it to the oak grove before her racing heart gave out; she opted to stand granite-still.

"Good. I like that."

Wish he didn't look at me that way. As if he was starving and I was the last cream puff at the fair.

She rolled her eyes with enough dramatic flair to win an Oscar before she planted her fists on her hips and fought the smile that tugged at the corners of her mouth.

He stood close enough now for her to smell the peppermint he tucked in his cheek. "You're beautiful when you're annoyed."

Considering the state of her wind-whipped ponytail, faded lime green tee, and the dirt encrusted cut-offs. "And you're full of it. What do you want?"

"Permission to walk you back to the house?"

"What? Are you nuts? Get off my property. Now!"

He lowered his voice as if he spoke to a petulant child. "It's your grandparent's property and LouAnn said I could inspect it anytime I wanted." Then he offered his hand.

Lindsay's mouth dropped open. Was he insane? Was Gram? Why would Gram do that? How could she not see what a ratfink this guy was? And why in the world would he be chatting it up with Gram? Lindsay narrowed her eyes and considered his threatening good looks. She imagined the line of broken hearts he'd left and lowered her opinion of him a notch. As if that was possible. He probably scammed Gram somehow too. Well she wouldn't fall for him. It. Not for a second. He was just another Mark in a different colored suit.

But if business school taught her anything, it schooled her on the wisdom of knowing every angle. Taking in the beige polo with a placket of buttons at the throat that offset his tan and hugged his broad shoulders and biceps, she considered how few angles she knew about him. She should take a little time to see if she could sneak information out of him. It couldn't hurt, could it?

"I suppose if Gram gave you the go ahead. Fine. Walk wherever."

But the smile that revealed his Hollywood-perfect teeth unnerved her. She spun on her heel and started to walk back to the little clapboard farmhouse perching on the hill. Forget about those lips. Remember Gram. Conjuring the image of her Gramps in his favorite chair, Lindsay listened to Brandon's leather sandals crunch on the meadow's debris as he strode up beside her. Must be getting a lot of dirt and grass between his toes. Maybe she should walk him along the neighbor's field — the one Mr. Henderson allowed his dogs free to use as they pleased. Wonder if he'd consider that stretch breathtaking.

"This is a stunning farm."

"Is that why you want Oakville to steal it from an elderly couple?" she shot over her shoulder. "So you can look at it?"

"Is that what you think?" His brow creased. "That I want to steal your grandparents' farm?"

She stopped short, not because of his question, but because the touch of his hand on her elbow burned like a branding iron. Jerking it back, Lindsay cleared her throat and said, "No. I think your company is promising Hiriam the world but they'll change their tune once they have control over our property — my grandparents' farm that has been in our family for more generations than I know. That's what I think." *Ratfink.*

"That's not it at all." Brandon's concerned look faltered before he covered it with a smile more plastic than her garbage can. "C&D is always looking for the next best investment. We believe Oakville is that investment." He pulled his cell from his pants pocket, checked the screen, and typed a brief text.

Lindsay hmf'd and stomped toward the farmhouse, which seemed to fall farther away the longer she walked. "Toeing daddy's party line, eh? Got a spine?"

"Hey," he said as he matched her steps. "Don't you want Oakville to grow? We're planning on adding a multi-functional, state-of-the-art senior living development too. Your grandparents could be first on the list if they wanted. Wouldn't that be best for them? Come on. They've earned the right to relax. No more lawn care. Snow shoveling. Gardening. Someone else would repair anything that broke. They'd be set for life."

She turned on him then. "This," she swept her arm across the field, the glen that kept the pond fed, and the backyard, "this is their life. What you're offering is someone else's dream. A dream that comes at the cost of their own." Lindsay rubbed her forehead, then she stared at him in awe at his cluelessness. "Look. I need to run an errand. If Gram says you can stroll the meadow — great. But don't plan on doing it with me as your tour guide."

When he worked his phone a second time, Lindsay rolled her eyes and took off through the meadow, but instead of veering toward home, she headed down the driveway. Pastor Suchar lived in the little house next to the church, which was a bit of a walk, but worth the time to clear her head.

She needed the space and the time to argue with God. What was He thinking, anyway? Why yank her from her swank future, one she fully planned on serving Him through? She could have funded a myriad of missions' teams with the average city salary. Or better yet, raised the next generation of missionaries if only Mark had seen fit —

Oh what use was it to let her thoughts stray to a man who drank mojitos by the pail? Besides, she imagined him filling his free time with that female shark hungry for his bank account. It was best this way. At least she knew who Mark truly was before they were married.

Who was she kidding? She missed him. His future and potential. Brilliant. Brilliant in the sense that Mark could win any season of Donald Trump's Apprentice. And he never annoyed her like Brandon did. Mark was a balm whereas Brandon was the nettle that bit into her flesh.

Wait. Where's my head?

How could she be so self-focused? Whining about her love life — or lack of — did nothing to save her family's farm.

What should I do, God?

But God didn't answer before the Suchar residence rose over the hill. If only Pastor Mike could tell her what to do.

Answers she hoped Pastor Mike held.

Once Pastor Mike heard her family's tale in full — minus the part about Brandon or Mark — Pastor Mike agreed to pray for her wisdom and guidance, but he offered her none of his own.

"But what should I do?"

Pastor Mike offered her cookies from the plate his daughter, Ella placed in front of them then Ella took a book to the corner of the living room where she seemed to melt into the wallpaper.

"I can't tell you what to do," he said.

Lindsay's voice elevated to full whine. "But isn't that what pastors do? That's your job, isn't it?"

Ella smiled and said, "Only when they're talking to their daughters."

Flicking a half-eaten cookie in the girl's direction, Pastor Mike smiled despite the bite of sternness in his tone. "Ella."

"Sorry."

Pastor Mike shrugged before he continued. "Ella's right. Only a father can tell a daughter what to do. In this case, only God knows what He wants for your family. Have you asked Him?"

"Yah. I sort of left a message. But surely He doesn't want my grandparents homeless or that development company invading Oakville." Even the name of that company left a foul taste in her mouth, so she spit it out like stale gum.

Pastor Mike seemed unfazed. "Can I suggest a little Bible study for you?"

"What?"

"When you have a quiet moment tonight, read 1 John 2:15-17."

Ella hopped up and offered her a slip of paper with the verse scrawled in clean script. "Here you go. He gives me that one all the time. It'll challenge you."

Not one to be disrespectful, Lindsay

licked her lips and tucked the last bite of cookie into her mouth. "All right. I'll read it." As she left the modest house, she convinced herself that rather than resolving anything, more had been added to her plate. Now, she had to save the farm, stop Brandon — C&D Development — and discern God's will — alone.

God, I just don't get it. What do you want from us? From me? Why didn't you just give me that job at Blake and Middleton's? Life would have been so much better. Even if Mark left me, at least I would have somewhere else to live instead of being smack in the midst of this mess. And I could have paid for Gram and Gramp's taxes. Maybe even fixed Mom's financial mess. What's up with the rough road you've put in front of me?

Lindsay kicked the gravel at her feet and scowled at oncoming traffic. When a distinct honking pattern sent her eyes across the road, she nearly fell over.

Dad?

CHAPTER FIVE

Leaning into the driver's window, Lindsay kissed her father's cheek and beamed. "I'm so glad you're back. Does Mom know?"

"No darling. And you can't tell her. Not yet." Her heart sunk with the determination she saw in his eyes.

"But why not?"

"I can't tell you yet. Trust me?"

"Of course. I love you."

"Ditto, kiddo."

The phrase he'd used since she could remember brought the first real smile to her face in days. Dad could fix this.

"Where are you headed?" His gaze ran the length of the road that led to the farm.

"Gram's. Mom's clearing the house and helping with the mess with the farm. Have you heard about what's been going on?"

When he shook his head, she ran to the opposite side, yanked open the passenger door and slid in beside him, then she filled

him in on everything that had happened —
this time she left the Brandon part in.

"Oh," was all he said as he drove toward
the farm.

"You can fix this though, right Daddy?"

He tipped his head to the side and grimaced. "Linds, it's complicated. But I like
your organic farm idea. I have a friend who
runs a small land inspector's office. If
memory serves, he used to work with farms
and surveys. I don't know if he works with
organic farms, but I could ask."

Lindsay gripped his forearm and held her
breath. "Really? Could you?"

He shot her a sideways smile as he slowed.
"Sure. No problem. But I have to drop you
off here. I'm not ready to face your mom.
Or your grandparents."

Lindsay gazed at the farmhouse and nodded. But the chill that swept up Lindsay's
spine gripped her heart. "Don't you think
Mom deserves to know you're nearby? I
mean how long have you been here?"

"Not long."

"Where are you staying?"

"Doesn't matter. Can you keep my secret
or not?" The sideways glance he shot begged
for her silence.

"Fine."

His grin did nothing to convince her she'd

done the right thing by keeping such a secret from the others. She knew better than to lie to anyone — especially her mother. And to her, omission was akin to lying. "But for the record, I don't like it."

"I know. But it has to be this way. At least for a little while. If she knew I was here it would ruin everything."

"Dad, she thinks you stole money from her."

"What?"

"Well, you did clean out the accounts."

"Oh that. It'll all be cleared up in just a little while. I only need a few weeks."

"I hope you have a few weeks."

Her father's sigh hung as heavy as the June humidity when Lindsay leaned over and kissed her father's cheek. "Love you."

"Ditto, kiddo."

She shut the door and leaned over the open window before adding one last warning. "I hope you know what you're doing. Mom's going to be so ticked when she finds out you've been in Oakville without letting her know."

He nodded once before he pulled the car into a U-turn and headed back toward Oakville.

Her lunch, well-curdled and now acidic, tore at her insides. Fatherly espionage?

Really? What was next?

Only Andy's scratched face, remnants from the truck accident, pulled her from her reverie. "What's up, bud?" she called as she strolled within earshot.

"I've been looking all over for you." Andy met her and matched her steps toward the little white fence that bordered Gram's vegetable garden. Not tall enough to keep out a baby bunny, the fence was pure decoration, one of the only signs of Gramp's soft side. Maybe Gram had him wrapped around her finger. Lindsay couldn't figure out which.

"Are you listening to me?"

"Huh? Oh sorry. Guess all the stress is finally getting to me."

"Yeah, well, join the club." Andy held the screen door open, but let it bang against the frame, raising Gram's eyes from the puzzle she and Gramps were assembling on the coffee table. "Sorry, Gram."

Gram tsk'd and returned to her puzzle, but not before giving him a wink.

"I was telling you about the organic stuff I found online." Andy led the way down the hall toward their rooms.

"Online? How'd you get online? They don't even have a computer here."

When Andy shoved his bedroom door

162

wide, an open laptop rested atop the quilted spread.

"But, how?"

Andy shrugged. "My dad packed it in my stuff."

"And the Internet?"

Andy's hand plucked a small card from the side of the computer. Wireless.

"Man, I love your dad right now." As she plopped onto the bed, she noticed a shadow cross Andy's face. "You okay?"

With a wave of his hand, he dismissed her question and keyed up a couple web sites he'd bookmarked. "Look at this. We can have the farm certified as long as we meet all these requirements." Andy sat up a little bit straighter as he smiled like a kid on Christmas Eve.

She read down the lengthy list before she whistled low. "Do you see that price tag?" she asked, tapping the screen.

"Yeah, but check this out." A couple strokes more brought her to the certification regulations — the exceptions page. Midway from the top, in black and white, sat a sweet gift from God. "No way. If we sell less than five thousand dollars' worth of product all we need to do is stick with the organic practices?"

Andy sat up a little bit straighter. Lindsay

sighed. "Well, that's a gift."

"Yah. That just leaves us with seeds and other farm stuff we might need. Dad would probably front us the money if we promised to pay it back."

"Oh my gosh. I knew we could count on him!"

Giggling, she studied the other requirements listed on the screen. "What we need to verify is this treatment section. The ground cannot have been fertilized or received pesticide treatments that are chemically based in the last three years."

"Is that a problem?"

"I don't know. Want to find out?"

Slapping the laptop shut, Andy took two strides to the door and headed down the hall. Lindsay's smaller stride couldn't keep up, so by the time she arrived in the living room, he had their grandparents captivated with his story. Grandpa's eyes seemed to glow with excitement. He even smiled — lopsided, but broad.

"Nesson . . ."

Gram placed her hand on his forearm gently. "What about Mr. Nelson, dear?"

"Nesson's equipment."

"By golly, you're right. Lindsay. Andy. Our next-door neighbor, Mr. Nelson, has all the equipment you'd need to till, seed, and harvest any number of crops. And what he doesn't have, I'm sure the co-op would be willing to loan out just this once."

Lindsay's brow dipped as she tried to figure out how Gram read Grampa's mind like that. And Andy's eyes grew as wide as Gram's yarn balls.

"I can't use that equipment, Gram. And now that you mention it —" Lindsay swallowed hard. "We didn't even think about the actual farming part. All I've done is help pick beans."

A mix between a cackle and a cough burst from Gramp's chair. Only the twinkle in his eye told Lindsay he wasn't seizing. He laughed at her.

A shaky finger pointed her way as a tear clung to the side of his face. "Not you. You." This time he pointed at Andy, whose eyes grew wider — as if that was humanly possible.

"Oh no. Are you kidding? Look what I did to your truck. Now you want me to drive some tractor or something? No way."

"It's easy." Gram added. "Even I did it when all the children were grown and gone. If you're only planning on tilling the back meadow, you can have that cleared and seeded by the end of next week. No problem."

"But I have no idea how to run those." Panic began to creep around Lindsay's brain and it sucked all the hope she rode moments before.

"Don't worry. You'll want to plant when the season's right." Gram smiled brightly.

"What do you need?" Grandpa seemed to sober as he stared at her with a clarity she hadn't seen since she'd arrived.

"Well, we need seeds and whatever else you need to plant stuff. We figure we can hit up Uncle Art for those funds."

Grandpa's shaky hand rose to his brow and rubbed his forehead.

"What? What did I say?" Lindsay glanced from Gram whose shoulders shook and eyes looked to be on the verge of hysteria.

"Nothing honey. It's just your city-side is showing."

"Huh?"

"Let Grandpa and me take care of the farming supplies. Andy can do the tilling and planting with the help of Mr. Nelson and maybe we can persuade your dad to help out, eh?" Gram glanced at Andy, but her hopeful look didn't mirror the frown Andy sent to his shoes.

"I'll take care of the business end." Lindsay jumped in eager to recover a bit of that elusive hope from earlier. "There's book work to be done. We're at a bit of a disadvantage since we can only raise five thousand from the crop sales and that's only if Uncle Art agrees to buy the seeds."

"Seed."

"What, Gramps?"

Gram shot Grampa a smirk as she patted his arm. "Nothing dear. Continue."

"Oh-kay, we'll have some expenses, but I think I can cover some of that with odd jobs this summer."

"I can work a bit longer at the church to chip in if you'd like." Cheery and hopeful were not words Lindsay associated with Andy the last two days, but it fit his demeanor at the moment.

"That would be wonderful," Lindsay said. "But that still leaves such a huge deficit."

"Otto." Gram seemed to be discussing something with Grandpa without using a single word. Just the look in their eyes spoke as he nodded and she smiled. "Since you two are working so hard to raise the lion share of those darned taxes, then your grandpa and I will cover the last thousand. I guess if you all care so much, then we have to make it right. Oakville can't be allowed to take our — no, your — land."

"What?" Lindsay shrieked. "Really?"

Gram nodded. "If you two are willing to

work that hard for this farm, then I suppose it's worth paying that Hiriam Bakersfield so we can keep it in the family."

Lindsay yanked Andy off the edge of the table and spun him around — pushed him more or less. "Wha-hoo. We're really going to do this."

Early Monday morning Lindsay headed toward the town of Bakersfield's office to apply for the necessary organic permits or at least learn a bit more about them. She parked the truck in the only spot left. Not that the offices were busy, but they shared the small lot with the local vet. She cringed when she noticed the black SUV in the next stall. An SUV with Illinois tags. Whether the shudder that followed her discovery came from disgust or something else, she couldn't decide, which frustrated her even more.

Swinging the large glass doors wide, Lindsay entered the structure and took her place in line — directly behind Brandon. His voice reached her first, loud and syrupy. Turning her shoulder to them, Lindsay peeked beneath her bangs. Brandon stood with his elbow on the counter. He leaned on his side so he could watch the comings and goings of the office lobby, Lindsay suspected. And although he smiled and allowed the farm girl behind the counter to babble, his eyes seemed to scan the room continuously. Until they rammed into her.

With his mouth frozen in mid-word, his cheeks took on a red glow, which sent a thrill through Lindsay. *Pull it together, Lindsay Murphy.* She squared her shoulders and faced him. "Excuse me, I need to talk to —" Glancing down at the nameplate, Lindsay tried to slow the maniacal tread of her heart. "To Sharon. Are you two almost finished?"

Brandon's eyebrows rose as he stepped back and waved her forward.

"Thank you." Lindsay laid the note from her grandfather on the counter; annoyed that Brandon seemed to have no intention of leaving the area much less the office.

Eye candy shouldn't stay on the shelf that long.

"I need to find this information for my grandfather," she said tapping the note.

"Why on earth does he need the Ag tax variance and the Organic Farm Bureau pamphlet? He's not gonna farm again is he?" The tap-tap-tap of her pen sent a wave of heat to Lindsay's face.

Wonderful. A busy body. Just wonderful!

"Do you have those pamphlets?"

"Of course, but if your family is planning on farming what's left of their land, they're gonna need it rezoned."

"Rezoned? Why?"

"Well, after the last chunk sold, the property was rezoned R-2. I've heard they're hoping to develop that area soon." The last tidbit was for Brandon's benefit, but Lindsay would have none of it.

"And that means —" Her voice rose.

"It's zoned residential. No farming."

"Who in the world did that?" The heat from her cheeks flared in her ears and throbbed with the beat of her pulse.

"Hold on." Dropping her pen to the keyboard, Sharon punched a few buttons on her dinosaur of a desktop and handed Lindsay a printed sheet. The Chairman's signature entitling the town's decision told her all she needed to know.

"Hiriam. This can't be legal." Lindsay waved the sheaf in front of Sharon's nose like an oriental fan.

"I don't know anything about that. All I know is that you'll need to have that property rezoned if you want to farm it for anything other than yourselves."

"How do I do that?"

"Petition the board. They meet in a couple weeks."

"A couple weeks? I have to go to committee to work my own land? You have to be kidding."

"Be that as it may, you'll need to speak with the board. Now, if you'll excuse us, I believe Mr. Calloway still had business to conduct." The pitiful smile she flittered his way rang of desperation.

She's way too old for him. What is she thinking? Lindsay took a step back and glanced over her shoulder. She meant to send Brandon a scowl, but instead she lost herself in the softness of his eyes.

Without shifting his gaze, Brandon excused himself from Sharon and took a step toward Lindsay. "I'm sorry about that. Is there anything I can do to help?"

Brow furrowed, Lindsay sucked in a deep breath. "Help? You want to help me keep the family farm?"

"Is that what you're doing? Trying to raise funds to pay the taxes?"

Lindsay nodded.

With one hand outstretched and the other against the small of her back, Brandon led her toward the parking lot. "Lindsay, I'm not heartless. Whether it's your farm or the next isn't for me to determine. Besides we were told the farm was available."

Her back tingled with the electricity his

fingers sent to her spine, but his soft tone made her lean toward him. *Got. To. Get. My. Head. Together.*

"But it is for you to deny. You could refuse to get involved, couldn't you?" A straw. A lifeline?

"What difference would that make? Oakville will still annex the property. Don't you want someone you know to do the right thing with the development?"

I don't know you!

"Please don't do this to them — to me." Lindsay didn't intend to weave her fingers around his suit lapel any more than she intended to step close enough to smell the Irish spring soap that lingered on his skin.

Instead of stepping back, Brandon wrapped his fingers around hers as he stared straight to her soul. His voice lowered as he held her captive. "I'm not breathing down anyone's neck, yet."

As the last word sunk in, Lindsay unwound her fingers from his suit coat, but he wouldn't let them go.

"Sorry." Though her voice squeaked like a mouse, the word did the trick.

Brandon stepped back and dropped his arms to his sides. "Look Lindsay, we — C&D — need this project to go through."

"Why?"

Brandon sucked in a ragged breath. "If I can't make this project fly, our company is going to take a major hit. I can't go into it right now, but trust me. I have to make this work."

His phone buzzed in his pocket until he whipped it out and tinkered with the screen. An easy smile replaced the care she swore she saw a moment before. "You're a bright woman, Lindsay. A Summa Cum Laude graduate from Chicago University should be able to find your family's solution. Perhaps it won't."

"Wait. What? How did you know that?" When she took a step forward, he took a step back and raised his hands as a barrier between them.

"Just reading the latest edition of the Courier. Your picture was all over the front page. Bakersfield is quite proud of their big-town postgraduate. As they should be."

Right. Proud. A lot of good her fancy awards and graduate status did her now. She still ended up jobless, penniless, and soon-to-be homeless. But he did have a point. She could figure this out. All she needed was a little ingenuity and creativity. "Yah. Thanks."

"Anytime."

Lindsay told him good bye and slipped

into her grandma's "get-a-round" car, when a fledgling idea sprung to mind. It was ridiculous for certain, but wild enough to work. If he was game.

Opening her door, Lindsay scanned the parking lot hoping he hadn't escaped yet. When she spotted him dodging parked cars with his nose buried in his cell, she leaped from her door and jogged over to him.

"Brandon," she huffed.

Startled but composed, he turned. "Couldn't bear to be away from me? Really, Lindsay. What will folks say?"

The invitation poised on the tip of her tongue stuck like glue as she gritted her teeth. "That you're delusional? Seriously."

He grinned and reached up to tuck a wayward tendril behind her ear. It was all she could do to remember how to breathe. Clearing her throat, Lindsay reminded herself of the last time she got involved with a Chicago hotshot.

The plan — that's what this was about. Saving the farm. "Come to dinner, tonight." The words came fast and stilted and she wished she could suck them back in. "I mean, dinner with my family. On the farm. So you can see why we love it. Everyone will be there. It's not a date or anything. Just get to know them. You'll see."

Brandon leaned back and chuckled. "You want me to come to your grandparents' house for dinner?"

Lindsay stretched to her full five-foot, four-inch frame and crossed her arms over her chest. "Come or not, it's your choice," she said, sounding bored and every bit as pompous as he had. Bait cast.

With a flick of her hair and a spin on her heels, she headed back in the direction of her getaway car. "Dinner's at six," she called over her shoulder.

If she knew anything about men, she knew Brandon would be at dinner.

CHAPTER SIX

Grandmother's clock had just finished chiming when Brandon rapped on the door. Lindsay took a deep breath and sent her mother a be-nice glance before she opened it wide.

In a navy tee and jeans, he looked relaxed, normal almost. But Lindsay knew better. Underneath that athletic build beat the heart of a potentially ruthless businessman. Holding a bouquet of white roses, he flashed his Hollywood smile and leaned down to whisper in her ear. "You look stunning."

Stunning. In capris and an old blouse she'd had since her undergrad years? *Either he's terribly sweet or just terrible.* She slid a slow smile in place and stepped back to welcome him in — without adding the quip that sat on her tongue. Instead, she said, "Thank you."

Once inside, he handed the roses to Gram and slid into an easy discussion with Uncle

Art. By dessert, Lindsay noted the vein on the side of her mother's head beginning to throb. Her mom had barely added a word all night and she nearly ran to the kitchen once the food had been eaten. Never had Lindsay seen anyone so excited to clean the dishes before. She made a mental note to bug her mom later, but right now there were bigger fish to fry.

"So where are you staying?" Gram asked Brandon.

Lindsay returned her attention to the man beside her, leaning her elbow on the table and her chin in her palm.

"Well, I had been staying in East Bend, but the drive was killing me. Fortunately I bumped into the father of a former college mate, Jack Nelson. He offered to let me stay in Dan's room for the summer."

Lindsay's fork rattled against the Corelle. "Next door? You're staying next door?"

Brandon turned toward her and she swore he wore more sneer than smile. "Yup. So if you ever need anything, you can just holler out your window. At least that's what Mr. Nelson says."

While Gram asked Brandon about college and Dan, Lindsay considered the implications of his room and board. Next door? Steps away? All the time? Like some crazed stalker? What did he do at night, use binoculars to make sure they didn't ruin his future property? And Gram. Sitting there chatting with the enemy as if he was her new best friend. She even offered him a second piece of Mom's chocolate layered cake, which he refused, patting his trim belly. As if he ever needed to watch his weight. He probably spent the mornings jogging the perimeter of her farm. At least Andy had the good sense to leave the table and take his cake with him.

"Earth to Linds, dear." Gram's hand swam before her face.

"Huh?"

Brandon leaned closer. "I asked if you wouldn't mind showing me the pond. Your Grandmother says it's the most beautiful part of the farm, though I think she's wrong on that assumption." His pointed remark and steady gaze missed no one as all eyes turned her way.

Heat flooded her face like a lava wave. Escape. She needed to escape. "I should really help my mom with the dishes." But Gram beat her when she rose from the table with the dexterity of someone half her age. Then she waved her napkin toward the door. Lindsay looked to Uncle Art for backup, but he caught Gramp's attention with a new line of conversation. Something about the Packers' training camp.

"Fine." She threw her napkin on her half-eaten cake and rose. *Traitors. Each and every one of you.*

They walked along the edge of the glen in silence for about twenty minutes before Brandon spoke. "Your family is sweet."

Lindsay slid a careful glance toward his tan cheekbones. He kept his eyes on the setting sun and his step steady. "Yes, they are." As they neared a line of cattails that indicated they had arrived, the sun glinted off the water casting pink and rosy hues as though a painter drew his brush in reckless abandon across the sky. She led him to Gram's glider — the two-seater she had Gramps place by the edge of the pond so Gram could watch the sunset in comfort. Lindsay slipped her shoes off and curled her feet beneath her as Brandon set the rocker in motion. Again he pulled out his cell and punched in a text. Before he tucked it into his hand, she caught the texter's name — Rebecca.

A girl from home? A girlfriend? Don't be foolish, who he spends his time doting over is none of my business.

With an upward tilt to her chin, Lindsay watched the sun recede and though the night air cooled, she ran her finger beneath her collar and fanned her neck with her hand.

"I can see why you love this place." His voice lowered as Lindsay turned and searched his face for any sign of sarcasm or insincerity. An intense gaze bore through her, melting what little resolve she had left. *Girlfriend,* her inner voice whispered. *Remember what's-her-name.*

His fingers brushed against her cheek as he toyed with her hair. "But I still disagree with your Gram. The pond pales next to your beauty."

Flinching back, Lindsay narrowed her eyes. "What about Rebecca's? Is she as beautiful?"

Brandon blinked. "My Aunt Rebecca? I suppose. Why?"

"Oh." Smooth. Lindsay stared at the horizon. "No reason. Just curious. Heard she was a looker. That's all."

"Really? Huh. Didn't know anyone up here knew Aunt Becky. This is a small town."

With a tug to her restrictive collar, Lindsay smirked. "Yeah. One filled with busy bodies. Sorry."

"No, that's all right. I don't mind. Besides when you're not trying to bite my head off, I rather like telling you about my family."

Her eyes locked with his as a million warning bells rang in time with the pond frogs. Step away. But she couldn't. Not even Mark looked at her like this man did. As if he'd drown without her.

He leaned down and slid his hand around the nape of her neck as her breath caught in her throat.

"Whacha guys doing?" Andy ran through the meadow a little too eagerly. His obnoxious grin told her that Andy had seen it all and she'd never hear the end of this.

"Nothing. Watching the sunset. That's all." Barefoot, she rose and stepped away from the gliding rocker. From Brandon. The air cooled the second she left him and she couldn't decide if that was good or bad. She kept her eyes on her cousin's back, thanking him and wishing he'd never come.

Andy picked up a handful of pebbles and started tossing them into the water. Each plunk sent a dozen frogs clamoring for safer waters.

"Can you skip 'em?" Brandon's voice neared the edge of the pond and sent Lindsay clamoring for the safety of the bull rushes.

"Yeah. Any dork can do that."

Lindsay thought she saw a pink stain on Brandon's cheek.

"Not this dork," he said. "Teach me?"

Brandon picked up a handful of pebbles and plunked one into the water. It cast a small ripple, but sunk after hitting the surface. Andy fingered the rocks in his hand, chose one, and sent it skittering across the water.

"One. Two. Three. Four. Four skips. See? Easy."

Lindsay snickered at the edge in Andy's tone. But she swallowed her giggle when Brandon glanced back.

Turning back to the water's edge, Brandon tossed a rock wide where it landed in the midst of a white lily patch. "Real easy."

Lindsay returned to the glider and watched the two toss rocks for nearly an hour. Warmed by the easy conversation and the kindness Brandon showed Andy, Lindsay leaned her head against the back rail of the swing and yawned. She never would have guessed the evening would turn out like this and she surprised herself at how she didn't want it to end.

It was dark by the time the boys stopped, but Andy had thought to bring a camping lantern to light the return path. More like Gramps's idea, but Andy willingly took the praise Brandon offered for good thinking ahead. When they neared the back porch,

Andy waved and took the steps two at a time. As the door slammed behind him, they were left alone with the lantern and the crickets. Neither spoke a word as they faced the porch. Brandon didn't move toward his car. And oddly enough, she didn't want him to.

"There's one more place I'd like to show you. If you have the time." She placed her fingertips on his forearm which he covered with his own. Unsettled, she pulled them back and held the lantern before her as she traced the well-worn path to the west side of the barn.

His footfalls echoed in the darkness — near enough to bump into, should she turn around. She thought she heard him say, "I'm all yours," but she couldn't be sure with the rush of her blood drowning out every noise of the night.

"So farm girls really do like to roll in the hay." When she looked back he nodded toward the graying wood of the barn door and winked.

She rolled her eyes and picked up her pace.

"I wouldn't know anything about that." She rounded the corner of the barn and kept walking on the dirt path lit by her lantern. "We have straw."

His chuckle brought another warm rush to her face. She'd better stop doing that or she'd need her mother's high blood pressure medicine before the week was out. And if Brandon noticed, the last thing she needed was him thinking she fawned all over him. What she needed was to focus on showing him why their farm needed to be left alone.

"There." She shone the light on a small cemetery no more than two rows deep and five rows across. "This is the rest of my family. My great-grandpa Albert. My great-grandma Rose. Their son, William. My Uncle Otto."

"You have a family plot?"

She nodded, holding the lantern higher so it illuminated the second row. Their stones were older, worn down by years of weather and mourning hands. Some were crooked, having settled deeper on one side than the other. Still others stood proud and square.

"My Gram comes out here every June second and plants a fresh annual garden for Uncle Otto." Lindsay focused the beam of light on the newest stone. At its base, violets and impatiens rested and waited for the next day's sun. "It would kill her to change that." She found his eyes and begged him to see what she saw. Feel what she felt.

184

Brandon sighed. "Lindsay, you don't understand."

"What? What don't I understand?"

"If this fails, C&D will go under. Not even my dad knows how bad it's gotten. Oakville is our last chance to get back in the black." He stared off into the darkness until she rested her fingers on his shoulder. Then he turned to her with a pleading look on his face. "I've prayed. God knows I've tried to figure some other way. Aww! I wish I could help you, Lindsay. Really I do. But I can't."

"Maybe if we gave God more time."

"I don't have time, that's the thing. If my dad finds out — I don't see any other way."

Panic chilled her bones. "You're still going through with it? Leveling our home? None of this persuaded you otherwise? Not my grandparents or the sunset or Andy or this?" She swept her hand toward the stones wishing they would cry out with more wisdom than she had. Anything to change this man's heart. Tears choked what few words she did think of. But only three squeaked out. "How could you?"

She heard his calls as she dashed back to the safety of her home. She stumbled no less than twice on the way back and she hoped he fared worse on his trip home in the dark. Hope he gets lost forever out there.

As she tripped up the back steps she cried out to God. *Forgive me. I don't want him harmed; I just want him to understand. You understand don't you?*

Only the crickets sang in reply.

CHAPTER SEVEN

June turned into July and the heat rose to record-breaking levels. But Mr. Nelson managed to turn the meadow into neat rows of green stubble, hungry to grow faster than the weeds. Andy helped from time to time, but Lindsay noticed a distinct disappointment in her Uncle Art whenever the boy neared the farming equipment. Since the church demanded most of his time anyway, Andy had persuaded Mr. Nelson to finish the initial planting provided Andy would help Mr. Nelson paint his barn before he left for school.

Since Brandon had returned to Chicago, Lindsay could focus on encouraging those shoots to thrive. And keep an eye on her mom's new interest in Josh Calloway. An interest that gave Lindsay an uncomfortable nudge every time she caught her mom's interested glances and pinkening cheeks whenever that man came near. But even that paled compared to the discomfort Brandon brought around.

Seeing him sit two rows in front of her at church for the past few Sundays was painful enough. Not to mention the times he followed her down the aisle and out the front steps. As if she'd really have lunch with the enemy.

If only her first impression of him had been right. A pompous man she could toss aside without thinking twice, but Brandon? He didn't seem pompous anymore. Troubled, yes. Caring, at least toward her and Andy and even Mr. Nelson. But pompous? Ooh. She didn't need him living next door. It only confused matters.

Now that he'd moved back to Chicago, Uncle Art had talked the board into rezoning the property for hobby farming — perfect for what they needed. And Lindsay spent her days pinning flyers from East Bend to Milwaukee. So far she'd sold eight shares. Most because West Bend Appliance agreed to throw in a complimentary juicer slash peeler as a promotion. She shined her nails against her T-shirt. Slick business. She still had the knack. That left four shares to go. The time had come to use her Internet connections to beef up sales. It might mean shipping expenses, but if Uncle Art and

Andy finished fixing the truck soon enough, she could deliver the produce herself.

It was hardest to wait. Wait for share purchases. Wait for the plants to grow. Wait for God to work His miracle, which Lindsay didn't doubt would come, she just didn't know when. Or what form it would take. And with Pastor Mike telling her God's ways were not man's ways, well, her nerves were fried.

That afternoon, Lindsay decided to pull a few weeds. Gram always said gardening was therapeutic — it looked like work to Lindsay, but she promised to try it. Dragging a small wheel barrow to the edge of the meadow-turned-farm-field, Lindsay pulled on her gloves and knelt in the baked dirt. Gram told her to use a hoe, but that instrument did nothing but bite into her tennis shoes. Weed after weed flew either to the barrow or the pail by her knees. In time, thoughts of the farm shares and taxes melted away with the beat of the sun and the whir of the cicadas. In their place swam a tan face with melted-chocolate eyes. Eyes that seemed to see right through her.

Just last week, Lindsay caught him helping Gram's quilting cronies with their frames and bundles at the farmer's market. He'd laughed along with them as though he really cared. And when Esther told him about her feral cat that had eaten a field mouse and left the carcass on her linoleum, he sobered and nodded with interest. Esther was convinced her kitchen now bred the bubonic plague, but Brandon smiled reassuringly and offered to find just the right disinfectant to clear her kitchen from any threatening pathogens.

How could a man who offered such a kind-hearted act, turn around and take something so dear to her?

Dear to me?

Yes. Dear. What if she stayed on? Farm another season or two. Now that she'd done it once, she rather loved the feel of dirt under her nails and the sun on her back. And nothing beat driving a tractor through the countryside. No chance you could speed. Everything slowed to a manageable pace. Calming. Peaceful. Maybe she'd offer to buy the farm. On installment. That way Gram and Gramps could stay on and advise her. Yes. She could do that.

If Brandon didn't take the farm out from under them.

Forgive him.

As if the very breeze carried God's voice, she heard it again.

Forgive him.

"But he's trying to destroy our home. Our family."

Ephesians 4:32 came to mind, a verse she had memorized along with the fourth grade class she shepherded the year before. "Be kind to one another, tenderhearted, forgiving one another, as God in Christ forgave you."

"Even him?" she asked the sky.

"Even him, who?" His voice was soft and husky like a windblown kiss, but it slammed through her ears like a freight train's whistle.

"Brandon?"

He walked down the row and stopped when his shadow cooled her face. "In the flesh," he said, spreading his arms open wide and grinning like a fool. A stunningly handsome fool.

Flustered, Lindsay wiped her hair from her eyes and stared openly. The sun must have baked her good sense dry.

Brandon knelt one row in front of her and rested his chino-covered knees in the dirt. Without gloves, he pulled weed after weed, tossing them with ease into the bucket beside her. "Are you going to pull or sit there with your mouth open?"

Clamping her mouth shut, Lindsay rose with her bucket and dumped it in the barrow. How do you forgive someone like

191

Brandon? Someone who hasn't asked for it? Should she blurt it out? I forgive you. Just like that?

When Brandon walked up behind her, a fistful of thistles in hand and a grimace on his face, Lindsay couldn't bring herself to do it. Instead she said, "What are you doing here? I figured you'd be off to Chicago plotting the ruination of our family."

Brandon looked like she'd sucker-punched him. "Bit melodramatic, don't you think?"

"Perhaps." When a smirk lit his lips she wanted to slap it off, but instead she threw her pail in the barrow and grabbed the handles. "You're welcome to leave." Then she recalled the words of her Bible verse and groaned inwardly. Forgiveness would be easier if he weren't a part of it.

Exasperated more with herself than anything else, she slammed the barrow down and thrust her finger into his chest. "Why. Are. You. Here?"

Rubbing the spot she poked, he tossed a glance over the field. "I wanted to see how your farm was coming along."

"Really?" She narrowed her eyes and picked up the barrow again. This time she aimed the front wheel for his foot. "It's coming along fine. Peppers, tomatoes, and onions are all growing beautifully. Turns out, an organic make-your-own-salsa farm is just what the doctor ordered. We already have over half the money raised. You're not going to get this farm."

"Salsa farm?" His eyebrows arched in a curious manner. "Sounds delicious. I might have to buy a share."

"Buy a jar of pesos." She ran the wheel over his overly-shined Allen Edmonds and stomped off to the barn.

"But I like mine fresh and fiery."

Lindsay lowered the handles with great deliberation before she turned to face him. He'd followed her and stood no more than a step or two away.

"You confuse me to no end."

"Good. Then we're even." He crossed his arms over his chest and smiled.

Rubbing her forehead, Lindsay tried to capture a decent thought. "I confuse you?"

"Yes. One minute you invite me to dinner and to the pond. Then you bite my head off without hearing me out. I tell you my company is in dire straits and the responsibility of all those jobs lies in my hands and you seem bent on thinking this entire mess revolves around your family's farm as though I'm out to stick it to you. For fun. Yes, Lindsay Murphy, you confuse me."

She'd been wrong. It wasn't just Brandon

193

who needed forgiveness, it was her, too. Shame washed over her in waves heated by embarrassment. "I'm sorry." A mere whisper.

In one stride he covered the gap between them and tilted her head so she could meet his gaze. "That makes two of us. I'm so sorry. For my part — C&D's part in your misery. Can you forgive me?"

Nodding, Lindsay wore a lopsided grin. "If you can forgive me."

"Done."

Hovering inches above her, his lips curved into a delicious smile. His hand cupped her chin.

"Lindsay. Lindsay Murphy! Where are you girl?" Gram's voice cut through the summer heat like a river through the Grand Canyon. And darkened like the clouds gathering above.

Lindsay tipped her head down and giggled. "Sorry," she whispered again. Then she turned toward the barn and the direction of the house where Gram must be calling from. "In the field, Gram."

Before Gram rounded the barn, Brandon tipped his head and left her side. Some business matter or the other needed to be addressed, he'd said. It didn't matter anymore to Lindsay. Peace settled in her heart.

194

Brandon couldn't be the enemy. Not anymore. With the taxes paid, things would be different. She sensed a change more than knew it, but that was enough for now.

"Who was that I just heard?" Gram looking every minute of her seventy-some years as she stood at the barn's side door.

Concern filled her. "Are you okay, Gram?" Lindsay emptied the weeds into a black bag and parked the wheel barrow before she sat beside her on a blanket-covered bale. The barn was cool and smelled of dust and dirt. It once smelled of fine Holstein stock, but that had been years ago.

An odd look shadowed Gram's face, but it disappeared before Lindsay could name it. "I'm fine, darling. Just tired." Gram patted Lindsay's hand.

"Well, don't go getting sick on us. We need you too much."

"Yes, I know. It's been such a long day. Good, but long. Oh, I came out here to tell you Art sold three more shares while you were in the field."

"What?" Lindsay's hand flew to her mouth.

"Yup. A fellow from Milwaukee bought all three. Said he loved salsa and couldn't believe his luck when he saw your sign at his church. How many does that leave you with?"

"One, Gram. We only need to sell one more. I can't believe it."

Gram wakened a bit. "Well, one should be simple enough. Let me call a few of my quilting cronies. One of those old biddies should be able to pick up that last share. Goodness, they'll probably churn out enough salsa for the church picnic." Gram took her time standing. "Come to think of it, you'll probably end up having to till more ground next year. This is going to catch on, I tell you." She left the barn with a little more spring in her step.

"More?" Lindsay raised her eyes to the loft. "God, what are you doing? Every business door I knock on — You shut, but I till one field and it becomes more than I can handle."

A resounding peal of thunder shook dust from above. Lindsay glanced at her watch and figured it was time to stop anyway. Dodging golfball-size raindrops, Lindsay barged through the back door as Gram hung the phone back on the wall.

"You did it, Linds. Esther wants to buy the last share. They're all sold. You met your end of the bargain, so come Monday morning we'll march down to that town hall and pay the tax bill — as much as it sets my goat to pay that man."

"Oh Gram, that's wonderful." She threw her grimy arms around her grandmother and danced about the kitchen.

Dislodging herself, Gram stepped back and brushed her apron. "Easy now, I'm an old woman."

"Old my foot," Uncle Art said as he strolled into the room. "What's going on?" When Gram told him, he gave Lindsay a big hug and a kiss on the forehead. "You're like a fresh breath of air to this family, sweetheart." He turned to Gram. "We need to celebrate. Have a party."

Gram's head nodded with determination. "Wonderful plan. Call the pastor and have him send Andy home early. But tell him not to say a word. Let's make it a surprise for the boy. He's worked so hard, he deserves a bit of unexpected fun."

Plans took root as the clouds gathered outside and grew in intensity. Even the explosion of thunder seemed ready to celebrate the Hasmer Farm's win. Come someday soon, the farm would be theirs — free and clear. Maybe someday, hers.

CHAPTER EIGHT

Thunder and lightning bore down on the farm as if God himself threw them a party. But Lindsay knew better. The celebration had ended in a mess of frustration between Andy and Uncle Art. Andy hadn't taken to his father's interest in Dana London, but then again what kid would? Not that Dana carried any of the blame. She couldn't be kinder, but it had to be hard for a boy to lose his mom, and wonder if this stranger would try to fill her shoes. Lindsay's heart broke for her cousin, but what could she do?

Alone in the old farmhouse, Lindsay peeled the kitchen curtains back and tried to make heads or tails from the rain-blurred scenery. She wondered how Grandpa was. It had been an hour since Gram took him to the hospital to have his oxygen tank checked. The spare sat empty beside his recliner and the other seemed to have failed.

A flash of light called her back to the window. Despite the early hour, darkness followed the thick storm clouds making it hard to see to the barn.

It's going to be a doozy out there.

At least storms that violent didn't last long. As another boom rattled the window frames, she prayed the wind wouldn't bring the old oak's limbs down. The great branches swayed near the power lines that led to the house. Lindsay's gaze wandered toward her field of green that poked out from behind the barn and her heart stopped.

My crops!

All those onion shoots and thickening bushes of tomatoes. Would they survive? Hail began to fall, tinging against the glass pane. Hail could break her pepper plants, couldn't it? If Gram and Gramps were back from the hospital, they'd know. Lindsay ran from the house and stumbled over broken ice chunks the size of bouncy balls as she made her way toward the barn. Once inside, she searched frantically for something to cover the fledgling peppers. Boxes. Cartons. Pallets. Anything. But all she found were a pile of old horse blankets — moth-eaten and stiff.

Would that help?

She didn't know. She'd never come close

to farming before. If only Gram or Uncle Art were here. They'd know what to do. An explosive clap of thunder shook the barn and made the hair on her arms stand tall. Gathering the dusty blankets, Lindsay dashed for the back door — the one closest to her field. Outside the wind wiped her hair free from its rubber band, but the rain plastered it back against her cheeks. She trudged through the gale until she reached the field's edge.

Bent stalks of tomatoes and flattened pepper plants dotted the field for as far as she could see. But the onion patch was gone. Submerged beneath a small pond that had formed in the center of the old meadow.

She dropped the blankets and took off toward the onions. Gone. All gone. Not one spindly top could be seen above the knee-high water she stood in.

Lord. No. Please, no.

She reached through the ice-cold water and wrapped her fingers around a limp piece of growth. Tugging she freed the onion from the mud and held it to her heart.

What good would the blankets do if the onions fail?

Maybe I could harvest them. Dry them and include them in the boxes that way.

Lindsay sunk into the mud and water and

pulled at the stalks. She'd gathered an armful before she heard his voice.

"Lindsay!"

"I have to save them." *Pull. Pull. Pull.*

"Save what?" He crouched beside her, soaked to the core. Then he cradled her head in his hands and lowered his voice so it hung just above the cry of the wind. "You have to come inside." As if to prove his point, thunder punctuated his command. "Please. Stop. I'll help you tomorrow, but you have to get out of this storm."

She couldn't tell where her tears stopped and the rain began, either way his face hovered over hers. So close.

"Please," he said.

Lindsay's shoulders slouched as she dropped the wilted sprigs and sunk her knees deep in the mud.

"They win," she whispered.

Pulling her up by her forearms, Brandon shielded her from most of the hail as he led them back to the barn. Once inside, he pressed for an answer. "Win? Who wins?"

She sniffed. "Bakersfield. Hiriam. He wins. No one will want shares in a salsa farm that doesn't have all the ingredients. I'll have to refund the money. All the money. Checkmate. He wins." Her shoulders shook with the sobs that took over her body.

"Can't you find the money some other way?"

She turned wild eyes toward him. "No. There is no other way. I wouldn't have done this if there had been another option."

Brandon stroked his chin with a faraway stare as he walked over to an unused horses stall. "There might be another way."

"Really?" Hope flickered sending a warm rush through her rain soaked body.

"Yes really."

"But how?"

Brandon returned to her side and shook his head. "Can't tell you, yet. I have to see if I can work it out, but you'll be the first to know when everything is set."

Lindsay hugged him, like a drowning woman to a life vest. "Thank you."

"You're very welcome." Tipping her head up with a finger beneath her chin, he lowered his head until his lips brushed hers.

"Lindsay Murphy! What are you doing?" Her mother's anger echoed through the rafters.

Lindsay shoved against Brandon's chest and faced the flashing glare her mother shot them. "Mom?"

"Get away from that liar." Her mother pointed at him as though he had brought the plagues of God to Oakville.

Shock froze in Lindsay's gut like a greasy pizza. "Mom."

"Don't Mom me. That man knows this farm is perched on a goldmine and he's doing everything in his power to steal it from you. From all of us." Her mother stepped forward like an angered mother-elephant. "Don't dare deny it, Calloway. I just spoke to your father."

"But —"

"No buts. Get off our farm."

"What is this about?" Lindsay turned her eyes on Brandon and watched a flurry of emotions fly across his face.

His fingers wrapped around her biceps as he furrowed his brow. "Your mom is right. Your farm sits atop an untapped artesian spring. The reports confirmed it last week. If tapped and bottled, the opportunities are endless."

Lindsay shrugged free from his grip as the all-to-familiar icy feeling snaked from her gut to her heart. "So what was all this? Get on my good side so I'll sell — we'll sell you the land ourselves? Then you'll sell it to your cronies at C&D? Brandon?"

When he didn't answer right away, she reached for her mother's hand and yanked her toward the farm house door. "How could you?" she cried before she slipped through the wooden door.

"Lindsay. Give me a —" The slam of the door cut him short and shredded her last nerve.

"Honestly, Lindsay. I thought you were wiser than that. Kissing that man. What were you thinking. Don't trust a Calloway. Just ask your father." Her mother droned as they walked from the barn to the farmhouse. Even going as far as following Lindsay past Uncle Art and Andy who stepped back looking perplexed. Her mom trailed her to her bedroom, bent on imparting words of Calloway wisdom.

Resting her forehead against the hand she placed on the door frame, Lindsay moaned. "I'm sorry. I had no idea. Look, Mom, I'm really whipped. Do you mind if we finish this conversation in the morning? What I really want right now is a hot shower and some dry clothes."

Her mother stroked her forearm. "Of course, sweetheart. I'll be in the kitchen if you need me."

"Thanks mom." She planted a kiss on her mother's forehead and closed the door as mom walked away.

What had she been thinking? That he'd changed? Brandon went from arrogant businessman bent on buying her apparently priceless family farm to sweetest man this side of Chicago? *I must be nuts.* Not even Mark peeled back her skin and left her so raw with emotion. Not even Mark. What was she saying? Comparing the feelings she had for Mark to those she had for Brandon. She'd loved Mark. But Brandon? No. Did she love Brandon?

"No. No way," she told the framed faces on the wall. Relatives, all of them, although their names escaped her. Each stared back at her as if to confirm her fear. "But it can't be."

CHAPTER NINE

Saturday passed in a haze of depression and dark foreboding clouds. More storms were headed their way, but what did it matter with nothing but a pond for an onion field? Surely that crop's destruction was already complete. To make matters worse, she seemed to be the only one who cared. Her mom grew more distracted by the minute and Uncle Art couldn't be found. At least not until an hour ago. Now Lindsay hovered over the freezer searching for a frozen pizza which she doubted anyone would eat. Uncle Art's voice drifted into the kitchen. And if she knew her cousin, the silence from his side didn't bode well, either.

Ah well. When it rained it poured. Or so the saying went. Her fingers collided with the frozen disk she knew to be her target and twenty minutes later, Lindsay headed down the farmhouse hall to call Andy to dinner. When she barged into his room after knocking again and again, her breath caught in her throat. His room lay trashed with pillows thrown about and the screen from his window lying against the wall. Lindsay dialed her cell and rambled the news to her uncle.

"Stay put Linds. I'll start looking around, but call if you hear anything. I'll do the same." His voice faltered before he finished. "Don't worry, I'm sure he's fine."

But she worried anyway.

For four and a half hours, Lindsay worried. She wrapped up the uneaten pizza, cleaned the kitchen and vacuumed the living room. Still she'd heard nothing. Had they forgotten to call? What was Andy thinking, taking off like that? She rang Gram's cell, but it went to voicemail. Maybe her grandparents were on their way home.

Walking the vacuum to her room, Lindsay tossed a couple wayward socks on her bed and lost herself in the noise of the machine. She flicked the switch off and jumped as her door rattled beneath a tap, tap, tap.

Andy's smiling face filled the door frame when she yanked the door wide. With a sigh and a slump of her shoulders, she pulled him into a hug. "Andy."

His face looked flushed, but he seemed in

207

good condition. "You look awful. Are you okay?"

Releasing a huff she stepped back and planted her fists on her hips in her best Gram imitation. "I should be asking you the same question."

"Yeah. I'm fine. Ella got in a bit of trouble, but I saved her." The smile that filled his face and consumed his eyes grew irresistible.

Lindsay invited him to sit down. "Really. Is that why you took off? What kind of trouble? Is she all right? You should've told me."

Chuckling, Andy plunked down on her bed and leaned back on his elbows. "Yup. She's fine. No major damage. She's so amazing." His eyes wandered to the window and filled with a gauzy look.

Lindsay wandered over to the chair opposite him and nudged his foot with her own when she sat. "Uh huh. Amazing. Sounds to me like you like her. As in like, like." Despite her own emotional state, Lindsay managed to raise a teasing smile for him.

Which he returned with a blush. "Yeah. I really do. I didn't want to fall for her, 'cause she could be so irritating, you know? Man that girl could annoy me more than anyone

I know — she even beat my dad." He tipped his head toward the window and sighed. "Between you and me, I think that's what clued me in. I started missing it when she wasn't bugging me."

Andy had it bad. Then again, his story sounded a lot like hers and Brandon's. But how could she care about someone so callous? So . . .

Andy's hand waved in front of her face. "Earth to Linds. Where are you, girl?"

"Lost. That's where."

"Talk." Raising on one elbow, Andy narrowed his eyes.

"You know Brandon Calloway?"

Andy nodded and rolled his wrist to keep her talking.

"Well, for the longest time, I thought I hated him. He threatened our family heritage."

Andy held up his hand to stop her. "Hold on, 'cuz. He never did that. Oakville threatened to take the place. Brandon's company happened to be the developer they brought in. That's not his fault."

"It could be. That's the part I don't get. He's been all over this property, taking notes and carrying sample things around. Then I find out we're sitting on top of an artesian spring."

"A what?" Andy wrinkled his nose.

"I don't know. Something C&D is willing to develop for a lot of money." Lindsay flopped back against the soft curve of the Queen Anne chair.

"So you think Brandon wanted to take the land for the water rights?"

"That's the thing. Mom thinks so, and on the surface it looks like it. But right before Mom caught us in the barn, Brandon tried to tell me he had some plan. A plan he hoped would save the farm."

Andy moved his elbow to his bent leg and inched forward. "No way."

"Oh yeah. He even said he'd help find a way to pay the tax bill since we lost the onion crop."

Shaking his head, Andy looked puzzled. "What? The onions are gone?"

"Yah. It's a swamp out there."

"Sorry."

Lindsay threaded her fingers through her hair and gazed out the window. "Why would he help us save the farm if he wanted to buy it? It doesn't make sense." She turned to study Andy. "Does it?"

"I don't know. Why don't you ask him?"

Shaking her head hard enough to snap it off, Lindsay balked. "Oh no. I couldn't do that."

"Why not?" Andy stood up and strode toward the door. "Then you could ask him what he really did. Either that or you're gonna spend an awful lot of time wondering. I'm just saying . . ." In two seconds he disappeared around the corner, leaving her alone with her twisted thoughts.

Lord, now what?

As Lindsay made her way to the kitchen the next morning, the sun beat through every window as though it mocked her depression.

"Mornin'," Gram announced when Lindsay stopped near the kitchen's archway.

Lindsay shuffled her slippered feet over to her spot at the kitchen table and plopped into the hard chair.

Gram placed a ceramic mug of steaming liquid before her. "Someone woke up on the wrong side of the bed this morning."

Gram's smile rubbed Lindsay the wrong way. And the mug. The "make-everyday-a-happy-day" mug made her want to break something. With a deep breath, Lindsay reminded herself that Gram had been gone. She didn't know.

With a cup in her own hand, Gram blew across the top and sat across from her. "Want to tell me about it?"

Lindsay huffed, just this side of disrespect. "Where do I start? The onion field is gone. Obliterated. Who wants salsa without onions?" Lindsay flung her arms wide and groaned.

"You're right about one thing, if that meadow doesn't drain soon, those onions are goners."

"I'm going to have to return all the money." She picked up her cup and swallowed a scalding mouthful. "Where does that leave us? The taxes are due next week and I'm back to square one."

Gram stared into her cup.

"Gram?"

When her eyes rose to meet Lindsay's, there were tears collecting along the lower rims, but fire flashed, nonetheless. "You've worked so hard. You all have. Grandpa and I are so grateful, but this is our fight, not yours." She reached across the table and patted Lindsay's hand. "I wish we could do more. Maybe last month we could have, but the thousand we promised once you raise the first five for the taxes was a stretch considering Grandpa's mounting medical bills. Medicare doesn't even begin to cover the expenses." Then, as if renewed by indignation, she planted her fist on her side and hrmpf'd. "Ethel said we fell into some donut hole. Don't have a clue what that means, other than we have to pay out the nose."

Lindsay worried over the redness that filled her Gram's face, so she patted her hand and stretched a smile over her tired lips. "Don't worry Gram, I'll find another way."

"Another way for what?" her mother asked as she strolled through the back door. "And what in the world are the two of you doing in your pajamas? You'll be late for church."

Lindsay jumped forward like a schnauzer stung by a bee. "Mom! What about your fundraising connections? You know the people who helped you raise all that money for the library a few years back. Maybe they could — I don't know — organize a community benefit or something."

Grabbing the coffee pot, her mom poured herself a cup, sipped from the mug, and then turned to face them. "The Stanton Group? No. They only work with non-profits. Why? I thought you had everything covered."

"Have you seen the field?"

When her mother shook her head, Lindsay rolled her eyes. "Didn't you see it last night?"

Mom and Gram exchanged glances.

"Sorry, sweetheart. I've been a little distracted. Why don't you just fill me in?"

Lindsay rambled through the story once more, banging her mug against the table with more gusto this time. When she finished, Mom rubbed her temples with her fingertips.

"Well, darlings," Gram rose to rinse her cup once the story ran its course, "none of that worrying is going to do any of us a bit of good. Get up, both of you. We better get that boy up too. And you need to get dressed, Lindsay girl, or your mom will be right. We'll be later than the Bakers to church. We don't want that, now."

Lindsay nodded and deposited her cup alongside Gram's. "I don't think we'll have any problem getting Andy to go to church this morning. Or any morning, for that matter." She sidled up between her mom and Gram.

"And why would that be?" her mother asked with one eyebrow raised.

Lindsay sidestepped them both before hesitating under the arch. "Oh I think you know."

When the distinct odor of teen boy cologne floated into the room before Andy did, Lindsay couldn't help but snicker.

"What's so funny?" Andy asked.

"Nothing, dear. Sit down and I'll get you something to eat." Gram whipped out a frying pan and the carton of eggs. Then she placed a full glass of milk before Andy. "P-ew! What is that stink?" Ducking down the hall, Lindsay swallowed a giggle. At least life would go on. Whether it would be here on the farm or somewhere else.

CHAPTER TEN

There he sat — two rows up and four heads to the right. With his arm resting over the back edge of the bench, Brandon appeared relaxed. Relaxed, of all things. As if he didn't have a care in the world. If she stared hard enough perhaps his hair would catch fire and then he wouldn't be so distractingly handsome — just bald.

Lindsay Murphy!

With a shake of her head she attempted to rid her mind of his broad shoulders and replace his image with Pastor Mike's sermon. But the hum of the ceiling fan and the swish of Esther's paper fan didn't help her concentration one bit.

Besides, what use was that? She caught the shift of Brandon's head and met the gaze he sent her way. With lightning speed, she brought her eyes forward and fanned at the warmth that flooded her face.

Uncle Art shifted beside her as he crossed

his legs and nudged Andy in the side. Didn't look like Andy would win the sermon quiz later, either. Staring like a daydreamer, Andy kept a love-sick smile on his face which widened every time Ella turned around to peek at him. Lindsay rolled her eyes before she checked the back of ratfink's head again. Only it wasn't the back he presented. Brandon had pivoted in his bench and craned his neck until his glance collided with hers. Only this time neither looked away.

Lindsay lost all track of time. How long had they stared at each other? Seconds? Minutes? She swallowed hard and lowered her gaze to her lap as she imagined tomorrow's wagging church tongues.

How much longer could one church service last, anyway? When the last hymn died, Lindsay mumbled an excuse to Gramps, slid past her mother's childhood friends and sprinted for the door. She shook the pastor's hand with a brevity that surprised her as she rushed through the doors and into the stifling July heat.

"Where's the fire?" Brandon called from the air-conditioned cabin of his SUV which he idled feet from the church's front door. How'd he do that — escape before she had?

"None of your business." She wasn't

ready. Not to confront. Or forgive. Or whatever God wanted her to do. She just wasn't ready. So she stomped down the three front steps, around the side of the church, and down the back path that led toward the little Suchar house and the forest beyond.

"Lindsay! Slow down."

Behind her a car door slammed shut and the crunch of gravel grew louder. When his fingers encircled her elbow and spun her around, she yanked her arm free, though he barely held it. Every sleepless moment darkened her scratchy eyes and cranky mood. She'd listened last night and what did that get her? More confused, that's what. "Leave me alone."

"Please let me explain."

With her hands planted on her hips, she squared off with him. "Explain what? Why you would want my farm last month and not want it now? Why you want to help me pay the taxes, but you have to have the spring under our property? Well, I'm not interested. Nor do I have the time. You see, I have to figure out how to move a dozen grave sites from our meadow. So just go back to Chicago and leave me alone."

Her throat constricted as if an anaconda ensnared her. All she could do was look away before he could catch the tears welling in her eyes. But they weren't for him. They'd never be for him.

"But I do want to help. I think there's a way for both of us to win here."

"No there isn't. You just think there is. People don't always win, Brandon. Sometimes they lose. Ooh, you're just like Mark."

"Mark? Who's Mark?"

"A ratfink who ditched me when the next best thing came along. So I'm saving you the effort. Consider yourself ditched."

He reached for her hand. "Win or lose, I'm not like Mark. I wouldn't hurt you like that."

She shook her head before she started down the gravel path that would lead her home the long way. "You can't know that, Brandon. Oh, it just doesn't matter anymore." Her feet were running by the time the last word left her mouth. Running like the frightened wimp that she was.

When she hit the forest's edge, she turned left on the path and slowed her pace. He didn't follow her and if she were a betting girl, she figured he would be standing right where she left him. Stunned, maybe? Confused, definitely. And why not? She couldn't figure herself out, why should he get the privilege?

She blamed it on Mark. If he had loved her like he should have. Returned her care with his own instead of dumping her like last year's textbook, she'd be playing house in a high rise north of Michigan Avenue. But that wasn't the case.

And Brandon wasn't Mark. Brandon never told her what to wear or what to do with her hair. He didn't seem to mind her preference for jeans and flip-flops. And he wanted her to listen, as if he cared about her opinion. Even the way he looked at her was different. Mark never made her insides melt with one glance nor could he get under her skin the way Brandon did.

But what did it matter? She'd ruined it with Mark. He preferred the undergrad with high expectations and even higher heels over Lindsay. Now she'd ruined it with Brandon. If she could boast in anything it would be her grand ability to scare off anything male.

CHAPTER ELEVEN

It took a week for the onion field to dry out enough to walk through and as Lindsay suspected, the young shoots did not survive the days under water. Covered in silt and grime, most lay pressed to the ground. A few stragglers tried to reach for the sun, but there would never be enough.

The tomatoes fared better and she only lost half the pepper crop, but there was no getting around it. July thirty-first dawned with Lindsay's accounting work spread before her and the phone numbers of her shareholders close at hand. Each buyer thanked her for her honesty and told her they would return next year, but yes, they wanted their money back. Everyone except for Gram's friend Ethel. She was willing to purchase a larger share of the tomatoes to can for sauce. Said she'd corner the fall farmer's market. Sweet Ethel. Still the books fell far from the necessary funding.

Wandering amidst the broken and bent tomato plants, Lindsay thanked God for the month Hiriam offered them to remain on the farm provided they sell to Bakersfield. To the end of August, he told them. It should be enough time to pack their boxes and their memories along with a bushel of tomatoes, maybe a nice basketful of peppers, too. Uncle Arthur had called a local excavator to relocate the family cemetery, but Gram nearly burst a blood vessel when she found out.

"Not a chance this side of heaven those folks are going to make us move our family."

"But Mamma, you don't want the developers to dig them up, do you?" Uncle Art asked in a hushed tone.

Gram turned several shades of green before she agreed to let him make the calls. With the move scheduled for late August, Hiriam had no choice but to let them stay.

She ran her hand through her hair, knelt beside a row of peppers and yanked a series of dandelions free from their encroachment. Lindsay spent the rest of the morning praying, clearing the weeds and tying the weaker plants to stakes until they could recover from their bruising. By the time she'd finished, Lindsay dripped of sweat and smelled like dirt, but felt like she'd accomplished something useful — peaceful even. When she heard Gram call her for lunch, she was more than ready to return.

"Now, what possessed you to pick the weeds from that infernal patch?" Gram pulled a casserole dish of crumb-topped macaroni and cheese from the oven and dropped it on the stove before she spun around and planted her mitt-covered fists on her hips.

"Isn't that what good farmers do? Take care of their crops?" Lindsay couldn't help the smirk that lit across her face.

Imagine, me a farmer.

"Yes. If they planned on harvesting, but we'll be long-gone by the time the last of those plants are plowed under by the town bully."

Lindsay snickered as she pulled the silverware from the drawer and set them around the table, one for her, for Andy, for Gramps, and for Gram. The others were too busy arranging the move to come home for lunch. "Gram, I don't think it'll be the town bully who'll be knocking down our tomatoes."

"No? Then who, little one?" Yanking the stuck utensil drawer free from the cupboard, Gram pulled out the big scooper and dug it deep inside the steaming noodle dish.

Lindsay threw her arms wide in amazement and lost all threads of her humor. "That development company, that's who. With Brandon Calloway leading them all."

Gram spun around with such finesse, Lindsay stumbled backward and landed in her Grandpa's chair. "Now see here," Gram said. "Did you ever bother to hear that poor boy out?"

Lindsay rolled her eyes. "Poor boy? Really Gram."

"Don't you roll your eyes at me, young lady. And yes, poor boy. You've hardly been kind to him."

With one hand on the table, Lindsay tried to push herself up, but Gram swiped her hand and sent her back to the seat. "Listen closely, Lindsay Murphy. This farm issue is not Brandon's fault. It isn't even Oakville's fault. Your grandfather and I made the decision to withhold those taxes. It is our fault." She wiped a tear from her reddened cheek. "Don't take it out on Brandon. He did nothing but attempt to develop the land according to his company's plan."

"But the water."

"We knew about the spring. Have known for years. Why do you think I let him wander around the property? He tested it for us."

Shocked, Lindsay could only blink.

"We thought if they discovered the spring, they wouldn't level the place and turn it into a trailer park. We hoped they would let us stay on if we sold them the right to tap the spring. But . . ." Gram plopped into the chair opposite Lindsay and laid her head in her palm.

"But Hiriam found out," Lindsay guessed. "And thought it would be a goldmine for the town."

Gram nodded. "By the time we learned that little truth, it was too late. I'm so tired of hiding the truth. Of fighting this battle alone." She let the tears fall in earnest. Each plinked softly on the table.

Lindsay rose and reached over to stroke Gram's back. "Gram?"

With red-rimmed eyes, she glanced up. "Can you ever forgive me, love?"

Wrapping her arms around her shoulders, Lindsay whispered into her silken, gray hair. "Yes. As long as you forgive me."

"For what? What could you need forgiveness for?"

"Being such a pig-headed woman. I've done nothing but badger everyone about this farm."

Gram craned her head to flash a knowing smile. "Especially . . ."

"Especially Brandon. If I ever see him again."

"Oh you will," Gram smiled through her tears as though she knew more than she should. "I have faith that you will."

Lindsay clung to those words. Why, she couldn't quite answer, but she clung to them nonetheless. As she wandered down the hall to call Andy to lunch, she couldn't think of anything she wanted to do more than talk to a certain Chicagoan. She'd been so crass. So foolish. Pig-headed, too. And if she ever saw him again, she'd be the first to apologize.

CHAPTER TWELVE

With the evening free, Lindsay decided to wander down to the pond's edge to feed the geese who seemed to have adopted the wilted salsa fields as their buffet and the pond as their resort. The sunset glowed a magenta hue, setting the water aflame with golden flashes. The air grew silent except for the occasional croak from the bull frogs or the flutter of a bird's wings.

When her bread supply ran empty, Lindsay set the glider in motion and rested the back of her head against the hard, wooden slats. Her mind drained as she fell into a methodical rhythm.

"May I join you?" Brandon strolled up beside her, cautious as if he thought she might take flight like the frightened geese.

"Suit yourself." Too embarrassed to say more, Lindsay scooched over.

If she was honest, she'd admit how she missed him. Every night since that Sunday service a week ago, she watched Mr. Nelson's house for the tell-tale glow of the house lights. Two sets if Brandon stayed on, one if he'd returned to Chicago. Brandon had arrived in Oakville last night.

"The view is magnificent." His languid voice sent ripples through her nerves. Even the slight motion he maintained with the swing did nothing to calm her.

"Mm-hmm." She bit back a smart remark about the beauty of a nice bottling plant against the horizon's backdrop.

"I missed you."

Lindsay's head snapped up.

He chuckled. "Hard to believe, I know. But you bring life into every moment we share. I missed that."

Smiling, Lindsay said, "Glad you see it that way. I sorta missed you too."

"Sorta?" He nudged her side with his elbow while he kept his eyes on the setting sun.

"Okay, so I missed you."

"I have something for you." He pulled a letter from his pocket and held it in front of her.

"For me?" Though she had no idea what he could have brought her, a thrill still fluttered her heart.

Nodding, he pulled it closer to his chest

instead of offering it to her. "But you have to promise not to get mad."

"I don't make promises I can't keep."

He grinned like Andy in Ella's presence as the weakening sunlight twinkled in his eyes. "No doubt. Nonetheless, promise you'll hear me out before you attack."

Narrowing her eyes, she agreed although she wondered if she had walked into some kind of trap. He handed the sheaf to her which she peeled open with care. Across the top, "The Township of Bakersfield" had been typed in bold letters with red ink spelling out "Paid-In-Full" beneath her grandparent's address. In awe, she raised her eyes to his.

"Before you say a word, you have to know I never wanted to hurt you or your family. I was told to expect your farm to be available by the end of summer, so once the test samples came back positive for artesian springs, we were more than agreeable to their investment terms. I had no idea they were forcing you out. As soon as I learned about their tactics I set about finding another solution."

"But how?" her voice wavered as she sniffed.

He brushed a tear from her cheek and left his hand there an extra moment. "Mr.

Nelson. There are two springs, one of which runs under Mr. Nelson's back acreage. He couldn't sell the property fast enough. Especially when he saw our offer."

"So our farm . . . ?"

"Is yours free and clear. But there is one thing you should know." His hand dropped to toy with a wisp of hair that hung near her shoulder.

Distracted by the heat sent from the hand that seared her skin, Lindsay could only stare at him.

"You'll have to put up with a new neighbor." He thumped his chest with his free hand before he tossed his thumb in the direction of the Nelson's farm.

A choking sound caught in her throat. "You want the Nelson house?"

His nod melted the remains of her heart and she flung her arms around his neck.

"Welcome to the neighborhood."

Brandon pulled back only far enough to cradle her head in his palms. "Is that the best you can do?" Then he lowered his head until his lips found hers. Not until they were both breathless and flushed, did he release her and tuck her in the crook of his arm. "I think I could get used to farm life."

"I could teach you all I know," she said with a playful smile tugging at her mouth.

Brandon craned his neck over his far shoulder as if he took in the woeful sight left by her salsa fields, then he turned back to flick the tip of her nose. "I think I'll stick to water rights and watching sunsets."

Lindsay pushed against his side before she wedged her elbow there. "What's the matter with my farming? I have wicked tractor skills. Surely you can't blame me for the weather. Of all things, Brandon Calloway."

Brandon pulled her against him and smothered her next words with a kiss that left her tingling. "I'm not interested in your farming skills, although I would be interested in your business skills. As my partner perhaps?"

Her eyes grew wide as the impact of his words sunk deep. "That is if you're willing to be my wife."

Then with a flash of indignation mixed with a bit of humor, she pursed her lips and stuck her chin in the air. "If that's your idea of a proposal, you'll have to do better than that."

She never expected him to move from the swing to the ground before her. But he did. On one bended knee. He pulled a red velvet box from his pocket and reached for her hand. "Lindsay, I was miserable every time I left Bakersfield — and you. Being with you is like breathing, I can't live without you. I love you Lindsay Murphy. Will you marry me?"

Too choked to speak, Lindsay nodded. When she gathered her wits once more, she opened the box and stared open-mouthed at the solitaire ring, glimmering. "It's beautiful."

"And still, you outshine it." Tugging it free from its cushion, Brandon slipped the ring on her finger and kissed her hand.

Then she wove her fingers through the hair at the nape of his neck. "I love you, too. I have since we first met in the parking lot."

"You have a funny way of showing it, my dear." His voice had grown husky and his face rosy.

"Can you ever forgive me for being such a ninny?"

"Done. I would expect nothing less from someone as passionate as you. If anything, I find that fire irresistible." He pulled her to her feet and held her close. "Now," he whispered against her hair. "I think we better head back to the farmhouse. Your father was rather pleased to have you off his hands, but your mother looked a bit doubtful. Maybe you could persuade her to see me as more than a money-hungry lout?"

Lindsay chuckled at the thought of her mother's reaction. And as she walked beside him, warmed by the arm that held her close, Lindsay prayed that in time, her mother would come around.

■ ■ ■ ■

Andy's Story

■ ■ ■ ■

Proverbs 15:1 "A gentle answer
turns away wrath, but a harsh word
stirs up anger."

CHAPTER ONE

The rumble of the truck's diesel motor beneath his feet gave way to a sensation of raw power that ignited Andy's brain. One week in this outhouse of a town might be survivable as long as he could street race. With a glance over his left shoulder, Andy eyed the 1989 Pontiac Trans Am Turbo that roared beside him. Despite the rust along the frame's edge, the motor sounded juiced. No way did Will pull that off the junk heap behind his father's barn. That beast smelled like a well-loved grease monkey. Andy was sunk.

Pressing his right foot heavy to the floor while his left stayed like a brick on the brake, Andy tried the old intimidation factor. His grandpa's truck didn't shine like the Trans Am, but it had guts. Maybe just enough. Will's smirk brought a sneer to Andy's lips. Country fool.

"Lower the flag already," Andy yelled out

the window. If he hadn't ticked off his dad, he'd be racing the streets of Madison, Wisconsin with Cutler and his friends. And instead of some bony farm boy lowering the flag, Analiese or Crystal would've been waving their —

"Whad ya say?" The kid they called Henry or Hank or something like that stood fifty feet in front of them. He lowered his arms to cup his mouth. *Close enough to a start signal for me.*

His right foot stomped the pedal hard. Tar and sulfur smells filled the truck's cabin, but not for long. Andy tore down the empty road, zipping past Will before the hick boy knew what hit him. But Will was better than Andy gave him credit. Faster too. Before Andy hit a quarter mile, Will's front bumper slid along the side of Grandpa's truck, making it squeal like a stuck pig. *Yah. That'll take some explaining.*

Andy weaved to the left, cutting Will off. But Will hit his breaks, feather-light. Andy flicked his eyes into the rearview mirror. Will's car dropped back, shifted right, and punched forward for the front spot. *If he gets it before the half mile turn.*

Jerk right. Jerk right!

With flash-fire reaction, Andy drove the old pick-up into Will's back bumper, rip-

238

ping the thing half clear of the frame. Sparks flew as it bounced off the asphalt. The added drag gave Andy what he hoped was the upper hand. As he rounded the half-mile marker, Andy pulled into position — the treasured front spot. If he got enough force, cornering alone might give him the lead.

But something caught his bumper. He spun wide with the back of his truck whipping like an alligator's tail. Will zipped past him, but Andy didn't care anymore. He gripped the wheel to steady the truck sliding toward the gravel's edge. And a long row of huge oak trees. He pumped the breaks. Jerked hard on the wheel. But the driver's side tire caught in the gravel and the rear of the truck pitched around with enough force to send him straight for the nearest tree. By its size, Andy figured it had to be a hundred years old. And here he'd never make it past seventeen.

I'm gonna see my mom. His mom who'd been gone for more than a year, now. The crunch of bending metal against an unforgiving pillar of wood filled his ears as he watched the passenger side of the truck buckle toward him. *No. No way are you gonna make it to Heaven.*

That thought hurt worse than the shower

of glass that rained on him from the crumpled windshield and the side window that exploded. Grandpa's truck predated airbags, so the last thing Andy remembered was the salty taste of blood and the ache of never seeing his mom again.

"Dude. Dude, you alive?"

Andy's hand rose to his face which ached as if he'd been attacked by a porcupine. "Huh?"

"Hey, Will, the kid's alive."

"Can't say the same for his truck." Will snorted in the background before he drew up beside Andy's window and peered in. "Can you get out?"

Breathing hurt. Moving hurt. Living hurt. Reaching for the door handle, Andy managed to pop the door open a crack. But that was it. Anymore would have killed him, he could feel it. Will must have sensed it too, because he grabbed the door handle with both hands and yanked the door open about a foot, maybe two. Good thing Andy stayed trim. When he unclicked the seatbelt, he slid out the door and fell to his knees on the gravel.

"Hey, you all right?" It was a girl's voice. Soft, not whiny like some.

It reminded Andy of his mother's, but he

couldn't crane his neck that far to see who it belonged to.

"Hey, Ella. What's up?" Will glanced away as her shadow fell across Andy's face.

"Nothing Will. Is he all right?"

"Yeah, no sweat. Dude's just fine."

Andy raised his head enough to catch the sunlight glint off her long hair — straight like a match stick. I'm losing my mind.

"He's not okay. Look at his face."

Then her hands, soft in some places, calloused in others, cupped his chin and tipped his head from side to side. The movement sent rivulets of pain down his spine and through his head. All he could do was shut his eyes and moan.

"Will, call the police. Get an ambulance. Do something! He's hurt."

"No way. I ain't calling nobody. Hank, let's get outta here." Will's shadow disappeared before Andy heard the rev of the Trans Am's motor.

She grunted in disgust. "Don't worry. I have my cell phone."

Andy's sweet angel helped him lay back. She'd placed a folded cloth beneath his head and stroked his hair as she fiddled with her phone.

"Hi. Officer Montgomery? This is Ella Suchar. There's been an accident on Highway

P. Yes, right before the Summit turn-off."
When she glanced down, her face shielded
the sun from his eyes.

Hers were hazel and gorgeous. Even his
pain couldn't distract him from the gold
and green flecks sparking from the dark
centers like fireworks.

"Yes, sir. There's one injured person. He's
about my age, and his face is covered in
blood."

Covered in blood? Andy's hands flew to
his face. Sticky goo and shards of what he
figured must have been glass covered his
cheeks. When Ella pulled his hands away,
he shut his eyes against the horror he read
in her face.

"Thank you, Officer."

She thinks I'm a monster.

"Just lay still. The police and EMTs will
be here soon. They said you shouldn't be
moved." Her eyes flitted to the busted
driver's door and back to his face. "Well, I
guess you shouldn't move anymore." A faint
smile played at the corners of her mouth.

Andy ran his tongue over his lips and
caught the edge of a glass fragment there,
too. Wincing, he cleared his throat and said,
"Thanks."

Ella placed her hand on his shoulder.
"Don't talk. Just stay still."

"I'm Andy. Andy Hasmer."

A flash of dawning flickered across her face as she tilted her head. "You're not Otto and LouAnn's Andy are you?"

He tried to grin, but it felt like knives scraped the skin off his face. Before he answered, he waited for the sting of tears to stop burning the back of his throat. "Yah. That's me. And that's their truck."

She craned her neck to get a better view of the twisted metal and then she whistled low. "Not good."

"I'll say."

"What happened? Did Will and Hank shove you off the road?"

"Guess you could say that, but it was more a mutual shove. I lost."

"What?"

"Never mind." He could feel his brain righting itself again. "You look familiar. Do I know you?"

Ella swept a stray strand behind her ear and smiled. The gesture sent ripples of electricity through Andy's skin, unnerving him. Sure, he liked to play with the girls back home, but none of them affected him the way this girl did. He wrinkled his nose, hoping the pain would clear his girl-muddied brain.

Ella shrugged. "You might have seen me

243

around town. Or at church. Do you go? To church that is?"

That's why she's driving me nuts. "No. I don't go to church." As soon as the words were spit from his mouth he wanted to suck them back. He didn't mean to sound so harsh. Especially not to her. But he couldn't help it. Church was a dirty word in his mind.

Ella flinched and dropped her hand from his forehead. "Sorry. I didn't mean to make you uncomfortable. I just thought —"

"Yeah? What did you think? Come on. Tell me what you really think."

"What?"

"That's something you church people do so very well, isn't it? Tell us what you really think? All the while, you're just as messed up on the inside as the rest of us. The only difference is that you're better at hiding it." His eyes cornered hers and held them hostage.

She blushed the cutest shade of pink, but her eyes flashed with an intensity that should have turned her face blood-red. "Andy, I don't know what you're talking about, but I think you need to settle down. Your face is starting to bleed again."

When the air filled with the sirens from Oakville's only ambulance and Bakersfield's volunteer fire and rescue vehicle, Andy decided to keep his mouth shut for the remainder of their time alone. He found it more fun to watch her avoid eye contact than listen to any preachy pretense she'd probably start spouting.

"Hey Ella," the first EMT said as he walked up beside her. "Who do we have here?" He plunked his box of gear beside Andy's ear and started unpacking as Ella filled him in on everything that had happened. From her detailed story, Andy knew she'd witnessed pretty much the whole thing. Why she acted like she hadn't was beyond him. But lucky for him, she didn't tell the racing part. Instead she left it at "he seemed to make a sloppy, wide corner and lost control." Street racing wasn't encouraged in Madison. Oakville probably didn't like it much either, so he decided to leave the storytelling to her.

Ella and the other EMT chatted a bit, laughing about someone's lost cat and a squirrel who liked another lady's chimney. Twice Andy had to moan just to get a little attention. And after a brief examination, the EMT and his partner declared Andy ready for transport. They promised to extricate the glass shards at the hospital since they thought it might take a while. *Great!*

As the gurney rose to its full height and bounced along the rocks and asphalt on its way to the ambulance, Ella grabbed Andy's hand and said, "I'm glad you'll be okay. And don't worry, I'll call your grandparents to let them know where you are and that you're gonna be fine." She sent him a cheerful grin that had begun to grate on his last layer of skin.

"Don't do me any favors."

Ella took a step back as if he'd taken a swipe at her and the exchange brought a scowl to the EMT's lips.

"Hey, friend. Ella did you one. Don't you think you should be a little grateful?" he said.

"Thanks, Ella." Andy didn't even try to make it sound authentic. He could see it hurt her, and he didn't want to do that, but it was self-preservation. At least that's what he told himself.

"Anytime, Andy." She spun on her heel and walked away.

As he rode in the ambulance to the hospital, Andy wondered if he'd been too harsh. What if she was different? Yeah, and what if I hadn't wrapped my grandpa's truck around a tree? He shook his head. No sense in thinking on the "what if's."

"Buddy, you're one lucky kid," the EMT

said as he looked over Andy's face one more time. "Another inch to the right and your eye would've been in serious trouble. Not too many people survive a wreck into one of those old oaks." Then he shook his head and tsk'd.

Yeah, I could've been killed. Like my mother. Killed. In a mangled car. Could've been killed.

What would his father say?

CHAPTER TWO

Hospitals reeked. Antiseptic cleaner and burnt fried chicken stench hung in the air like the June humidity. Couldn't someone spray a little air freshener around?

"Hi there. Feeling any better?" Raine asked. She'd been Andy's nurse since he arrived three hours earlier.

"Yeah. Super." He added an eye roll for good measure.

Raine laughed and checked the machines that beeped behind his head before she placed her hand on his scalp and shifted his head from side to side. "Dr. Thomson did a wonderful job with your stitches. You might have a slight scar above your right eye, but the rest should fade nicely. None of these other scratches are deep so we won't wrap your head tonight."

Andy snorted. Now that would be something to see. Andy, the walking mummy. Not a bad idea actually. "Aw come on,

Raine. Let's play up the sympathy card."

With a giggle and a toss of her hair she jotted down a note or two before leaving the way she came. Then she paused at the curtained door and looked back. "Ooh, I almost forgot. You have a visitor. Would you like me to send her in now that the doctor's finished?"

Andy grimaced as he wrinkled his forehead. "Who is it?"

Checking the clipboard in her hand, Raine said, "Lindsay Murphy."

"Yeah. You can let her in." He breathed a little easier knowing it was just his cousin. She'd be cool. At least he hoped she would.

When Lindsay peeked around the door, her face paled and then her hands shook as she covered her mouth with her fingertips. "What did you do?" she mumbled over and over for a full minute.

Andy didn't have a good answer. Racing sounded stupid now that Grandpa's truck was wrapped around a tree. "I'm not hurt. At least not that bad. It's just scratches."

Lindsay rolled her eyes and plopped into the vinyl chair beside him. "Honestly, Andy." She blew the bangs from her face and stared out the window.

"Is Grandpa ticked?"

When she brought her eyes to his, he

249

didn't need to hear the answer, but she said it anyway. "No. He's crushed. I mean he's glad you're fine and all, but it's just such a mess."

" 'Cause he loved the old thing?" Andy's gut began to throw lava waves as he thought about the truck his grandpa had fixed with his dad. He'd heard story after story about how that truck made his dad the man he was. Long before his uncle had died.

How stupid can I be? The last thing he wanted to do was hurt his gramps. He didn't want to hurt his dad either. But hurt seemed to follow him everywhere he went. Andy closed his eyes and leaned his head back.

Lindsay didn't seem to notice as she piled the guilt high. "Sure he loved that old truck, but don't forget about the farm stuff and his health. Having to pay for a new truck wasn't something any of us planned on."

Andy inched the upper part of the bed into a reclined position. "Oh."

Lindsay stared out the window and shook her head. "I did get some good news today."

"Yah?"

"The back meadow looked plowable and great for growing crops. Just have to check with Gram and Gramps."

"That's awesome." Right. Even though

he'd suggested the organic farm project the night before, the project sounded like it had more holes than patches.

"I just wish they had a computer. I really need to research the organic part."

"Mmm." Andy thought about the computer his dad left with him. A sluggish laptop with a few games — it was meant to be a pity gift since Gramps didn't have cable, but Andy wondered if they had Wi-Fi or something he could tap into. He decided to check as soon as he got home.

Not that he loved the farm or anything. He'd visited a handful of times when he was younger, but to hear his cousin and Aunt Tess talk about it, you'd think it was better than a waterpark. Personally, he wasn't so convinced. No action. No game systems. No TV. The whole community seemed a bit hokey. Don't get him started on the nightmare he had to deal with when Gram took him shopping at the five and dime that morning. Besides, Gramps and Gram would be better off in some cushy senior center where they never had to worry about shoveling snow or tending gardens. "Linds, are you sure we should try to save the farm? I mean wouldn't it be a good thing for them to move to something else?"

Lindsay opened her mouth as if to answer

his question when the phone rang. She scurried over to the bedside table to answer it before Andy rolled within reach. "Hello?" she said while she stared at Andy's face. "Hey, Uncle Art. How are you?"

Uncle Art. His father. A shudder racked Andy's shoulders. Here it comes.

When Lindsay handed him the heavy hospital phone, he glanced up and noticed her pressed-lip smile. With a deep breath, he held the phone to his ear and said hello.

"What happened? Tell me you weren't street racing again. Andy, honestly. You didn't do that with Grandpa's truck, did you?"

"Yeah, Dad, I'm fine. How are you?"

"Don't get smart with me."

"Heaven forbid."

"Andrew!"

Andy could hear his father's heavy sigh through the line and it broke something deep inside him. "Sorry. Look. I'll make it up to Grandpa. I promise."

"Oh yes you will. You'll need to pay for the damages. That's what you'll do."

Andy shot upright, a picture of the mangled truck burning his brain. "What? No way. How'm I going to do that?"

"Grandpa has a friend at the auto shop and the guy gave Grandpa a quote for a couple grand. You're lucky. Doesn't seem you bent the frame of that old heap, you just pushed in the door and broke out a couple windows. It could have been a whole lot worse."

"Yeah. Like I could've gotten hurt or something."

A mumbled grunt responded to Andy's sarcasm before Art continued. "Can you at least keep your nose clean for a little while?"

"Yeah. Sure. But there's nothing to do here."

Andy heard a car horn in the distance and white noise that sounded like traffic, but before he could ask his father continued his rant.

"Look, I've gotta go. Do me a favor and don't give your grandparents any grief. They have enough to deal with right now."

Andy's voice dropped low. "Sure. No trouble."

"I'll see you soon."

"Whatever."

His dad's line clicked off and buzzed in his ear for a moment before Lindsay plucked it from his hand.

"Are you okay?" she asked as she fussed over his covers.

Andy avoided her glance so she wouldn't catch the tears that stung his eyes. "He didn't even ask me how I was." He sniffed.

Then she avoided his gaze as she answered. "He's probably gotten all the news from Gram and the doctors. Not to mention the call I made before I got here. That's all."

"But he didn't ask me." He caught her eye then and pleaded with her to see his side.

Laying her hand on his, she chewed her lower lip for a second. "He loves you, Andy. Don't doubt that. You just scared him."

Andy dropped his chin to his chest and shrugged. "I guess." She didn't get it. None of them did.

"He told me he's coming soon. Do you realize he hasn't been on the farm in years? Since the accident. If that doesn't show how much he loves you, well then I don't know what would."

The accident. A story his mother told him about each June when his father disappeared for a day. Something about his father's twin brother and a farm machine. His father lived and Andy's uncle didn't. But it had happened so long ago. Well before Andy came along at least and not once had his father returned to the farm in all those years. Maybe it did mean something if his dad returned now. For him.

Will poked his head through the door. "Safe to visit?" he said with a grin. The boy looked like a high school quarterback. Tight T-shirt stretched over thick muscles. And clean cut — the kind of short buzz cut Andy's father would love. Andy ran his hand through his own tangled mop. Looks weren't everything — or so the line goes.

"Sure. Andy could use a friend right about now," Lindsay said. Then she turned to Andy and handed him the TV controller. "I'll go see about checking you out while you talk with Will."

As her footsteps echoed down the hall, Will leered. "She ain't half bad."

"Back off. She's my cousin and she's about ten years older than you."

Will snickered. "Yah, well, I like 'em older."

"Older my foot. You just like 'em."

Will laughed in earnest that time. "True, that."

"By the way. Nice going, slick."

With an offended look as real as the stick-on wood coating that clung to the bed tray, Will lifted his hands. "What? Wha'd I do?"

"You left me. Bleeding. On the side of the road with some girl for a nursemaid."

"Ella? Dude you were in good hands. That

girl helps the homeless and the busted. You were fine. Besides, no sense in all of us getting into trouble, right? You wouldn't do that to your friends, would you?"

Andy rolled his eyes. He hadn't known Will for long, but Andy knew his type. They met earlier that morning when Gram "treated" Andy to breakfast at the little diner. Andy spied Will leaning against a fine piece of ride in the diner's parking lot. While Gram paid the bill, Andy raced outside to grab a smoke and see about meeting the kid. Just his luck, Will still stood beside his car and had a pack to share. They'd been comrades since that morning.

Turns out Will's folks lived down the lane from his grandparent's. "A stone's throw," his grandma would say. Oh he played the good-boy role in front of folks, but behind their backs he loved to raise trouble. It's what made him interesting. Someone to keep Andy from going nuts when there wasn't a thing to do but watch the weeds grow.

"You feeling up to a little fun?" Will grabbed the remote and flung it onto the chair Lindsay left.

"Do I look like it?" Andy raised his hand to highlight his face.

"Never judge a book by its cover." The

snigger that played with Will's lips never voiced itself, but it brought a grin to Andy's face.

"Whatever. I've gotta lay low," Andy said.

"What?"

"Yah. I have to find a job and pay for the truck repairs and probably smooth things over with Gramps. I'm busted. At least for a couple days."

"Get a job? Here? So you're staying longer than just a week?"

"Yeah. Looks like I'm here for a while. Dad says I need a babysitter and my grand-parents get stuck with the job. I'm all yours dude."

"Cool. It'll be sweet. Just wait and see."

"Riiight. First I have to find a job. Got any leads?"

Will tilted his head and stroked his chin, but after a few seconds he shook his head. "Naw man. I've got nothing. I'm working at the mill, but they're not hiring. Hank's at the Qwik-y-Mart, and they're not hiring either."

"What else is there?"

With a flick of his eyebrow, Will flashed his famous grin. "Not much, man. There's the diner or there's farm work."

Dropping his head to the pillow, Andy raised his eyes to the tiled ceiling. "No way am I spending my summer as a farm hand." Then he thought of his promise to Lindsay and her organic farming venture. *Oh man. There's no way out of it.*

Just then Lindsay walked back through the doors with an attendant in tow. "Time to go, Andy. Will, it was nice seeing you again."

"Likewise." The glassy-eyed smile he threw Lindsay made Andy's eyes roll. Lucky for her, Lindsay seemed to miss Will's sickening expression as she gathered Andy's stuff into a hospital bag.

Will took off while the attendant plucked every hair off Andy's wrist along with the IV tape he peeled free. When the soft tap of a visitor's shoe neared, Andy didn't pay the visitor any attention as he focused on the bald spot that stung on his wrist.

Until the visitor spoke.

"Good evening, Lindsay," Ella said.

CHAPTER THREE

Ella stood by the door and held a cellophane covered weight attached to a "Get Well Soon" balloon. Gaping, Andy froze at the sight of her.

"May I take that for you?" Lindsay snickered as she reached for Ella's outstretched gift.

"Yes. That would be fine." Although Ella handed the gift to Lindsay, her gaze stayed locked on Andy. Cherry-red blotches crept up her neck and colored her cheeks while her right hand fiddled with her watch.

Of course Andy couldn't move or breathe with the weight that settled on his chest. Maybe the accident had done more damage than the doctors thought, since his chest seemed to constrict the second Ella showed up. Maybe he shouldn't go home, yet.

Lindsay stepped in front of Ella, blocking his view and freeing his breath. "Thank you —"

"Ella Suchar. I'm Pastor Suchar's daughter."

Lindsay moved the balloon to the small pile of belongings resting on the vinyl chair in the corner. "Oh yes. I think we've met."

"In passing. I wanted to see how Andy was doing." Ella stepped closer.

As she inched near, Andy's heart thumped a crazy rhythm against his ribcage. Thankfully, the attendant had removed the heart monitor from his finger and his forearm. He imagined the wild chirping they'd have made as his face heated. Great. I'm feverish, too.

"Hi," Ella said when she'd reached his bedside. "I brought you a gift."

"Thanks." Why did she have to look at him that way? As if she cared.

She swayed on her heels and glanced around the room. "Are you feeling any better?"

Andy swiped the hair from his eyes. "Yeah."

"Oh. Good. Well, I guess I'll just head out." She hesitated at the end of the bed, fiddling with the drawstring that hung from the collar of her sleeveless hoodie.

She glanced up with an expectant look, one that seemed to plead for some type of remark, so Andy flashed a shaky grin. "Okay."

Then she left. No formal goodbye. No gushing thanks. She just slipped through the curtain and out the door. He couldn't even hear her footfalls down the hall through the loud pounding in his ears. Had he really acted like a love-struck drama king? Maybe if he tried hard enough he could imagine that she'd never been there. But when Lindsay waved the brightly colored balloon in front of him, he knew that would never happen. Lindsay's snorted laugh raked across his nerves like the truck's glass on his face.

"What?" His harsh bark stopped her giggles, but it did nothing for the know-it-all expression she brandished.

"Not a thing, Andy, my dear. Not a thing."

By the time they arrived back at the farmhouse, Andy's mood dove south. The pain medication had worn off and his side ached. But that paled in comparison to the discomfort he felt every time he thought about her, which was way too often. The Madison-Andy would've schmoozed her. Told her he loved balloons and sleeveless sweatshirts. Knocked her off her feet with a joke or quick comeback, but his brain turned to mush every time she showed up.

For all she knew, he had the IQ of a barn door. *Nice, Hasmer. Really nice.*

By the time Lindsay pulled into their grandparent's gravel drive, an extra car crouched in the round-a-bout. His dad's Corolla.

Part of Andy sighed with relief. His dad came. He cared. He'd take Andy home. Then again, he was bound to yell at Andy for the truck thing. And if his father found out about he'd been racing . . .

Andy shivered when he considered a summer without his cell or his laptop or his iPod.

Lindsay must have spotted the Corolla, too. "No way. Look who's here." Her elbow found his rib cage, sending a jolt through nerves that stretched like piano wire.

"Yay." Did he come to chew Andy out or to make sure he'd survived?

Lindsay threw him a sideways glance. "I thought you wanted him to show you he cared."

"Yeah. Cared. But you know he'll just harp on the truck. Why'd he have to come down?" Slamming the car door, Andy sidled up beside her and blocked their trek inside. "He's just going to yell at me. Then what? Huh?"

After Lindsay strung the hospital take-home bag on her wrist, she took hold of both his shoulders. "Relax. He won't yell. Gram's in there. She'll keep him in tow. Besides, he's here — on the farm — I told you he loves you." She waltzed right past him and flung the screen door wide.

"Yah, but does he care? There's a difference you know." Andy stared at his shoes and trudged behind Lindsay until they went inside.

God? You up there? If so, I think I'm gonna need you. Soon.

Prayer hadn't been something he did often. At least not since his mother died, but she always said God listened. Since he missed her more than his friends at the moment, he thought he'd try it. Once. Swallowing hard, he hoped she had been right.

Gram met him at the door with a bear hug that smelled like Ben Gay and Chanel No. 5, the perfume he bought her every Christmas and she wore it every time he saw her. "Honey, I'm so glad you're alright. Are you hurting much?" Leave it to Gram to care.

"Naw, I'm fine. It just looks worse than it is." Making his way inside, Andy hesitated at the overstuffed rocker that cradled his Grandpa. "Gramps, I'm so sorry about your truck. I'll get it fixed. I promise."

Grandpa Otto's crystalline eyes gazed at

Andy as a line of drool trickled from the left corner of his mouth to his chin where it glistened with the rays of the fading summer sun. When Gramps rolled his head to the side and mumbled, Andy leaned forward so he could hear the hoarse whisper. "As long as you're alive."

That's it. A simple line that drew the tears Andy had been quelling since he'd collided with the ancient oak. But the familiar clearing of a throat forced those tears to stand their ground. Andy turned to face his father. As he did so, Gramps grabbed Andy's hand with his good one and squeezed as if to give the boy the strength he needed to face what Andy knew he'd earned.

As Andy turned, the warm rush of grace he'd felt from his Gramps fell away as the steely cold radiating from his father's face replaced it.

"Andrew." His father's suit shone dark but professional, and his wing tipped shoes didn't have a fleck of gravel dust on them. Andy hadn't noticed him standing in the kitchen archway. But there he stood beside a woman Andy didn't recognize. He ran his aging hand over his chin, which seemed to be missing even the stubble a normal man would wear at the end of the day. His father, the perfect man, stood feet in front of him as though he hadn't a clue what to do next.

Then again, neither did Andy. "Dad."

Fluttering about like a butterfly, Gram waltzed in with a plate of cookies and a glass of milk for Andy. "Art, darling, would you like another glass of iced tea? Or lemonade?"

Without taking his eyes from Andy's face, Art answered her in a tone he must have saved just for her, since Andy had never heard him use it — not even with Andy's mom. "No thanks, Mom. I can't stay long." He smiled. When was the last time he'd smiled?

Her face fell. "You're going to leave? Already? But you just got here."

It must have taken the slight whine in her voice to break the hold his father had on Andy's eyes, because Art turned to hug her close. "I know, Mom, but I promised Dana we'd catch up before it got too late."

"Dana?" The stranger? Who was she? And why does Dad care when she gets home? Andy took a step forward and stared into the stranger's pewter-gray eyes. She wore a kind smile, one Andy couldn't return.

But his father did. "She's a friend from the past." He cast a peculiar glance in her direction.

Aunt Tessa walked in with a lemonade of

her own and gave Dana a shoulder hug and a wink. "A very good friend from the past." The grin on her face told Andy he'd missed something. And if the creepy way the hair on the back of his neck stood up was any indication, he figured he had missed something important.

"Oh." Andy couldn't help the anger that crept into his voice and hushed the room. Sure he'd been the one to tell his Dad it was time to move on — his mother had been gone for a year and Andy thought it was time. But packing old sweaters and clearing Mom's closet was a whole lot different than dating. Dating? Even the word left his mouth puckering.

"Never mind all that. What you should be concerned with is rectifying the mess you made today. And you're in luck." His dad looked him in the eye.

"Yeah. It seems to be my lucky day." Andy shrugged his shoulders and gulped from his tea glass. *Ask me. I dare you to ask me how I feel. Come on, Dad . . .*

"Andrew!" Grandma LouAnn said in her whispered voice she used when you knew you were in trouble. She had taken the wingback chair beside Gramps and sipped her lemonade while she watched their argument like a tennis match.

"Sorry, Gram." Andy fumed. Not only was he the last to know about his father's girl pal, but he'd lost Gram's support. With wide eyes and half-open mouths, Aunt Tess and Lindsay wore the same expression Gram did. They had chosen their side and it wasn't his. With a deep sigh that started somewhere deep in his gut, Andy knew defeat. All he wanted was one question from his dad. Just one.

Instead Dad drew in a ragged breath. "Your Grandma managed to find you a job."

"What?" Andy dropped the glass he held on the nearby end table, sloshing sticky tan liquid over the edge. What kind of job would Gram find? Didn't they trust him enough to find a job on his own, for crying out loud? His mouth hung open when his father continued.

"You should be grateful. It's not as if you'll be cleaning someone's stalls or baling hay all summer. It's a nice job." His father shot him a watch-it glance.

He'd never hurt Gram — at least not on purpose.

When he found his tongue, Andy blurted, "I would be grateful if I knew what to be grateful for. I mean what is this job?"

"Community Church is looking for someone to fill in while their custodian recovers from a broken leg," Aunt Tess said.

Andy could tell by the overly cheery tone that she was trying to smooth things over. But what did these people take him for? A custodian? He didn't have the faintest idea what that job entailed.

"I'm not great at fixing things, so if that's what this is count me out." Andy averted his scratchy eyes to the mess on the end table. Busying his hands, he mopped at the liquid with his napkin, but Gram swatted him away as she wiped it clean.

When he looked up, Aunt Tess shook her head and raised her palms, while his dad rubbed his forehead until it turned red.

"Oh no," Aunt Tess said. "No fixing necessary. They'll save those items for when Edgar is feeling up to it. Right now they need someone to mow the grounds, weed . . ."

"Dust and clean the sanctuary, care for the offices, and do general upkeep where it's needed," Gram finished as she walked the dripping rag into the kitchen.

Andy swallowed hard. The job had merit. It wouldn't be like some of his friend's jobs at the mall in Madison. No cute girls hanging over the register waiting for him to get off work. No movie theatre to blow his pay check at when he finished a shift. But it did keep him off the farms. Besides he wouldn't have to listen to the people and their self-effacing advice, not while he cleaned their floors. Custodians had a way of disappearing into the paneling of a place. But still, it should have been his choice.

When she returned, Gram took Andy's hand in hers. "Honey, I'm sorry. I should have asked you before I spoke with Mike. You're old enough to find a job on your own, but forgive an old lady. I didn't want to miss this opportunity for you."

Andy leaned over and gave his Gram a kiss on the forehead. Gram had his back, even if his dad didn't. "You're not an old lady. Don't let anyone call you that." He leaned in and whispered, "Especially you." When he pulled back she smiled, letting him know all was right between them.

"Thank you. I do appreciate it, Gram." Then as the moment cooled, the pain in Andy's face began to throb and his neck grew stiff and sore.

"Maybe we should go." His father leaned into Dana and with a nod of her head, she headed toward the door.

As his father passed Andy's frozen figure, he paused. But Andy averted his gaze and pretended to be deep in thought over the ice floating inside his glass. The air bristled with the electricity of the moment, until Art brushed past him and headed to the door.

Then he was gone. Art, the perfect man, stunk as a dad. "Gram, Gramps, I'm pretty wiped. If you don't mind I think I'm going to go to bed." Then he moved down the hall toward the small back room they'd fixed up for him.

As he lumbered away, his grandmother's voice followed him. "All right, sweetheart. Do you think you'll be ready for an interview tomorrow?"

In slow motion, Andy turned and met her hopeful gaze. "Sure, Gram. I'll be up for it."

"Wonderful." Her face lit like the Fourth of July sky. "I'll wake you around eight-thirty."

Eight-thirty AM? His head thumped on the closed bedroom door. On a Sunday? In the summer?

"Pick something nice to wear, but pack something to work in. When Pastor Suchar finishes the interview, you'll want to be ready in case he puts you to work right away. He might need something done before first service."

Andy's head jerked back as the name flashed a familiar face to mind. A female face.

Chapter Four

Gram's wake-up call came before sleep ever did and Andy's mood soured with each passing minute. When he stepped up to the bathroom mirror, he inspected the damage. Not too bad. The scratches scabbed over and the stitches made him look rugged, cool even. They only stung when he squished up his face. His side hurt the most and when he lifted his T-shirt to inspect it, he discovered a bruise about the width of the seatbelt that must have caught him just right. He shrugged. Doctors told him he'd survive, so he wasn't concerned.

As he finished up his shower, Andy considered his father's visit. At least he'd gone back to Madison so Andy could suffer at the hands of Ella's father — and Ella — without his father around to see it. Ella's memory brought a flutter to his gut. One that warmed him and made him eager to get to church — weird.

At five minutes to nine, Lindsay dropped him off in front of the ancient white-steepled church. Andy began to doubt his ability to tolerate the people who were bound to fill the place within the hour. The same ice that froze his veins once Ella told him she was a Christian, began to flow again as he opened the door and walked down the aisle of the small one room sanctuary. The smell of candle wax and wood polish filled his brain with memories of his mother and youth group meetings. He shook his head to clear the emotion that threatened to take him places he had no intention of revisiting.

Wood benches — one after another — filled the room along with bright colors created by the sun's rays through the stain glass windows. Still, Andy thought the place looked creepy. Or lonely. He shivered for good measure.

"Cold?"

Ella.

Andy spun around and caught himself before he slipped into a pew, sideways. Ella leaned against the edge of a bench with her hands curled over the dark wood. Pink and red squares of light cast from the windows bejeweled her hair like a princess' crown. She appeared more beautiful than an artist's rendition. Except for the dark red triangle that colored her nose like a clown's. He raised an eyebrow and tried to hold back the twitch of his lips.

"Something funny?" she asked, shifting forward until the triangle decorated her eye.

He laughed, deep and guttural till his face hurt from the strain. When he finished she just stood there, triangle in place along with a smile and a knowing look in her eye.

"Perhaps this is better," she said, stepping to her right and forward three feet. She stiffened her back and let her face relax as it became a screen for the colored lights that shifted and danced. When all stilled, she morphed into a giant blue Smurf not unlike the reruns of an old cartoon he'd watched at his Gram's house. Even her teeth shined with the color.

Except she looked more like a mermaid, elusive and mythical. His breath caught in his throat and his hands turned moist as he stared.

"Ella, you're not frightening the new custodian, are you, precious?" From the shadows of the room emerged a man no older than Andy's father, but his aged eyes seemed kinder. He placed a wiry arm around Ella and hugged her close, freeing her from the ocean of blue that colored her skin. With the mermaid's spell broken, Andy took a step forward and introduced himself.

"Yes. Yes, Andy. You have no idea what an answer to prayer you are." Pastor Suchar released his hold on Ella and gripped Andy's hand in a strong shake, uncharacteristic for one with such thin limbs.

Andy smiled into his kind face and decided he liked this man, even if he was one of them. When the pastor let go, he leaned down and kissed the top of Ella's head. "Sweetheart, would you mind pulling some treats and some tea together for us, please? No sense in fellowshipping without a little food, don't you think Andy?"

"Yes. Sir." Andy didn't care if he ate a thing, but something tugged at his core, begging him to stay in this man's presence. Never had he felt so close to someone he'd never met. It was as if he had to get to know him. Weird.

Ella smiled up at her father and nodded. "The little sugar cookies from Mrs. Hanson?"

A dreamy look crossed the pastor's face as he licked his lips. "Yes, I think that will do. But you better bring extras, this boy looks hungry." He smiled down at Andy. Even though no one believed the cookies were for Andy, Ella giggled and skittered down the aisle, disappearing into the shadows where the pastor emerged not more than a few minutes before.

Then Pastor Suchar gave him a sideways glance as he led him on a short tour of the grounds. They visited the inner sanctuary, the storage rooms, the basement and the classrooms. They toured the grounds and the equipment shed until they ended their tour in the back offices that hid in the shadows. Only twenty minutes had passed by the time they returned to the comforts of the air conditioned office and a plate heaped with dainty cookies in the shape of iced crosses waited for them. By the time they sat down, Andy's appetite had returned and he reached for both a cookie and a glass of iced tea, consuming them both in a fraction of a minute. The second cookie melted in his mouth as he spent time chewing and savoring its sweetness. Not too sweet like his Aunt Tess's rich wedding cookies, but not dull tasting like the store-bought kind his dad picked up. Andy decided church-people or not, he needed to meet Mrs. Hanson.

"They're amazing aren't they?" Pastor Suchar said as he munched on the edge of his own cookie. A few crumbs made their way to his dark shirt, but he brushed them aside and smiled. "Guess I should watch that, if you're planning on cleaning this office, eh?" He smiled before he gulped down the cool tea.

"Is the job mine?" Andy asked. All along, the man had behaved as if it was, but an agreement hadn't been approached.

"Oh goodness," he said, laying the cookie on his plate before placing it on the small coffee table in front of them. "Of course. That custodian's ad has been in the bulletin for at least a month and we've had no takers until your grandma called. Everyone is too busy with the planting and growing seasons to care for an old church. And I'm sure you've noticed the sorry state our church is in because of it."

Andy nodded. He had noticed the layers of white dust that coated most of the wooden surfaces and the pieces of paper and fuzz that gathered in the corners of every room. He wasn't one to pick up on stuff like that, but he wanted to know what he was getting into so he'd been watching.

"It'll be hard work, but if you like to work at your own pace and work alone most of the time, you'll enjoy it." Pastor Suchar gave Andy a moment to think on the offer as the man reached for his half-eaten cookie and polished it off.

Andy breathed slowly as he thought about the hard work — at a church nonetheless. He'd run into a few church people as they began to file in for the morning services. They seemed kind enough. And the pastor offered to pay for the repairs in full if Andy worked until the end of July. Six weeks. Then his obligation to the pastor and his Dad would be complete. He could do that, couldn't he?

"Yes. Thank you, I'll take it." They shook hands, sealing the deal just as Ella waltzed in with two fresh glasses of tea.

Ella. He'd forgotten about her.

Once she placed the tray on the table she fidgeted with the cookie platter and empty glasses. "Did you need anything else, Andy?" she asked, returning his stare.

Embarrassed, Andy dropped his gaze to the tea glasses as he stuffed another cookie into his mouth. "No," he mumbled through the crumbs.

"Oh. Well. Dad, can I go into Oakville this afternoon, please?"

Andy tried to block out their exchange, but he couldn't help but hear. Besides, his ears burned with her presence, so he figured he was entitled to a little eavesdropping to soothe his discomfort. When Pastor Mike directed a question his way, he startled hard, upsetting the fresh glass of tea.

"Sorry," he said as he rushed to stem the flow over the table's edge.

Before he could say otherwise, Ella jumped in with a dishrag that materialized out of nowhere.

He grabbed at the rag and replied in a tone more irritated than he intended. "I can get this." When she flinched back as if he'd stung her, the guilt that swept through him fueled his frustration, so he lowered his voice and tried again. "I've got this. It's my job now anyway. Really Ella. Leave it."

Her face flushed deeper than the red plate she carried and she sputtered as she apologized. This wasn't going well at all and Andy had no idea how to salvage any of it.

"Ella, could you go check on the choir practice for me? Mrs. Bakersfield had a question about her alto part in the new arrangement of Amazing Grace. I'll set Andy up with his new chores. Thank you so much for bringing the cookies and tea, honey. You are such a dear for taking care of your old dad," Pastor Mike said. He rose up and encircled his daughter in a hug that brought the first smile to her face since they'd met in the sanctuary.

"Thanks Dad." Then she disappeared through a side door, leaving the dripping table and a flustered Andy behind.

"She has a heart of gold, that one does." Pastor Mike gathered up a few soaked napkins and dumped them into the trash can before he returned with fresh ones retrieved from his desk drawer. As if sensing Andy's question, he said, "I eat up here often, so I keep a stash handy." Then he drew in a slow breath before he finished. "You can start in the sanctuary tomorrow. It needs a good dusting and polishing, not to mention the mess the floor is in. I think that should keep you more than busy for a while. Did you bring work clothes when you came to visit?"

When Andy nodded, Pastor Mike showed him where the supplies were and where he could change should he ever need to. Then he led them to the parking lot where church-goers began to arrive in earnest.

"One more thing, Andy. Ella's mom died when she was five. She's all I have this side of heaven and I intend to protect her as Christ would protect you. Just thought you should know that." Then he turned on his heel and followed an aging couple into the sanctuary.

What did that mean? He got the part about being an over protective father; Andy had met a few of those types before. But the idea of Christ protecting him? That sounded nuts, especially when he compared it to the way the pastor seemed to dote on Ella. Pastor Suchar couldn't mean Christ doted on Andy, could he? Well, Andy didn't buy it.

CHAPTER FIVE

Four miles. That's how far he walked every day since he'd started working at the church. Two miles there and two miles back. Once in a while Lindsay would drop him off or pick him up, but most days she rushed off to gather farm supplies, set up inspections, or hang out with Brandon. Okay, so they didn't really "hang out," more like yell at each other until one of them stormed off, but still it kept Lindsay from carting Andy to the church. As for the truck, the repair shop still hadn't finished with Grandpa's truck. A few weeks passed and they'd done little more than bang out the side, leaving pockmarked indents across the passenger door. Sort of looked like his face — healed but marked by pink-spotted skin.

The windshield they ordered hadn't arrived and wouldn't for another two weeks. Since his dad moved into Aunt Tessa's, he decided to make the truck a pet project, so the two of them worked on applying Bondo to the larger dents and sanding them smooth. Far from perfect, still it looked better. And it hadn't been too horrible working with his dad. Surprised, Andy pressed his lips together as he realized he'd enjoyed the time with his dad.

But that still left Andy with a long walk every day. Except for Sundays. At least he got those days off.

Today had been exceptional. Andy spent eight hours scraping peeled paint from the steeple in ninety degree heat and humidity. Lucky for him, Ella had the foresight to send him water and tea every hour.

Ella.

That's all it took to fill his mind with her image. One stray thought and everything but her sweet face faded to black. Ella with the round eyes that flashed when he annoyed her — which was often. Ella with back-draping hair the color of summer squash. No not summer squash, more like yellow wax beans. No those are too yellowy. Her hair carried deeper tones of gold like . . . like. *Oh, I don't know what color it is, I'd just love to touch it.* Or torch, depending on his mood.

It bothered him to be so controlled by anyone, but a girl? That thought unhinged him. Andy wavered between asking her out and telling her to take a hike every time she entered the room. The whole thing put him in a sour mood, so much so he wondered if the long walk home blessed him with a chance to cool off.

Blessed him. A phrase he'd heard tossed around the church so often it became a part of his vocabulary of late. No matter how hard he tried to keep the whole Christian thing from seeping into his being, he couldn't help the tug that pulled him right into the crook of its arm. Even on his day off, he spent the better part of Sunday mornings at church.

Gram never pressed. She didn't have to since his self-inflicted guilt won week after week. If Gramps could pull it together to go with his lop-sided limp and his air tank dragging through the parking lot, then Andy could wipe the sad look from Gram's face by attending a simple service. But when his father caught wind of his new devotion, Andy's simple service turned into a "new leaf" that could lead him home, except Andy didn't want to go home anymore. Not since home meant seeing his father with his new girlfriend. Andy couldn't stomach that. Not in the home his mother had made and still lived in if anyone asked him, which they didn't. So here he stood on the edge of a cornfield. Nowhere to go. No one to care. Alone with the memory of his mother. She still cared, he could feel it. Just this morning, Pastor Mike hummed a few bars of an old hymn, the one his mother used to sing. *Be Thou My Vision.* Even now, the words filled his mind as the tune played on his lips.

Be Thou my Vision, O Lord of my heart;
Naught be all else to me, save that Thou
    art
Thou my best Thought, by day or by
    night,
Waking or sleeping, Thy presence my
    light.

He could picture her flour-caked and cheery, singing to him from the edge of the field. Reminding him of days when he would have sung along, too.

Be Thou my Wisdom, and Thou my true
    Word;
I ever with Thee and Thou with me, Lord;
Thou my great Father, I Thy true son;
Thou in me dwelling, and I with Thee one.

But not any longer.
"No! It's not true. I don't have any father

except the iceman in Madison. Besides where was God the night your helicopter crashed, Mom? Huh? Where was He then?" His fist pummeled the sky as his shout echoed where no one could hear.

Andy, weary from a hard day's work and his rolling emotions, sunk into the shade beneath a hedge-size wall of corn. His head, cradled in his hands, ached and left him feeling drained as the last of the lyrics played over and over in his mind. Was his mom trying to tell him something? Could God really be here? Now? Gooseflesh rippled along his forearms. Andy hoped God wasn't hanging around, not the way he'd been acting. More than anything he wanted to conjure up Ella's image to wash away the press of what he felt sure was God's shame, but he couldn't.

Thou my great Father, I Thy true son;
Thou in me dwelling, and I with Thee one.

"I want a great Father. I want that so bad." He spoke to no one in particular, but Andy sensed his words didn't fall on deaf ears. "God, is it too late?"

"Too late for what?"

Andy startled. When he raised his head to find a shadowy Will standing in front of him and Will's fired up Trans Am purring not more than a few feet away. Shock widened Andy's eyes.

"If you're late, I can give you a ride. Anyplace you want, just say the word."

A "no thanks" poised at the tip of Andy's tongue, but exhaustion made him think twice. He could still see the church's steeple in the distance and Andy didn't relish another trek in the heat. The heat. That's what all this deep thinking came from. Heat exposure. With a shake of his head, he wiped the last of the song from his mind.

"Yeah. Thanks Will. I could use a ride."

"Where do you wanna go?"

"Home." Andy rose on shaky legs and brushed the dregs of last year's harvest from his work clothes.

"Your babysitter is gonna have a cow if they see me pull in." Will shot the comment over his shoulder with a knowing wink.

Andy gave thought to Will's statement and realized he was right. His father made Aunt Tess swear that Andy wouldn't hang with Will any longer. "So he'll keep his nose clean," his dad had said. He couldn't show up on the farm with Will playing chauffeur.

Besides now that Andy sat with the air-conditioner blasting cool tendrils at his face, Andy didn't feel so inclined to head home.

"On second thought, I've got time. Let's go do something."

CHAPTER SIX

Andy leaned against the head rest and drained his mind. The cool air helped, but Ella's face kept popping up with his mother's voice singing in the background.

"What do you want to do?" Andy turned to Will. No sooner had the words died away than Will's smirk filled the rearview mirror.

"Can you keep a secret?"

"Yeah. Why?"

"You know this is my last summer in hodunksville and I plan on leaving an impression before I go."

Andy tried to keep the curiosity from sounding too childish, but he couldn't help the grin that slipped through. "What kind of impression?"

"A big one. You see that barn over there?"

Who could miss it? The behemoth stood as long as a swimming pool, as wide as a baseball diamond and at least a couple stories high. The roof caved in the middle

288

and if the wind blew just right the greying slats would peel right off the cross beams. The whole frame would collapse down the center. Andy pictured the barn in a Hollywood horror movie instead of sitting in the middle of some farmer's back lot.

"I'm gonna torch it."

Andy's head snapped back around. "You're gonna what?"

"Gonna do old man Nelson a favor and send the whole thing up in smoke. Ever see a barn burn?"

When Andy's head stopped shaking, Will continued. "A barn burned about a mile east of here last year. The whole town showed up to watch. Those things are so old they flare like fireworks. Man, they send off some cool colors, too. Must be the paint or something, but it's awesome." Will's face grew animated and flushed as the words rushed from his mouth. "Now that barn was nothing compared to this one. Nelson has the biggest barn around, that oughta raise the stakes. Don't you think?"

They'd slowed to a crawl as Will seemed bent on letting Andy get a good look at the barn from every angle. When they turned up the next block, Andy got a better look at how the barn stood in relation to the other outbuildings and the farmhouse.

"Dude, you can't torch that. It's too close to the house."

"Who says? You some fire chief?"

"No, but I'm not an idiot either. Look."

Will hit the brakes and leaned toward Andy's pointed finger. The house couldn't have been more than two car lengths away from the back porch of the building. And that didn't account for the tall oak that shaded both the corner of the barn and the corner of the house. It didn't take a computer whiz to see how things would shake out.

Will shrugged his shoulders and pressed on the gas. "Eh. That's what the fire department's for. Gives them something to do besides polishing their shiny pumper."

Andy leaned back and crossed his arms over his chest. "It's nuts, man. Stupid nuts."

Will's ear reddened while his knuckles whitened. "I ain't stupid, chump."

"I didn't say you were stupid. But setting that fire is."

"Whatever."

The Trans Am pulled into Andy's driveway before Will grew any redder, but when Andy crossed in front of the car and past the driver's door, Will shoved it open, catching Andy in the thigh with the handle. Doubled over and breathing raggedly through the pain, Andy glowered at Will as he stood, bent beside him, and hissed in his ear.

"You say one word about this to anyone and I'll —"

"You'll what?" Andy's challenge fell on deaf ears as Will drifted away from his side, wearing the dumbest looking grin Andy had ever seen. When he followed his path with his eyes, his heart sunk.

There in his grandmother's garden, Ella bent over a pair of rose bushes. Her hair had been swept back in a fancy braid that fell over her shoulder from time to time as she stooped over to free another bloom from the bush.

"No!" Andy ground out.

Will winked back before he covered the ground to the rose garden in three quick strides. "Why, Ella Suchar. It's been a while."

Ella startled, but she managed to smile. It seemed to waver at the corners. "Will. How are you?"

"Fine. Thanks for asking. You look amazing." He'd arrived at her side before Andy and his bruised thigh hobbled to the garden's mini-picket fence.

Andy steadied himself against the corner of the white-washed wood and tried to control his raging emotions.

"Thanks," Ella said as she wiped her gloved hands against the gardening apron she wore. Slipping off the hardened canvas, Ella tucked a wayward strand of hair behind her ear and smiled into Will's baby blues. Andy hadn't realized how much like the quintessential football star Will looked, until the blush from Ella's face opened his eyes. Blond and built, Will seemed to attract the very rays of the sun.

No way can I compete with that.

Why did he want to anyway? He didn't want Ella, if anything he wanted to be rid of her and the ridiculous power she had over his every thought. Didn't he? As Andy watched Will tuck a second strand behind Ella's ear, he realized he did. Badly.

"Ella." Andy moved away from the post and waved with the cheeriest smile he could muster, but between his stiffening knees and the ivy vines near his feet, Andy only managed to squeak out her name and stumble into a patch of wood violets.

"Oh, Andy. Are you all right?"

She was at his side before he could finish standing and as she dusted the dead leaves from his shoulder, she snickered. Though she tried to hide it behind her hand, Andy didn't miss a beat.

"I'm sorry. I shouldn't be laughing, but

you. You."

An all too familiar frustration ate away his gut like acid. "I what?" He knew it sounded harsh, but so did her laughter.

"You look like a scarecrow."

Snorts and giggles came from Will and Ella and grew as she picked twigs from his hair and elbow.

With a scowl, Andy brushed away her hand and the last of the garden's debris. "Thanks." It was all he trusted himself to say.

"I'm sorry, Andy." Ella cleared her throat and tried to wipe the grin from her face, but only managed to smear black dirt across her chin. Her sweet, upturned chin.

Agh.

When Andy looked away, Ella excused herself and walked off in search of his grandmother, or so she said. As the last of her flowery scent drifted away, Andy sucked in a few deep breaths.

"You like her." There was no missing Will's narrowed eyes and clenched jaw.

"You're nuts."

"You do. And if you don't help me with my plan, she'll regret it." His finger penetrated the air at her retreating back.

Pain, as sharp as any injection, raced through his ribcage and stabbed his heart.

"What do you mean?" he growled.

"I can't light Nelson's barn alone. So you're gonna help. And if you don't help, I'll make sure your girlfriend gets to know a side of me you won't like."

CHAPTER SEVEN

Sleepless nights and days of mowing, weeding and painting in temperatures hotter than the Sahara stripped Andy down to a sparking bundle of nerves. Will appeared at the church from time to time, always at just the right moment for Andy to catch him sidling up to Ella. Afterward, Will squinted his eyes and smiled in Andy's direction, heating Andy's cheeks until they bested the July heat, no contest.

But the dreams curdled Andy even more. It was the same night after night. Ella sat alone in the sanctuary, relaxed on the front bench as the moonlight cast rosy shadows through the stained glass. From the back hall a figure strolled forward with a cocky swagger until he towered over her from behind. Unaware, Ella looked to be in prayer and no matter how hard Andy screamed or how fast he raced up the aisle, she remained still, eyes closed, lips murmuring. Just as the shadowy man laced his fingers through the back of her hair, Ella's eyes would fly open clouded over in fear and pleading to him for help, but his legs that raced moments before became glued to the floorboards and his screams became mute.

Night after night he had witnessed the shadow-man's torment until it woke Andy in a sweaty mess.

Not even the long walks to the church and back soothed his muddled brain these days, so when he arrived early Friday morning, it was all he could do to pretend civility. In the sanctuary, Ella replaced dried flowers with fresh stems and chatted amicably with Will who lounged against the front bench, like a stretching cat. Andy's tongue held between his pressed teeth, but he didn't know how long that would last.

"Oh. Hey, Andy." Will sounded overly friendly and far too confident.

"Will."

Ella turned in his direction and flashed a sweet smile, but they'd kept their exchanges short and brief, since he barked at her in the garden. Try as he did, he couldn't return her smile with anything more than a nod. A frown crossed her brow as she tucked the last bouquet in the vase near the choir stands. Gathering the debris from her efforts, Ella disappeared behind the screen to toss the garbage in the only can around. Andy took the opportunity to sidle up to Will.

"What are you doing?" he whispered.

Will raised his hands in surrender. "Nothing, man. Can't a guy spend a little time in church?"

"Yeah, but your case'll need more than a little time. What are you after?"

Will sat up and let a sinister grin spread across his face. "I was hoping to catch you, my friend. The time has come man. All the supplies for the torching are waiting in my garage. I'm thinking we strike tomorrow night. It's supposed to be cloudy, perfect weather for a little night fun. What do you say?" He leaned into Andy's personal space until Andy could smell eggs and coffee on his breath, making Andy want to gag.

In a gravelly voice, Andy answered. "No way."

Will shrugged and rose to his feet as if he'd expected that answer or didn't care, but Andy sensed it wasn't the last he'd hear about the matter. Brushing past Andy's shoulder, Will leaned around the screen and called to Ella.

"Yes?" she said, peeking out from behind

the material until her head almost collided with his shoulder. Giggling she took a step to the side and gazed up at Will in a way that stirred up Andy's already nauseated stomach.

"Did you need something, Will?"

Before he said another word, Will placed his hand against the wall behind her and leaned closer. Despite his hushed voice, Andy heard every inflection and every note. "I was wondering if you're free tomorrow night. My schedule just cleared."

Ella's eyes moved over the floor as she chewed her lip. "I don't know. I prefer group things." Then her eyes flew to Andy sending a ripple of electricity down his back. "Andy, are you busy? I could ask Sarah if she'd like to come along."

Will's sideways glance did not look like he appreciated the added company. "No, Andy's busy. Aren't you, man? He just told me he couldn't hang out tomorrow night. But hey, I don't bite. Besides, I wanted to ask you about something I read online the other day. About Jesus and salvation, but I kind of wanted to talk to you privately." He lowered his voice as though he had a pressing question, but Andy didn't buy it.

Will had stepped away from Ella, but just enough to give her breathing room. Upon hearing Will's curiosity and his longing — fake or real — for Christ, her face lit like a lighthouse.

"Sure, Will. I'll talk to my dad, but I'm sure if you'd like to meet me here tomorrow, we can find some time to talk about whatever questions you have. You don't mind coming to the church do you? I don't feel right about going on a date alone." Her words came fast and furious and seemed to take Will off guard with their speed.

Will recovered in time to agree to a time before he sauntered past Andy. He nailed Andy's shoulder with his in the process. An animal-like growl rumbled through Andy's chest, catching Ella's attention.

"How could you be so foolish?" Andy asked when Will strode out of ear shot.

Ella's face tightened as she drew in a sharp breath. "Excuse me?"

Again, he seemed to have said the wrong thing. *Recover. Recover.* "Don't you see what he's doing?"

"No, Andrew Hasmer, I don't. Enlighten me. Please." She added a flip of her arms to punctuate her manners.

"He's coming after you to get to me." Her cheeks reddened along with her scalp and ears, but Andy pushed on. "He doesn't want to know about Jesus any more than he wants to chit-chat with you."

Ella licked her lips and breathed through her teeth before she spoke the next words, carefully as if each had been chosen with care. "So there is nothing desirable about me? No reason someone like Will would want to spend time with me? Not to mention the possibility Will might actually want to learn about Christianity? You are the end all — the only thing worth anyone's time. Is that it?"

The heat from his anger seeped from his body like water through a three-inch hole. With his mouth agape Andy blinked.

When he failed to answer, Ella brushed past him and followed Will's trail. It wasn't until the sanctuary door slid shut behind her that Andy noticed Pastor Mike leaning against the office archway. His arms crossed over his chest and he looked content if not smug. He smiled.

Andy lumbered up beside him.

"She's a quick thinker, that one." Pastor Mike's smile deepened.

"I didn't mean to imply she wasn't likeable. She's really likeable. I like her. She's cute actually. And I'm sure Will thinks so, too. I just . . ." The words poured from his mouth as if a watershed had broken.

Pastor Mike held up both hands. "Hold

on. Hold on, there. I didn't hear the whole thing. What happened?"

Filling Pastor Mike in took several minutes and still Andy left out Will's fire threat. He did mention Will's questionable intentions, though.

"Andy my friend, you never know when someone feels a prodding of the Spirit. Even if Will doesn't believe it yet, his falsified interest might lead to something real. If Ella asked him to meet her here, it's because she knows I'm always around and she feels safe. What I'd really like to know is why this is so upsetting for you." Pastor Mike led them toward an empty bench where he turned to face Andy. With his chin cradled between his index finger and his thumb, Mike stared into Andy's eyes with an intensity that made Andy run his finger beneath his collar.

Because I think Ella is the most beautiful creature ever to walk the earth. Because I want a father who cares as much about me as you do for Ella. Because I want a faith strong enough to face Will and not worry what will happen when I tell him no.

Andy jerked his eyes toward the stained glass and swallowed hard. "I don't know."

"Andy, where does Jesus belong in your life?"

Wishing he knew the answer, Andy could

feel the sting of emotion cramp his throat as a strong female voice sang the first chords of Be Thou My Vision. The song came from the balcony above their heads and it filled the room as the pianist joined in.

Mike leaned forward. "Sorry. I can ask Mrs. Castor to stop. She's practicing for tomorrow's service." Pastor Mike rose, but Andy's hand on his wrist stopped him short.

"Please." His voice choked through the lump that threatened to block any sound. "Let her play. My mom loved that song."

"She was a Christian, your mom?"

Andy nodded. "Me, too. But I just couldn't believe after she died."

"Didn't get along with God after that, eh?"

Andy shot a suspicious sideways glance at the man wondering what kind of pastor talked like that.

"I get it, Andy." The man pulled out his wallet and flipped to a photo of a woman holding a young Ella's hand. The woman smiled into the camera, broad and open as though she was about to say something. Despite the joy that sparkled in her eyes, something was off. Her cheekbones were sharp and prominent while her pallor bordered on bluish-grey. Andy doubted the cause was laid in the film development because Ella looked flushed if not a bit sun-kissed. When Andy held the photo closer, he noticed the woman's clothes seemed to hang off her in droopy swags.

Pastor Mike reached for the picture with a softened gaze. "God took Ella's mom about ten years ago and not a day goes by that I don't miss that woman dearly." His thumb brushed the wind-swept hair from the woman's frozen face before he locked eyes with Andy again. "There's no knowing God's ways, not this side of heaven. I wonder sometimes if that's not why He allows us to wail and whine like David does throughout the Psalms. He knows this life hurts."

Andy's voice dropped to a whisper. "How do you do it? Believe in a God who does this?"

"Because God didn't take my wife, a congenital heart defect did," Pastor Mike said as a wispy smile curled his lips. "Besides, I don't see it as God taking my wife, I see it as God carrying me through the months and years of grief that followed. I wouldn't have made it without Him."

The ache in Andy's head crescendoed leaving him nauseous and disgusted. "I guess it's how you look at it, but either way, He doesn't seem to give a care about me so I'd just as soon do the same for Him." Andy rose and started down the aisle until Pastor Mike reached out a hand and rested it on his shoulder.

"Can I give you a word of advice — about my daughter, that is?"

Andy twisted his body around and shrugged.

" 'A kind answer soothes angry feelings, but harsh words stir them up.' Proverbs 15:1. You might fare better if you kept that in mind."

"Easier said than done."

"So true." Then Pastor Mike turned up the row and headed toward the offices. After a couple feet, he jabbed his finger in the air and called Andy's name. "I almost forgot. Lindsay called and wanted to tell you she got the last of the shares taken care of. She's making a celebratory dinner tonight, so don't be late. But all things considered, why don't you take the day off. You've got the inside sparkling and it'll be far too hot to work outside, so start your celebration early."

At last, a good break. "Thanks, Pastor Mike." Mike had already turned back toward the hall and walked into the shadows, but his hand waved in the air to signal his response.

"Congratulations on your success," he

called as he slipped through the door.

"Yes!" Andy hissed, pumping his fist in the air.

Now to find Will. Pastor Mike might think Will could be trusted, but Andy knew better. Andy had to keep Will away from Ella.

CHAPTER EIGHT

It didn't take long to find Will. Stunting his dirt bike, Will scattered no less than three people leaving the Community Center as he rode it up the handicap ramp and jumped the steps on the back tire. Then he'd circle back as if he'd do it again.

"Will!"

The bike spit gravel to the side as Andy sprinted beside him. "So what'll it take?" Andy asked once he had Will's attention and his lop-sided grin.

"Andy. My man." Will back-slapped Andy hard enough to send the thwack to the onlookers across the street. "I don't want nothing from you."

"I ain't playing, Will. Leave the girl alone. She's done nothing to you."

"Yet." The sneer on his face curdled Andy's breakfast making him drop his gaze until Pastor Mike's verse about kind words reminded him how to turn this in his favor.

Andy brought his eyes from his shoes to Will's face. "I get you want to go out with a bang, but why Nelson's barn? Why not something else?"

"Like what?" Will drew out each word as he furrowed his brow and stared at Andy with open suspicion.

"Ever tagged?"

"That's old."

"Not if it's a masterpiece. Unless you're not good."

Will slapped his chest. "I can school you any day."

"Then go out with something that sticks, man. A little aerosol art will last longer than a burnt barn."

Nodding slowly, Will thrust out his chin and paused. "Not a horrendous idea. Got a place in mind?"

"No dude. You're the one who lives here."

"I got just the place. Hop on."

Andy placed both feet on the rider posts of Will's dirt bike and held onto the boy's shoulders as they took off down Main St. They passed through Oakville and started down a quiet country road. It didn't take long before Will slid to a stop and pointed at a beat-up van parked beside the railroad tracks. Andy's heart sank. He'd expected a water tower or an overpass, something

307

buried in the middle of the country where no one would care if they added a little graffiti art, but some guy's ride? Not cool.

"Will, are you nuts?"

Will turned to him as the smile on his face washed away faster than a kids day-after-Christmas joy. "What's the matter?"

"It's someone's van."

"Yeah. So."

Andy rolled his eyes and slapped his forehead.

"Look, Andy. Either we tag or we burn. Your choice. Of course if I'm bored, I could always call Ella."

"Tag. We tag." A hollow ring captured Andy's voice as he spoke. Between the van and Ella, the van lost, hands down.

They made a quick trip back to Will's for his car and a bag of spray paint Will nabbed from his dad's garage. Back at the van, Will tagged the far-side while Andy covered the other. Not one passerby interrupted their work and after an hour or so, Will announced his master piece complete. When Andy walked around to inspect the paint, he sucked in his breath and tried hard not to grimace. Will described the picture as a fresh rendition of old man Bakersfield holding a pitchfork in one hand and a flapping chicken in the other. Will entitled it "Hiriam's Gothic" before he capped the last can and threw the last empty in a plastic bag.

Andy cocked his head to the side trying to see the pitchfork or the chicken, but he only succeeded to pick out Hiriam as the largest stick figure.

Who teaches art around here?

"No evidence," Will said.

Andy nodded before he retreated to his side of the van.

By the time Andy finished it was well past lunch and the heat turned unbearable. Will dropped Andy off and waved like a five year-old school girl on his way down the drive. At least he wouldn't be burning anything or hanging on Ella anymore. Andy ran his hands through his sweaty hair as he walked through the back door and headed for the utility sink to wash up.

"Andrew Hasmer!"

Andy turned in the direction of his grand-mother's voice. Her eyes flashed and her hands formed fists that whitened as they perched on her hips. "What have you done?"

What? No way could she have found out about the van. Could she? No one caught them and they only just finished. No. No way. Had he done something else? He shrugged.

"Get yourself into that living room,

right now."

Dried paint tightened the skin on his hands. Can't wash. She'll know. He shoved his hands into his pockets. Sweat trickled down his temple. It itched, but his hands stayed put.

"Go on," she said. "Get in there."

I should pray. Pray? Why would God help him now? After what he'd just done? He shuffled past her.

Then he stepped into the living room. Silence. With his head dipped, he glanced up and noticed Aunt Tess and Lindsay. Oh man. His heart thumped against his ribs. He'd give anything to wipe the drip from the side of his face.

"Surprise!" Aunt Tess and Lindsay clapped and shouted. Even Grandpa managed to throw a handful of colored bits of paper into the air.

"What?" When Grandma stood beside him, he sent her a quizzical glance which she parried with a denture-flicking smile.

"The last four farm shares came through this morning." Lindsay hugged him until his lungs ached.

"I know. Pastor Mike told me. But this?" He held his hand up displaying the bits of paper he'd caught in mid-air.

Lindsay grinned through watery eyes.

"Half the shares sold came from those you pitched last week. We made it because of you." She held him by the shoulders just like his mother used to do. It brought the sting of tears to his eyes which he quickly sniffed back.

"Aw man. That's cool."

"Yeah that's cool. Andy, we couldn't have done it without you," Aunt Tess said. "And Grandpa has something to say to you. He's been practicing all morning."

Andy closed the distance between Gramp's recliner and himself. "Gramps?"

Through a lopsided smirk, he spoke in a gravelly voice. "Thank you."

Andy let the tears come as he embraced Gramps. "You're welcome," he whispered into his grandpa's ear. Andy coughed on the joy and laughter that vied for space in his mouth.

"What's so funny?" Andy's father stood in the front door glancing from the mess on the floor to Andy's moist face.

"Art, darling," Gram squealed as she ran toward him and hugged him close. "How was your ride?"

"Wonderful, but I'm more interested in what brought that laughter out of my sullen boy's mouth."

Andy chuckled as he approached his

father, but just as he did a woman rounded the door's corner and poked her head inside. Andy froze.

"Hello," she said.

"Dana!" Aunt Tess said as she moved to welcome the woman inside.

But it wasn't until Andy's father placed his hand on the small of the woman's back and guided her forward that Andy sensed the crumbling of the world he and his dad had just started to rebuild. Dating. That's what people did when they were . . .

A heavy drape settled on Andy's shoulders more oppressive than the mid-summer's humidity. Somewhere in the distance thunder exploded before Gram closed the front door. Voices chattered and laughed all around him, but Andy could only stare at that hand. His father's. The one still resting on that woman's back. The room closed in, sucking out every last molecule of air. He had to get out. Run. Escape. Anything but stay here and watch that woman fill his mother's space.

Andy bolted through the room and out the back door. His father's voice followed him down the back yard all the way to the field near the pond.

"Andy. Come back. What's wrong? Let's talk."

He was done talking. Done trying. Go back to your laptop or the TV. Now that some stranger stood at his side — the very same side his mother used to occupy — his father wanted to talk. Oh no. That wasn't happening.

Despite the rolling clouds and the distant rumbles, Andy ran. He passed the barn and the baby plants. He ran through the over- grown outfields and the neighbor's lot. He didn't stop until the rain cooled his face and the sound of distant cars sloshed through the downpour.

"Why God?" Andy demanded. He raised his fist to the sky when a crack of thunder rumbled so loud it made his heart jump. "Why my mom? Take my dad instead. Please, give me back my mom! Please." Andy sunk to his knees and mixed fresh tears with the rain. There he remained until his throat ached and his energy slipped away with the passing of the storm. He couldn't face that woman or his dad, yet. So when he got to his feet, he let them lead the way.

They took him down a familiar gravel road. Sure enough, the lights in the church office told him Pastor Mike was still in. With a long, slow breath, Andy placed his hand on the sanctuary door and pushed it open and headed for Pastor Mike's private room.

When he knocked, the man threw open the door and pulled Andy inside with such force Andy had to brace himself against one of the wingback chairs.

The pastor slapped Andy's shoulder. "So glad you're here. Your dad is beside himself with worry. Said you ran out the minute he got home and they couldn't find you. Worried sick with this storm. Got more coming, too. I hear we're in for a doozy of a weekend. Come on in. Sit down. I'll go get a dry towel."

He disappeared for a moment and returned with a towel and a small tray of food. Before the pastor set the tray on the table, Andy cradled his head in his hands and moaned. "I don't want to be a mess any more. I'm tired of being angry all the time."

"I know." Mike's voice lowered as he patted Andy's shoulder.

"How do I make it stop?" He begged Mike with his eyes.

"You have to give it up. Give it to God every day. Every hour. Every second if you have to, but you give it to Him. He knows what it's like to lose a loved one."

"Yeah but He got His son back."

"True. You mentioned once before that your mother loved God."

"Mmm-hmm."

"And you? Is Jesus part of your life, too?"

Andy hesitated, considering the past year. "Yes. I haven't been the best at it, but He was — is — part of my life. I just don't know what part."

Mike nodded. And waited.

"I mean, I asked Him to be my Savior."

"Tell me about it."

"My mom and I talked about everything. Jesus included. So when I caught her on the couch one afternoon — crying — she told me the tears were happy tears. Tears because she couldn't believe how much Jesus loved her. I wanted that, too. So she prayed with me. Look, I know the spiel. Jesus is in my heart, my BFF. But I haven't been His anything. Doesn't that take away from my relationship? Anger Him or something?"

Mike tilted his head and eased back into his chair. "Andy, clasp your hands together."

"Huh?"

With a knowing smile, Mike showed him by clasping his hands in front of his chest with his fingers woven together. "Like this."

"Okay." Andy complied.

"Now, release one hand, but only one. Like this." Mike wiggled the fingers of his right hand but gripped with his left until his fingertips whitened. "Can you pull your loose hand free?"

Andy shook his head.

"It's like that with God, too. He holds onto us, even when we've slipped or let go. All He asks is that we come back."

"Even if I've done awful stuff?"

"You only need to ask for forgiveness."

A smirk broke through Andy's tear-stained façade. "Some of those old church ladies told me the same thing. Right after they told me how disappointed my mother would be with me."

"Andy. Church people are no more perfect than you or I. What they said may have been unkind, but their hearts may have been in the right place."

"Maybe." Andy shook his head trying to clear the guilt those women had heaped upon him. "But it still hurt."

"I'm sure it did."

"Who's hurt?" Ella's voice lilted around the corner before the rest of her waltzed through the shadows. "Oh. Andy. I didn't mean to interrupt. I just saw the light and thought —"

Standing, Andy wiped his hands on his jeans and cleared his throat. "No. No, it's okay."

Ella smiled and Andy could swear he saw a darkening touch her cheeks, but she recovered quickly and spun to face her father. "I came to ask you who painted the church van."

"What do you mean?"

"Well, Mrs. McGerty just called and said she passed it on her way out of Oakville. Said the side with Jesus touching the man's head was amazing. She wanted to see if the artist painted murals, too."

Andy fell back against the couch as his blood drained to his feet.

The church's van?

"I have no idea what she's talking about, honey."

"I do," Andy squeaked.

CHAPTER NINE

"And it's not Jesus' hand, it's my mom's, but I suppose it might look like His since it's reaching through heaven's floor." Andy's hands covered his face as he groaned. "I'm so sorry. I did it to protect Ella."

"Protect me? Whatever from? A wayward can of paint?"

Gazing up, Andy shook his head. "From Will. I figured he'd leave you alone if I did this."

"Andy Hasmer, I can take care of myself. I don't need you breaking the law to save me from some kid's prank."

"But —"

"But, nothing. Will wants to hear about Jesus and so he shall. In the church with my father nearby. And I don't need saving from anyone but Jesus. Now, if you'll excuse me, I think I'm going to head off to bed. I'd like to get up early to see the damage you've done to the van for myself." Red-faced and out of breath, Ella stormed from the room. Only the sound of a soft chuckle reminded him he wasn't alone.

"What are you laughing at?" he asked Pastor Mike.

"Just remembering her mother. Full of spit and fire, that one was. Glad to see Ella takes after her."

"Me, too." Andy huffed.

"Look Andy, I'll be here tomorrow night when Will comes by. Don't worry about a thing."

Taking a few shaky long breaths, Andy calmed down enough to nod. "I'm really sorry about the van. I really didn't know."

"I'm not worried. That old thing rusted out long ago, any art has to have improved its value. We'll check it out in the morning. Why don't you head home to your family."

"Uhh" Andy slapped his forehead. "I almost forgot about that mess."

"Andy, your dad loves you. He's trying to figure out how life works without your mom in it, just like you are. Cut him some slack and see if you can't start over."

"Did you and Ella ever go through that?"

"Nope. Ella was too little. We did all our mourning cuddled in a rocking chair."

"And we yelled our fool heads off."

With a cheeky grin, Pastor Mike rose and

headed toward the door. "We all have our special ways."

Telling his grandparents and his dad about the tag graffiti took longer than Andy imagined last night, but it felt so good. They took it well, too. They grounded him, took away the laptop he'd been using and worked out a payment plan with Pastor Mike for the repairs. Then at daybreak he and his dad met with Pastor Mike and Ella by the tracks.

Pastor Mike stared at the paint while he stroked his chin. His dad kept making weird guttural sounds, but Ella's reaction topped them all. She stood with her mouth agape, her hands on her hips, and her eyes blinking in rapid succession.

"It's amazing," Pastor Mike said. "I'm not sure what those black hash marks are on the other side, but this — this is amazing." His hand waved in front of Andy's work. A shadowy man stooped over one knee where he braced one hand against the ground. The other extended toward the clouds as if to beg, but his face remained downturned. Through the clouds a hand reached out, open as if it were going to touch the man's head. When Andy tipped his head, he could understand why Mrs. McGerty thought it was God's hand. It didn't look feminine at all, something Andy hadn't noticed as he painted.

"The other side's Will's addition." Andy's voice rose just above a whisper as he waited for the other two opinions.

"I suppose it's nice enough." Ella glanced over the painted van door one last time before she turned and walked away.

She must think I'm some paint-happy thug. As he stared at her back, he wondered if he could ever change her mind about him. Probably not. Besides, why did he care? *Because I do. A lot.* With the admission came a wave of remorse as though he'd found her and lost her in one stroke.

"Andrew." His father's voice sounded tight, but warm as he stared at Andy's tag. "You have your mother's gift. How is it I never noticed this before?"

"You haven't noticed a lot of things." There I said it. Out loud. And as he studied his dad he grew amazed.

Shock registered on his father's face and he opened his mouth as if to answer, but instead he sucked in a breath and ran his hand through his hair. "You're right, son. I'm sorry about that. I want to change if you'll let me."

"Won't you be too busy with Dana?" Then

he kicked at the gravel.

His father grabbed Andy's shoulder and forced Andy to face him. "I'll never be too busy for you. Never again. I promise."

"That'll have to be seen."

Sighing, Andy's dad released him. "You're right. I'll have to earn that back. Just like you'll have to earn my trust back. I'll talk to Pastor Mike about what he wants done with the van." His dad glanced around. "You're not to go near Will anymore, got it?"

"Yeah, Dad. I got it last night when you grounded me."

"But this is specific. No more Will. At all. For any reason."

Almost relieved not to see Will, Andy agreed. "All right. Say, I've gotta get to work. I left a lot undone yesterday. Would you mind giving me a ride?"

"Yeah. Sure." He ruffled Andy's hair and dropped his hand as though he'd made a mistake, but his face still looked eager.

Andy smiled. This would take work, but somehow, he'd make Mom proud again.

Voices from the church's back door slowed Andy's trek to the back garden.

"Why can't you come, Will? My mom's making her famous chili pizza and everything."

Andy ducked behind the church dumpster when he recognized the voice of Will's crony, Hank. As he moved to the far side, Andy caught a glimpse of Will's holey tennis shoes.

"Cause I've got me a date."

"Really? Who's the girl? Tracy? Anna? Who is it man?"

Feet grated across the gravel parking lot skittering rocks that rolled to Andy's feet. Holding his breath, Andy tried to shove himself between the metal container and the wooden slats meant to keep the coyotes and raccoons out of the bin. All the while he wondered why he didn't feel a sense of relief at Will's admission. Shouldn't he feel good that Will had moved on? Found some other girl to pester? If so, why did his arms breakout with goose flesh?

"I'm heading out with the preacher's daughter."

That's why.

"No way. She doesn't date. How'd you manage that one?"

"Easy." Andy imagined the sneer on Will's face as he listened to his story. "Just had to ask her about that religious junk."

Snickering rang through the lot before a meaty thunk stopped the noise. "Don't laugh. What do you have planned for tonight? Soggy pizza and cards? With your mommy?"

"Hey!"

"The way I got if figured, that girl is ready for a fun time. You know what I mean?"

"Yeah. Yeah, I get it. Where ya going to take her? Bristol's Point?"

"Naw. We're going to meet here tonight."

The gasp that rent the air could have been heard inside the sanctuary had the windows been open. "In the church? Man, you're sick. Won't her dad be around?"

"Nope. I've got that covered."

"Huh?"

In the course of a few minutes the voices receded too far for Andy to hear Will's plan, but whatever it was, it couldn't be good. Lifting his head from behind the dumpster, Andy peered around. They'd disappeared. Andy dashed for the sanctuary, fiddled with his key ring until he found the master key and slid it into the lock.

"Ella!" he yelled as he raced through the sanctuary and then to the offices. "Ella!" It wasn't until he had sprinted out back again that he spotted her in the garden. Sun glinting off her hair, turning it auburn in the shadows. The sight of her stopped him cold, but raced his heart. This was his fault. If he hadn't gotten tied up with Will. If he hadn't

324

gotten involved with Ella.

He threw the back door wide. "Ella!"

Her head snapped up and the peaceful look she wore faded to confusion or frustration, Andy couldn't tell which. Before she could speak, he strode up beside her and pleaded with her to listen. "Look, I know I've messed up before. I've been nothing but mean to you and I'm really sorry about that. But you've got to listen to me. Please."

Her eyes blinked in rapid succession. "Okay. Consider yourself forgiven. What's got you so worked up, anyway?"

Without thinking, Andy grabbed Ella's forearms and squeezed. "You have to tell Will no. Don't meet with him tonight."

Ella's face contorted until it looked angrier than Gram's when Gramp's ate all her chocolate-striped cookies. With a shrug and a step back, Ella freed herself from his grasp. "Andy, don't tell me what to do. You're hardly one to be giving dating advice, or any advice for that matter. And second, what Will and I do is none of your business. I have lived here all my life here, and I've known Will and his family since we were toddlers. I think I can deal with his questions."

"But that's just the thing. He doesn't want to ask a few questions. I overheard him talking to Hank about wanting nothing to do with your religion. He's planning something way worse."

"Like what?" she asked, planting her hand on her hip and tilting her head.

"I don't know what, but it isn't about Jesus."

"Well, you have nothing to fear, my dad is planning on staying in his office until Will and I are done. Just in case Will has a question I can't answer."

"Well if he's here, why doesn't he join you guys? Couldn't he answer the questions better? Then it wouldn't be a real date, either."

Ella narrowed her eyes. "That's what this is really about, isn't it? You don't want me to date Will?"

Andy searched the garden for some escape. How could he tell her something he only just admitted it to himself?

"I'm right, aren't I?" Her features softened until her eyes turned liquid gold and her lips curled into a relaxed smile.

Andy unhinged. "I don't care who you date. Just make sure someone is here with you tonight." He spun on his heels and stomped from the garden.

Never had the wooden benches shined like they did after he polished them that afternoon. He'd rubbed until his arms ached and his brain numbed from the rush of emotions. There. Maybe they'll both slide right off those silly benches and crash so hard; he'll have to go home. With one last look back, Andy closed the sanctuary doors and thought his heart felt as heavy and wooden as they did.

He did care. *Why can't I just tell her?* If he had the choice, he'd be the one in the church with her, asking her about how Jesus kept her from missing her mom. Ella with the soft voice and the fiery eyes that flashed when he pushed her too far. But she was always quick to forgive him. Even now after battling her about her date, he knew she wouldn't hold his ornery behavior against him. She'd even forgive Will and whatever plan he had up his sleeve. He gritted his teeth as his breathing grew ragged. No way could he let that louse hurt her. No matter what, Andy had to be there tonight to stop him. He just had to be.

Jogging the rest of the way to Gram's, Andy thought through his plan. He'd tell his father everything. But when he rounded Gram's drive, he chickened out. Even though they'd gotten along recently, didn't mean he'd understand Andy's need to save Ella. Ella didn't even think she needed saving. How could he convince his dad she did?

Nope. This was on him.

"Andy? Is that you?" Lindsay called through the screen.

Andy took a slow and steady breath. "Yes. It's me." He whipped open the door and walked inside before the wooden frame banged against the house.

"Come on in. You must be starving." Lindsay rose and disappeared around the kitchen door before Andy could flop on Gramp's chair.

As he sunk into the cushions, an odd realization struck him. "Where're Gramps and Gram?"

"Grandpa had to go in to have his oxygen tank checked. Gram took him. They should be back soon." His father's smile didn't fade, but it lost some of its strength.

"On a Saturday?" Andy asked, leaning forward.

Lindsay buzzed around the corner carrying a bag of chips and lemonade. "Yes. Don't panic, but Gramps was having trouble breathing. The hospital said it was nothing to worry about, but they needed to keep him for a couple hours."

"What? Why didn't someone get me?"

Andy's father rubbed his hands on his pant legs as if he needed to warm them up — or wipe them dry. "He's fine. Doc thinks

328

it was just a clogged oxygen tube on his tank. He'll be back in no time."

Andy checked his watch before running his hand through his hair. Not before Ella's date. "Um. Dad? Could I talk to you?"

CHAPTER TEN

Dad's smile disappeared as Lindsay hustled from the room mumbling something about finding a frozen pizza.

"Can you make it quick? I'd like to check on Grampa before I — well, I have some unfinished business in Oakville," his dad said when they were alone.

Staring at his father, Andy began to doubt the wisdom of involving the man. What if his dad didn't believe him? Or like Ella, thought Will had turned some corner?

"I forgot my extra work shirt at church. Could I pick it up after dinner?" It wasn't a total lie, Andy reasoned, he had left his shirt behind. Might as well pick it up and bring it home for Gram to wash. And while he was there, he could stay out of sight, but within earshot in case Ella needed him.

"A work shirt? Why don't you leave that for tomorrow? You must be exhausted. Kick back and take a night off." When Andy huffed the hair that hung over his brow, his dad walked over gathered his shoulders in a quick hug. Then his dad headed toward the door. "Why don't you go see if Lindsay found that pizza."

Before he headed into the kitchen, his dad headed outside and Andy listened to the gravel spit beneath his father's tires. Now what?

Pray.

As clear as the church bell, Andy heard the word ring through his brain. *Pray.* He shoved the impulse deep, thinking it hadn't helped in the past.

"Andy? Uncle Art? I have the pizza in the oven." Lindsay walked into the room and glanced around. "Where's your dad?"

"He had to go."

"Oh. Everything okay?"

"Sure. I'm not hungry right now, Linds. Mind if I go crash instead?"

Lindsay furrowed her brow and placed a gentle hand on his shoulder. "Sure. You'll holler if there's anything you need, right?"

"Yeah." Andy sighed as he walked down the hall to his room. Escape consumed his mind and he hated lying to Lindsay, but he couldn't get her into trouble. Besides, his dad told him not to give her any grief, and telling would definitely bring her grief. Andy

331

shut his door behind him and shuffled the pillows under his covers like he'd seen a thousand times on TV. It didn't look like a human, not even close. Maybe if Lindsay didn't look too close? No. Andy swiped the pillows from the bed, letting them pile on the floor. She was too smart for that ruse.

Yanking the wooden frame of his window wider, Andy wriggled his way through it, replaced the screen, and jogged through the yard until he was far enough away to hit the road. With thunder cracking in the distance, Andy figured it would take him at least twenty minutes if he walked fast and he only had fifteen according to his watch.

Twenty-five minutes later, Andy rounded the corner of the church's parking lot and launched himself up the back steps. What was he doing? Sneaking around a church after hours. Andy gripped the railing and lowered himself to the top step. If Ella knew, he'd be sunk for sure. But did he dare leave her with Will? Even if her dad was in the rectory? Pastor!

Andy scanned the lot noting two cars, the one Ella used and Will's Trans Am. Pastor Mike's Toyota Camry was gone. He left them?

Now what?

Pray.

This time the word seared his brain like a flash of lightning.

God. I don't know if you're listening or not. I don't even know if you care, but I can't do this alone. Ella's in there with a guy that's gonna hurt her. If I go in she's gonna write me off as a nut. If I don't, well, I can't bear to think of what could happen. What am I supposed to do?

With a groan he cradled his head in his hands.

I'm so tired. Tired of being angry and fighting with my dad. Tired of getting into trouble, but trouble seems to find me. Help. Please.

Sitting on the top step, Andy's heart skipped a beat before it slowed into a relaxed rhythm — a rhythm that matched the patter of rain that began to fall against his face. For the first time in months, his shoulders loosened and he sensed a peace fill him.

As he rolled his eyes heavenward in wonder, Ella's voice seeped through the door and rolled over the rain, but her words blurred together. Her anger was clear enough, though.

Andy unlocked the door and slipped inside. God, give me strength. Please. The back hall, darkened by shadows, loomed

333

longer than Andy remembered, but he made his way toward the voices as quiet as possible considering the brooms and Christmas props he dodged along the way. No one seemed to notice him, while Ella continued to argue.

By the time he'd reached the screen that separated the back rooms from the altar of the sanctuary, Andy could hear Will's voice match Ella's tone.

"Come on girl. You know you like me."

"I said leave! Will. Now!"

"But you haven't explained everything to my satisfaction." Although Andy couldn't see Will's face, the sneer in his voice painted a clear enough picture.

"I should have trusted Andy. He knew you were up to something."

Andy shifted around the screen, hiding behind the oak podium. Ella had backed against the stained glass wall while Will turned. He wore a mischievous grin that didn't light his eyes. If anything, it darkened them.

"Well. Andy isn't your concern right now, sweetheart. I am." Will sidled up beside Ella where he leaned his hand on the wall over her right shoulder and leaned in.

"Actually," Andy said as he stepped out

from behind the podium. "I am your concern."

Will jerked back, shooting Andy with a glare.

"Are you okay?" Andy kept his eyes on Will, but moved to fill the space between Ella and the weasel.

"I'm fine. Thank you." Her voice hovered between a shaky whisper and a coarse rasp.

Andy glanced back and noted the pallor of her face which boiled his blood. "You're going to pay for this," he hissed in Will's direction.

Will backed away. "For what? A little fun? I didn't hurt anyone. No harm no foul, right girly?" Throwing his palms in the air, he copped a cock-eyed smile and winked. "See ya." Then he turned and ran toward the front doors like a squirrel up a tree.

CHAPTER ELEVEN

"Where's the fire, Will?" Andy's father pushed the door open for Dana as Will whipped past him.

Will's head bounced from Art to Andy to Ella and back again. In a shot, he sprinted past Lindsay, shoving Dana into the door frame as he escaped into the wind that had kicked up.

"Andy?" Accusation and questioning mingled in his father's voice as the group headed toward him.

Panic nibbled Andy's bravado until he glanced at Ella. She had slid down the wall and sat on the floor hugging her knees where the receding light of the sun cast gold-colored rays through the stained glass. Like a halo, it ignited her hair and made her face glow. In awe, Andy approached her. He crouched down and swept the hair that had fallen into her eyes.

"Are you okay, El? You look pretty

shaken."

Andy looked up to meet his father's gaze. Then Ella captured his attention with the touch of her hand which she rested on his wrist. The burning it created coursed through his arm and flooded his face until he thought his scalp would ignite. His lips curled in what he knew must look like a stupid grin, but it had a mind of its own.

Ella returned his smile and patted his hand before she glanced around. "I'm fine. Andy's a real lifesaver — a hero, really." She caught Andy's eyes once more and held them. "I hate to think what would have happened if you didn't walk in. Thank you. And I'm really sorry."

"Sorry?" he asked. "For what?"

"For not believing you this afternoon. You were right. Will didn't want to talk about God. He —" Tears began to pool in her eyes.

Andy's heart shredded as his mind bent with anger. "You have nothing to be sorry for. But Will does. Don't worry about a thing. I'll make sure he never does anything like that again." Each word spit from his mouth with a bitter rage fueled by Will's callousness and a year's worth of pent up frustration.

But Ella shook her head and reached for him. "No, Andy. Don't. He needs your —

our forgiveness, not anger."

He looked at her as if she'd eaten a handful of worms. "What?"

Sniffing, Ella rose and walked over to the bench in front of her. She pulled out the Bible that snuggled in a little shelf beneath the seat and riffled through the pages while his father found a seat nearby. But Dana sat several rows back.

"Here." Ella jabbed her index finger in the middle of the page and handed the text to Andy. "Read it. Verse 13."

So Andy read aloud. "Colossians 3:13 says, 'Bear with each other and forgive one another if any of you has a grievance against someone. Forgive as the Lord forgave you.'" He could only blink at what she intended to do. "But, Ella?"

"But nothing. Don't you see Andy? Forgiveness is a two-way street. If I forgive Will for being a jerk tonight, he receives the gift of grace. Maybe, just maybe someday that gift will be opened and he'll get it. He'll understand what Jesus has to offer. I don't think he'd get that if you pounded him." A merry twinkle danced in her eyes which only puzzled him more.

"How is that two-way? Sounds like he wins and you lose, and you're okay with that?" Andy looked to the others for help, but they seemed just as engrossed in what Ella said.

With a soft giggle, Ella took back the Bible and closed it with care. "It is two-way. When I forgive Will he gets that gift, but I receive a gift as well. An even bigger gift, if you ask me. I'm freed from holding that grievance in. That stuff only turns to anger and bitterness, neither of which sits well with me. Forgiving others also gives me a glimpse at what God does for me. The last line of that verse you read, where it said 'Forgive as the Lord forgave you,' tells me a ton about the God I serve.

"Just like I find it hard to forgive Will, God must find it hard to forgive me. Considering what He went through with Jesus — it must have been very hard, but He did it anyway. Why? Why would He do that, Andy?"

Again Andy glanced around, but no one answered her. So he shrugged. "I have no idea."

"Because God loves you. Because you and I and Will are so valuable to Him, that's why. We're precious to Him. I know that because when I forgive, I feel a connection to the person I forgive. I imagine when God pours forgiveness over us, He feels a connection too. Don't you think?"

"I don't know about that. I feel a connection to Will, but it isn't all warm and fuzzy."

Ella giggled. "No. You probably don't, but forgiveness isn't just a feeling, it's a decision to say that person is worth a second chance. It's that type of connection that makes me grateful God forgives me." Then her face sobered and her voice whispered. "Just as He's forgiven you."

As if a weighted gym ball thumped him in the chest, Andy released his breath and fell to the bench. Ella met him there in silence, waiting.

"It's right here in black and white. Past tense. You're forgiven. Done and over. The question is what are you going to do about it?"

Andy lowered his head to his palms as faces flashed before his mind's eye. Faces of people he'd begrudged for so long. His father's was first, then Will's, a couple kids at school, Brandon — Lindsay's friend, and Ella's. But the last face took his breath away and cramped his throat. His mother's.

God I'm so sorry. I couldn't forgive her for abandoning us. Me. Until now. Please tell her I'm sorry. I forgive her. I want to forgive like Ella. Like you. His anger ebbed as the weight from his shoulders lightened. Ella had been right; it felt so good to forgive — hard, but good.

Turning his moist face toward her, he asked, "Does it stay?"

Puzzlement flickered in her eyes. "Does what stay?"

"This feeling? The lightness?"

Grinning, she shook her head. "No. Not all the time. Sometimes I have to forgive the same person everyday. Scratch that, every hour of every day." Then she giggled again.

When Andy pointed a finger to his chest and raised his eyebrows, she laughed in earnest and nodded. He was growing to like the sound of her giggles, more so than the flash of her angry eyes.

"You're a wise girl, Ella Suchar." Art's voice startled them both. "I can only hope to be that wise and strong, someday."

"Oh it's not me, Mr. Hasmer. I have to ask God to help me all the time and my dad helps too."

"Speaking of which, where is he? I thought he said he'd be here tonight?" Andy asked as he glanced around.

Ella rolled her eyes. "Mr. Nelson called about an hour ago. Said he found a couple gas cans and a few fireworks in the field behind his barn. He called the police, but they just hauled the stuff away. Mr. Nelson was a bit shaken, so I told him I'd be fine for a while if he wanted to go help out. We figured he'd be back before Will arrived, so I'm not sure what's taking so long." She scratched her forehead and checked her watch. "I'm really glad you came tonight and that you didn't listen to me earlier."

Art chuckled. "Yeah, that's a gift of his. Not listening."

Andy raised an eyebrow and gave his dad's arm a playful flick of his head. "I learned it from the best."

Then before either of them realized what happened, Art stepped up to Andy and gathered him in a bear hug. "I love you, Andy. Don't ever forget that. And I'm so sorry I snapped at you."

Pulling back, Andy grinned. "You're for-given."

"See. You're getting the hang of it," Ella said with note of laughter behind her words.

His father's attention had wandered to the back pews where Dana's head bowed over her clasped hands. "I have some unfinished business."

Grimacing, Andy nodded. "I think I do, too." When Ella slid her hand into Andy's, his heart fluttered.

Asking Dana's forgiveness was by far the

easiest thus far, and when Andy finished, he left his father with her while he asked Ella to walk him out. Thickening clouds rolled over the countryside dumping rain in sheets. But inside the church foyer, Andy's mind calmed.

He faced Ella, intending to tell her how sorry he was. How grateful he was to have her in his life. How he cared for her. But every English word seemed to seep out his ears. He was lost in her smile and her gaze. Without a glimmer of frustration or anger, her eyes seemed to cast warm amber sparks that set his brain ablaze.

"What are you staring at?"

"The most beautiful girl I've ever seen."

"Then you're not angry at me?"

Flinching back, Andy rocked with shock. "Angry? Why would I be angry at you?"

"I don't know."

When she averted her gaze, he tipped her head up and recaptured it.

"I've been angry at a lot of things, but never you. I think we just got off on the wrong foot."

Ella stepped back, squared her shoulders, and offered her hand. "Hi, I'm Ella Suchar." Her smile broadened and filled with open promise.

Andy could barely contain his laughter as

he grasped her hand and said, "Hey, I'm Andy Hasmer. It's nice to meet you."

■ ■ ■ ■

Art's Story

■ ■ ■ ■

Ephesians 2:14 "For he himself is our peace, who has made us both one and has broken down in his flesh the dividing wall of hostility."

CHAPTER ONE

Art Hasmer revved the engine of his Corolla, impatient to move into the left lane as soon as the light changed. The sign pointing north to Wisconsin Dells caught his attention too late. The Dells wouldn't be the final destination; running was all that mattered.

The calendar page he flipped that morning seemed burned on his retinas. June second. Every year, no matter what, he drove until the gas gauge pointed empty. The direction was not important and rarely considered before he opened the car door and buckled in.

By Rhinelander he turned back, hungry, tired and drained.

Amy had married him twenty years ago, knowing this ritual. The need to run on June second had started the year he'd turned seventeen and torn in half. No therapy had been able to break him of his itch to flee. Last year — he shook his head and tapped the steering wheel, definitely not needing to go there. Now Andy was seventeen and apparently bent the same way. The meeting last night with Andy's principal confirmed the wild streak.

Art drove home to the cul-de-sac on Madison's west side in the warm darkness, having outrun his demons that late spring day. This year he'd had more than his old fears to burn. Amy had left him — them — a year ago last Tuesday. Andy had just gotten his driver's license at the time.

What could he say to Andy that didn't smack of hypocrisy? The school counselor should have steered his son clear of those losers. Andy's Blazer was parked crooked in their driveway. Art parked his car near the mailbox and walked up the front brick path. The music throbbed through the front door. Why hadn't Andy at least left a light on? Art had hated to pick too much at his son this past year, but he couldn't let Andy loose in the world without some attempt to teach him manners. Of course his mom or his sister Tessa would be much better at it. Tessa's two perfect girls, Robin and Lindsay, had grown to women and left the nest. Art hadn't done so well with his son. Tagging? Street racing? There had been no arrest, no police involvement — for now. Andy better have a good explanation.

Art turned his key in the lock and pushed open the door. "Andy!" The music was so loud. The neighbors would complain. "Andy! I'm back!"

He tossed his keys and wallet on the kitchen desk, noted the blinking answering machine and sniffed at the sweet and sour tang hanging in the air. White boxes of rice and General Tsao's chicken take-out spilled over Amy's blue-tiled counter. At least the kid had enough sense to eat. Art picked up the grease-stained credit slip and winced.

"Andy!" Art headed up the stairs of their colonial. The racket wasn't coming from his son's bedroom, but from his own. He stopped in the open doorway, stunned at the sight of piled clothes and shoes, boxes and garbage bags on the floor and the bed he had shared with his late wife.

"What's going on!" Art blinked, unsure how his hands got around Andy's shoulders so quick and so tight.

Andy stared back at him with startled deep blue eyes; the wounded and angry look that reminded him of Amy. Art blinked, released his grip and stepped back. He took a deep breath and shut off the blaring iPod docked in his clock-radio. He squared his shoulders before rounding on Andy.

"What in the world are you doing with your mother's things? Who said you could come in here and make a mess?" Art shut his eyes again briefly. Andy may have had his mother's eyes, but the rest of his features were so much like his twin brother Otto that it hurt. Otto'd had broad cattle and hay-wrangler shoulders where Andy was a sapling, but Andy had the Hasmer chin and cheekbones, no doubt about it. The mop of dusty hair that always looked like he'd just come in from the fields — despite the fact that Andy had never been to the farm except for a third grade school trip — was Otto's.

Art bit his lip. Tagging and racing some-how lost their places in the line of com-plaints. "Andy?"

Andy scowled at him with all the bravado of remembered seventeen-year-old angst. "It's time, Dad. You — we — have to move on. It's been long enough."

"And what made you decide this all on your own, without consulting me?"

Andy tossed his mother's red and brown reindeer sweater on the bed. "The counselor said a year — that we should give it a year." He sat next to the pile of winter sweaters and slapped his jeans-clad thighs. "It's been more than that."

Art felt like his heart was gripped in a surgeon's clamp. "Only by a couple days." He turned and accidentally caught sight of the photograph of Amy and Andy on the dusty dresser next to her hairbrush and wedding rings. Amy had given the photo to him for Father's Day the year Andy turned eleven. He couldn't look any more. "Son, you can't just decide to get over something, no matter what anyone says. Sometimes, especially when you love someone so deeply, it takes —"

"Don't pretend anymore, Dad!" Andy leapt to his feet. He picked up the reindeer sweater and threw it, red-faced, toward him.

Art held up his arms. What had gotten into Andy?

"I — heard — you!" Andy punctuated each word with the throw of another piece of his mother's clothing.

Art side-stepped like a Mexican jumping bean. "Heard what? What are you screaming about? And stop that, right now!"

"That night! She said she wasn't going to wait any longer. That you had to stop blaming yourself or leave! She wanted you to go to her graduation, but no — you couldn't postpone your little annual pity party."

The vice let go of Art's heart and squeezed his lungs instead. Amy had gotten her masters of nursing degree and wanted him to see her walk across the stage. Why had the ceremony had to have been held on June second? Weren't there any other days of the week to have a graduation? Then he tried not to drive. Tried so hard. His body hadn't obeyed him and he'd been in Dubuque before the sun rose. He'd called to apologize and say he'd be back for the reception, but she hadn't answered his repeated messages. "You heard that?"

"I tried to forget," Andy said. "All this past year I kept pretending I never heard, or that I heard wrong."

Art inventoried the chaos they'd managed to create. Anger oozed from him until only a grief-stricken shell remained.

"Why her?" Andy asked as he wrapped his sapling arms around his middle

"I know." Art's knees wouldn't bend. He couldn't take the first step toward Andy to hold and comfort him like he'd done when Andy had woken from a bad dream in the middle of the night when Amy had worked night shift at the hospital. The whole last year had been a nightmare. The grief of all the losses in his life swirled in the pit of his stomach along with the thought of what Andy had been holding in. Sure, he and his wife had argued once in a while. Didn't all married couples? They'd even visited her pastor for counseling. The same pastor had refused to answer his questions after her death. They were all alike, pretending to have answers to questions no one could ask until it was too late and nothing mattered any more. Even Andy had stopped attending the youth group after a few months without his mother's encouragement.

He forced himself to move toward his son. One step, then another. "I know, Andy. It should have been me. I'm so sorry." Art stood nose to nose with this angry, young man. Andy had grown several inches and he, the sorriest excuse for a father, hadn't even noticed. "I can't bring her back, but I will do everything I can to keep you safe."

Andy, who a second earlier had been trembling, went still. His spine stiffened. "You can't do that when you're not here."

"I begged her not to go on the Flight for Life trip that night," Art whispered, desperately trying to salvage the moment. "Did you hear that too?" The surgeon's clamp around his lungs squeezed out what little air remained. Fainting would not be in the best interest of the discussion. Art squeezed his temples in an attempt to get control of himself. "You can't decide to throw out her things."

"The way things have been going, I could get an emancipation decree in an instant." Andy stalked toward the door. "Don't make me do that, Dad."

Emancipation? Where did that come from?

"I pretty much live by myself right now. I do the laundry, buy the food. I take care of the energy bills and make sure I've done my own homework. I take on the stuff that Mom did." Andy clenched his fists. "She wanted us to be happy. We just wanted you to pay attention to us. But that was too much to ask, wasn't it?"

The principals' words swam before Art's eyes. "So you decided to get attention any way you could?"

Andy halted and turned around. "What?"

Art waved the wadded note in front of his son. "I received a message from school last night. Principal Emmerson claims you've been involved in a tagging incident. You were caught on surveillance tape on the school grounds with some other boys. The sound track captured you boys bragging about some kind of street racing? Is that right?"

Andy's face paled. "They can't make me do anything! No court would accept a phony setup like that. Anyone can fix —"

"Stop it."

"It's not fair!"

"I said stop it, Andy. This whole situation is out of control."

"I —"

"No more 'I'. From now till the end of the school year you are grounded —"

"You gotta be —"

"From the second you are finished with school —"

"What about —"

"You will accept the principal's offer to clean up the mess you made on the back wall of the school —"

"So how am I supposed —"

"I'm taking your phone and your car keys." Andy blinked in slow motion. His mouth opened and closed as his shoulders slumped.

"And I arranged to leave work early until school's out so I can pick you up. I'll take you in early so you can start scraping off that spray paint."

"You can't make me!" Andy sounded like one of the geriatric patients in Art's study group at the University Hospital lab.

"I talked to Grandma and Grandpa Hasmer this morning. As soon as school's out, you're going to stay with them."

The rage returned to stiffen his son's posture. The glare alone from his son's eyes would have fried bacon. "In hicksville? You have got to be —"

"You're going to Oakville, and that's all I have to say."

"I won't stay —"

"You will."

"For how long?"

Art cocked his head, wondering how much he could get away with. The folks had been cautiously enthusiastic, though Andy hadn't done more than spend a night or two at the farmhouse over the years. It was time Andy got to know his grandparents better. But Art couldn't inflict this mass of young male ego on his parents for too long.

"Three weeks."

"No way. I'll take off first."

Since Andy didn't move, Art figured he had some wiggle room. "Let's try a week. They're getting a little older and could use some help. Can I count on you to give them a week?"

Andy stayed still, although he folded his arms and jutted his lower lip.

Do not negotiate. This is too important.

"I do this, I get my phone back."

"When school's out."

Andy's eyebrows furrowed and he squinted. "How'm I sposed to get to no-wheresville since you can't seem to suck it up and go there yourself?"

Art hated the combine red hot prickles of anger meeting up with the icy fingers of disgust somewhere in his sternum. This was for Andy — nothing to do with himself. "I'll take you."

"That I'd like to see." His son sneered.

"Might hurt you worse than me." Andy grabbed his iPod and squeezed it. "Maybe they'll let me drive a tractor to town."

Through a haze of sudden apathy Art watched Andy leave the room. What a mess. And Art didn't mean the jumbled colorful piles of Amy's clothing. He mechanically picked up her dresses and eyed the closet. Sweating, he set them in an empty box. He took a few deep breaths before he gathered a blouse, the blue one she'd wear around the house because of a grease stain from a Fourth of July barbecue. He tossed it in the box and reached blindly for something else — and came up with a satiny nightshirt that still bore her scent. He closed his eyes and brought it to his cheek as he sunk onto the bed. *Why?*

CHAPTER TWO

The next morning an insufferably sullen Andy gulped a mug of black coffee and refused food. Art had taken the liberty of backing his son's Blazer into the garage, covering it, locking it and making sure he had all the keys. He'd locked up Andy's phone too, although he'd keep it charged, he decided. He checked his son's messages, something he'd fought his conscience over, but decided it was in both their best interests. A Crystal and an Analiese had left numerous somewhat earthy messages. He felt like calling their parents and letting them hear what their daughters said, but was afraid they'd turn around and show him similar messages from Andy. Three boys had left texts, some kind of code, it looked like. Well, Andy wouldn't be replying.

Art dropped Andy off in front of Monona Christian School, despite his protests, and watched until he sauntered in, head low and backpack shoving his slim shoulders forward. Art frowned. He should get the boy some pants that fit. And perhaps some shirts that didn't have holes in them.

Art checked the dash clock — too early for his first appointment with potential summer lab assistants. Each summer he hired university graduate students to help with his on-going research projects in gerontology. His lucrative grants gave him some leeway with the summer programs. He or his teaching assistants taught two courses during the school year, then did cognitive and therapeutic studies with the growing population of elderly. Art pursed his lips. Which he was rapidly catching up to, thanks to his wild child. Time for a chat with Amy.

Peace Cemetery stretched acres — prime land that Madison had grown around. After the ice-pick-to-the-gut shock of burying his wife grew less intense, Art had taken to spending his lunch hour here, a mile from work. Some days he changed clothes and ran the distance, circled her stone, and ran back. Some days he stayed long enough to set a pink tulip by her engraved name. He pulled into the narrow parking area and slung his summer suit jacket over the seat. It hadn't rained for a week so his shoes were safe.

Art had never been alone in the cemetery. People strolled the neat aisles, stopped to read some of the more colorful epitaphs or take rubbings of an ancestor's marker. Today was no exception. Art ignored them, intent on telling Amy what a lousy dad he was without her influence. Self-confession was good for the soul, right? He stopped in front of the reflective black marble etched with wedding rings and doves. Her name was on one side, his on the other. He'd brought no gift this time, just complaints.

"He's out of control, Ames." Art spoke out loud, not caring if anyone was in earshot. "He's doing all the things Otto did, and more. Girls these days who say things you would not believe. And the clothes." He stopped, swallowed. "Amy, I'm sending him to the farm. I know it's hard. But I think it's the right thing to do. Back at the farm, in Bakersfield, he —"

"Excuse me, did you say Bakersfield?"

Art blinked. He must be hearing things. Who in their right mind would interrupt a man's private —

"You're from that part of the state? Really? So am I."

Art put his hands on his hips and clenched his jaw, speaking out of the corner of his mouth as he pivoted. "Lady, this is a private

360

conver— oh, you've got to be kid—"

"Art? Arthur Hasmer, as I live and — Oh, I'm so sorry, you must be — this is — I heard about your wife, of course, but I —"

"Dana London." Art shook his head. Go figure. On the day he was confessing to his deceased wife what a lousy dad he made, out of the past comes more evidence of his loserhood. "Or did you get married? Dana . . ." He looked at her hands, which were stuck in the pockets of her cropped pants. He cocked his head. It was her, wasn't it? His former high school classmate and prom date?

"Still London."

It was her. She didn't elaborate. "So, uh, I didn't know you lived in Madison," he said.

"I don't."

She squinted. Maybe she needed new glasses. Or any glasses. She'd worn them in high school. Now what? Art checked his watch.

"Sorry, I was just out for a walk in between classes," she said and turned to walk away. "I didn't mean to disturb you. Excuse me."

"Uh —" Art forced his eyebrows back down to their normal positions and realized he'd been staring at the slight sashay of her hips beneath snug white pants. Amy had refused to wear white slacks outside the

361

hospital, claiming white made her look fat. Dana did not look fat. Or even much like she had in high school for that matter. How had he recognized her without the glasses and the — she was getting away.

"Dana!" Art hurried after her.

She stopped and looked over her shoulder. A ray of sun poked through the early mist and hit her hair, a tousled golden heap of swirls on her head. "Don't you have to be at work or something?"

"What?"

"You looked at your watch."

So he had, and promptly forgotten why. He looked again, but couldn't recall what he needed to be on time for. Must not have been that important. "Sorry. Habit. Do you have someplace you need to be? Maybe we could grab some coffee or something." *Idiot!* She'd written that huge paper on the evil effects of stimulants in society for civics, remember? "Or tea."

"Sure."

She was still squinting. Was that a good sign or not? "Did you want to ride with me? Or —"

"I'll meet you. Tell me where." Now she looked at her watch. "I have a class at ten."

Class? He shifted his feet. "Okay. How

about at Laugh a Latte?"

She rolled her eyes and agreed.

At the coffee shop Art replaced his wallet and followed Dana to an empty table by the window. The early sun had gone behind clouds again. Much-needed rain was predicted. Funny how the weather was still so important to him, even though he'd left the desire to work the family farm. Despite winning every Future Farmer of America award, he'd never given farming another thought after Otto.

"So, I heard you were some kind of doctor?"

Art focused on Dana. She'd started out friendly enough at the cemetery, even though she'd interrupted a private conversation. Once she knew who he was, her gray eyes sparkled like ice cubes rather than diamonds. He was saddened to hear she'd stayed single. On closer inspection, he noted fine lines around her eyes and on her throat. She was the same age as him — forty-four.

"PhD," he said. "In gerontology. That's the study of —"

"I know what it means, Arthur Hasmer. Your folks talk about it all the time. How you're going to find the cure for Alzheimer's disease, or something."

"Not exactly. I'm not a medical doctor."
So, the folks talked about him? Good grief.
He cleared his throat. "What are you doing
these days?"

"I'm the town clerk, you probably know."

He hadn't.

"I decided to finish my accounting degree
and get certified as a tax preparer."

Art cradled his Columbian dark roast and
inhaled. "I remember you did like statistics."

She tapped her ceramic mug of mint tea.
"I was a geek. Still am." She turned her
profile to him to stare out the window.

"So was I."

For some reason she smiled and faced him
again. "Yeah, weren't we a pair? Can you
believe it's been over twenty-five years since
high school?"

So, he hadn't gone to any reunions. No
one missed him, did they? "What else have
you been up to in all that time?" Now that
she seemed to have thawed, Art realized he
wanted to know. If things hadn't gotten so
messed up after Otto, Art would have made
things right between them after the prom
disaster. He'd always liked Dana, if she had
been — well, even geekier than he'd been.
But then there'd be no Andy, or at least not
a child like him. Would there?

They talked for a while. Art drank in the

local gossip he'd heard from his mother already, but Dana seemed to make it funnier. Two of the town board members weren't much older than they, and Dana made their crucial decisions on road repair and light districts sound as fascinating as a root canal on laughing gas. Finally she looked at her watch. "Gotta go. It was nice seeing you. Surreal, but nice," she said. "That's a line from one of my favorite moves."

"Oh." Art didn't get it, but he smiled anyway.

"Maybe we'll run into each other again sometime."

He got to his feet to follow her out. "Actually, I'm taking Andy to stay with the folks for a week after school's out."

"They'll like that. Lindsay's there now, but they're getting on, you know."

"My niece, Lindsay? Why is she there?"

He followed Dana to her car, a navy PT Cruiser. "I guess she's helping out while she looks for work. Tough all over." Dana got into the car and buckled up. "She's a smart girl. I think your sister likes having her close."

"Doing what? Watching the weeds grow?"

"Not exactly." Dana turned the key, then looked at him with her pussy-willow eyes. "I think you'd better catch up with your sister and your folks, Art. There's trouble com- ing."

CHAPTER THREE

The first trouble of Art's morning came in the form of Peggy Washington, Art's doctoral student, as soon as Art walked into his office at the University Hospital lab.

"Doc, honest to gracious, you have your phone turned off again? You missed the meeting with Steve Peterman, and he left, saying he was taking Harrison's offer."

Art reached into his pocket and pulled out a cell phone. Andy's. "Um . . . Steve?"

Peggy humpfed and gave him her best evil eye. Her braids jingled around her light brown puffy face, mocking the tough girl stance. All five-foot ten inches and one hundred seventy-five pounds of her were annoyed. Art could tell.

"I personally recommended you to Steve. He's the most promising researcher —"

"And cute too?"

Peggy folded her arms and cocked her head, swinging a braid across her cheek. "I will ignore that. So, now what are we going to do? I have my own work to do, you know."

He knew. Boy, did he know. She didn't have to go reminding him of it every other day. He sat and booted up his computer. Oh, yeah. There it was. He usually set his phone to beep at appointments. Art glanced sourly at Andy's phone.

"Don't worry, Peggy. I'm on it. I've got something up my sleeve."

Peggy tapped her foot. "Mmhmm, Doc. You usually do. And it usually involves me go-fering something."

Art's computer spreadsheet reminded him of another student interview at twelve-thirty. He glanced at his watch. Frowned, shook it. Must need a new battery, for the second hand stopped its sweep at 8:37 and forty-two seconds. Amy had changed the battery for him last time.

"Okay," he said, glancing at the office wall clock. "The next appointment's at twelve-thirty. Alana Richards. Hopefully she'll work out."

"Mm-hmm." Peggy turned and walked out.

Alana Richards had turned out to be a sincere young woman in the pre-med program. Spiked hair and black plastic glasses might have led him to believe otherwise until he took the time to listen to her calm sensible approach to taking oral history and documenting observation versus behavior. He'd been impressed at her suggestions for upgrading his questionnaire and his information-gathering points. Art had hired her that afternoon. After submitting the paperwork and getting her signed in, it was time to pick up Andy.

Andy hadn't been any more thrilled to see him now than this morning, even though Art had parked two blocks away per Andy's muttered parting shot. "How about picking up burgers or a pizza for supper?" Art asked, clueless about how to make amends with his son. What would Amy have done? Not allowed Andy to get into this predicament to begin with.

Andy shrugged. Art pulled into traffic and turned on Speedway. "Have much homework?"

"Nuh."

"I'll be around tonight, in case you need anything."

Andy shrugged again. Art took a deep breath and tried to remember being seventeen. Dad would have fixed his attitude with — it was a different time back then. Now kids talked about emancipation and rights.

369

Okay. "I hired a new lab assistant today."

"Great."

Art ignored what might have been sarcasm. "I thought maybe you could use some new clothes. We could go get something this weekend."

"I got plenty of stuff."

"Your pants are hanging. Have you lost weight?"

Andy shifted against the seat. "This is the way everybody's wearing them."

"Oh." Art got in line at the drive in. "What do you want?"

The conversation didn't improve much at home during their meal, which Art insisted they eat together at the kitchen table. He couldn't even remember how to set a table, that's how long it had been since the last time they sat there. He didn't protest when Andy went to his room.

As Art threw out the wrappers and washed their few dishes, he thought about the upcoming trip to Oakville. He hadn't gone back last Christmas. Andy had gone to Amy's parents and he'd worked. Interviewing folks at the mall.

The Town of Bakersfield, the country, the farm perched at the edge of Oakville, butting up the city limits. Gentrified estates cropping up like exotic produce. People pretending to live in the country, as long as they could see the nearest gas station. Art blinked and sighed out. Would the feel of holding Otto in those last moments of life never leave him? Otto's blood stained everything, the glazed and surprised look in his twin bother's eyes, the last breath he'd taken cycled with undiminished clarity every time he thought about the farm. Of course Otto thought he was invincible. Don't all teenaged boys believe that? Art hadn't, but maybe Andy did. Hence the street-racing.

Substitute thinking, the therapist had told him. Nothing worked up until now. Maybe the messy golden brown curls on Dana's head, her dove-soft eyes with crinkles around them when she smiled. Slowly her image replaced Otto's. Oakville — Dana London. Dana, who'd stayed around home and was now the town clerk. Had his mom mentioned that? Probably, but he'd never bothered to remember.

Dana commuted to Madison two days each week for her coursework. He guessed the clerk position wasn't a full-time job. Huh. As if the Town of Bakersfield could afford it anyway.

Art wiped his hands dry and hung up the dishtowel. He turned out the lights in the kitchen, listened for sounds from upstairs, then settled into a green recliner in the living room with the newspaper.

The lead article screamed about the poor economy and lack of jobs for the newly graduated class. He'd never insisted that Andy get a job. This last year had been too much of a mess anyway to think about it. But what had Dana said about Lindsay? Ah, yes. At home to help while she looked for work. He'd filed that last bit, about changes. He reached for the phone to call the folks. Mom answered.

"Hi, it's me," he said.

"So soon?" Mom replied. "We just talked yesterday. Don't tell me you changed your mind. We spent the day getting a room ready for Andy."

"No, no. We're still coming next week. Might need to get him some clothes though."

"Why don't you let me do that? It will give us something to do."

Art grinned at the thought of Mom taking Andy to the local general store for clothes. Oakville Mercantile was a dime store bargain basement of a shopping experience. He could just imagine the look on Andy's face when his grandma held up a pair of top-stitched front pocket jeans in front of him. "Yeah, sure. I'll send some money along with him."

"No need."

"Say, Mom, I ran into somebody today."

"Hope you didn't hurt 'em."

"Ha. Anyway, I heard Lindsay was with you? Why isn't she with her mother? And are you okay? I heard there might be some . . . some —"

"Some what?"

His mother's tone was definitely defensive. Prickles of dismay played up and down his spine. "What's going on, Mom?"

"Nothing we can't handle."

"We? You and Dad? How is he, by the way? Still using the walker?"

"Fine. We're fine. And Lindsay's just here 'til she lands a good job. Girl just got a fancy degree, you know. A master's something or other. Not quite like yours."

Art tuned out to the change in subject. His mother's rambling covered up something important. She only did that when she didn't want him to know she was nervous.

". . . that no-good Phillip Murphy. I could wring his neck."

Art shook his head to regain focus. "I thought everyone loved good old Phil."

"That was then. Things change, son. When

a man walks out on a marriage after twenty-eight years —"

"What? Phil left? What did Tessa say? What happened?"

"I think it best if you hear from her, Art. I don't go spreading gossip."

Art grinned. "Just not the family kind. Okay. I guess I have some catching up to do. And you better be prepared to tell me everything about the farm, or I'll be getting my information from Hiriam Bakersfield himself."

"Huh! That no-good —"

"Mom!"

"All right. We're expecting you and Andy next Friday."

"Yeah. I'll get to Tessa's —"

"Here. At home."

"I can't. And I'm not going to change that now."

He listened to a muffling sound over the line that meant she'd put her hand over the mouthpiece and was talking to someone in the background. "Thing is, son, there may not be anyone there to meet you."

A conspiracy, that's what this was. They were ganging up on him. A man had a right to some things, didn't he? Like his own feelings? *Now I sound like Andy.*

Art took a deep breath and ignored the

screaming obvious answer to the question about why his sister wouldn't be at her home. "We'll see what happens when we get there."

"Good enough for now."

They said goodbye and hung up.

Art pushed back the recliner's lever. Good old Phil. And what was going on with the place? He wished he'd gotten a number from Dana, but admitted he might not have had the nerve to use it. Andy was right. He really needed to get his life back. Sitting here in the dark was not healthy. Going to the farm could be a first step.

The real question loomed: was he man enough to go home again?

Andy and the other two boys caught tagging spent the weekend at Monona Christian finishing the scrubbing job. Andy's hands showed his efforts in red, chapped skin and ragged nails. The work wouldn't hurt the boy, and the doubled effort meant they could leave the day after school let out. At least Andy's grades hadn't tumbled any further since the drop from mostly B's to the solid and occasional lower C range. Art should encourage the boy to do better, but every effort at single parenting seemed to defeat both of them. Andy raged that his dad was picking on him, complaining that he couldn't do anything right, whenever Art questioned his grade reports. "So, maybe you had a kid who's not as smart as his parents, did you think of that?"

Andy was smart, and he did have the potential to do whatever he wanted. But how to get him to focus and make plans? They hadn't even discussed college, although Madison had plenty of opportunities. He assumed Andy would apply to the UW, but his latest report card pretty much nixed that idea. Barely above average grades wouldn't get him in. Art added "college" to the list of subjects the two of them needed to tackle when Andy came home. Maybe they'd better have some of these discussions in front of a counselor.

"Coming, Andy?" Art checked the time on his phone since he had yet to get his watch battery replaced. He stood beside the open hatch of his car. Andy had insisted on packing himself and refused the offer of new clothes.

"Yeah!" Andy sauntered through the garage, not even looking at the bulk of his car which hid under the canvas cover.

"That all you're taking?" Art frowned at Andy's back pack. Sure, it bulged, but still . . . "You have pajamas? Lindsay's going to be there and you're too old to —"

"Yeah, Dad. Like I'm going to prance around in my boxers. Don't sweat it. I got it."

Art slammed the trunk and buckled in. He handed Andy his cell phone before pressing the button to lower the garage door. "As promised. Although I wish your grades had been better."

Andy looked at him while plugging his ears with his iPod earbuds. "I tried." He closed his eyes.

Art hesitated. Amy would have insisted they pray before the trip. Art gripped the wheel before turning the key. "Lord, Lord . . ." Nothing but a pathetic "help me" came to mind. He pulled out of the driveway. The one and half-hour drive could be really long. He looked at his son's closed eyes. Or too short. One thing's for sure, they weren't going to waste any time bonding.

Too short, Art decided about an hour later. Andy hadn't changed position. As he exited the freeway and angled toward Highway P, Art's hands started to sweat. On Highway P, he began to tremble. He pulled off at the crossroads and headed into Oakville instead, hoping and praying Tessa at least had relented and would meet them at her house.

He turned into the driveway. The grass was too long; his first clue. The pulled drapes and locked doors were the second; no one answering the bell or his knocking, the final one. Art turned toward the car where Andy, now at full attention stared back at him through the windshield. Smirking.

Art sighed and pulled out the cell. "We're here," he told his sister. "Where are you?" Tessa's voice invited him to leave a message. He narrowed his eyes and managed not to slam the phone against Tessa and Phil's fake black lamp post. What now? He turned and looked over the neighborhood. Tessa and Phil lived on a cul-de-sac of other upscale homes on two acres of well-tended lots at the edge of Oakville. At least the other lots were well-tended. Tessa had never hurt him like this before. She'd been the one who defended him after Otto. She'd let him stay with her and Phil, even though they'd just gotten married, his senior year of high school. Things must be really bad if she'd gone back to Mom and Dad's.

Art walked back to the car. Hesitated. "Want me to drive?"

Andy was way too cheerful. Almost made Art mad, and the shot of adrenaline helped. He got in the car. Buckled up. "No thanks."

Turned the key. Wrestled the car back to Highway P. Back to the other side of Oakville and the outskirts of town where the blue house waited for him to come home. Today Arthur L. Hasmer took up the challenge.

"Speed limit's fifty-five," Andy observed, again with that nutcracker loud tone.

"It's a nice day and I'm not holding anyone up," Art snapped, although he nudged the gas pedal. Got up to forty. "Admiring the scenery." And he was too. Ancient oaks lined the road, fully leafed. Someone had planted waves of daffodils in the ditches and they glowed white and gold and yellow against the fresh grass. Locust trees were in bloom and weeping willow fronds waved. Sure, Madison had plenty of trees and flowers. It wasn't a towering, dark city like Milwaukee. There's no place like home. Silly movie.

Art nearly stopped at the mailbox before turning down the long gravel drive. Three cars were parked in front of the house. Tessa's big black Land Rover he knew. One of the others was probably Lindsay's.

"Dad. You stopped."

"Oh, yeah. Sorry."

"You want to let me out here?"

He could have. Would have been easy. Art

glanced again at the house. Great. Mom and Tessa stood on the lawn. And someone else with golden hair. Art groaned. Naturally. The owner of the third car, the Cruiser, stood there too with her arms folded. Watching. Waiting. Art forced himself to take deep slow breaths so he wouldn't hyperventilate.

"You're doing fine, Dad."

Art accepted Andy's encouragement for what it was. The boy's tone sounded sincere this time. Art managed to come to a stop three yards behind the Cruiser. He didn't want to scratch Dana's car. Why was she here? His thoughts slowed like cooling asphalt. He heard his pulse in his ears.

Andy climbed out before Art killed the engine. Art followed more slowly, feeling light-headed.

The first time. This was the first time in twenty-seven years that he'd walked on this driveway. First time. First time.

Men don't faint was the last thing he remembered thinking before an unnatural black dropped curtain across the landscape.

CHAPTER FOUR

"Art! Arthur, are you alright?"

Art lifted his face from the fine gravel next to his car and shook his head. "Yeah, Mom." He allowed her to help him sit up. Tessa pulled at his other arm.

A shadow crossed his legs. He looked up, and up, until the sun's glare blinded him. *Great, just great.* Dana's expression was lost in the white light haloing her head. Her arms were folded. How much of a fool did she think him now? He supposed he could have done something even more embarrassing than just kissing the ground.

Art pushed himself upright and dusted off his slacks. Andy stood a few yards away, watching, unsure as a young buck deciding which way to run. "You passed out. Just for a couple seconds," Andy said.

"You okay?" Tessa asked.

"Yeah, didn't eat much for breakfast." He grabbed the side of the car door.

Mom thrust a mug of coffee into his hands. "Here. There's some leftovers inside. Coffee cake."

Art sipped and made a smile. "Thanks." If there was one thing that could force Art inside, it would be Mom's raspberry coffee cheese cake. When his stomach settled. No one moved. Art glanced at Dana, who now looked at him cautiously, as if he might explode or vomit. Which was still an option. He pushed the mug into his sister's hands.

"Arthur, come inside," LouAnn Hasmer said firmly. At seventy-two, Art and Tessa's mother was still a tough, trim and tanned woman. Her weathered face sported a map of fine lines. Though her short hair was white, she wore it spiky, like one of her prized rooster's combs. Worn jeans wrapped around her narrow frame instead of the regulation apron other grandmothers dressed in. Andy was in for a strong dose of her no-nonsense, take no prisoners attitude. Hopefully a week would be enough. If they were fortunate, Andy might even decide to stay longer. Boy needed structure, something Art couldn't provide while his work kept him away odd hours.

Art rubbed his face and blinked. "Coming." He turned to breathe in the rolling hills and fields bounded by mature tree lines of oaks and locust, poplars and maple. Giant sumac would turn blood red in the late fall to contrast with brilliant snow. He frowned. The fields were green with weeds, not plowed and planted. "You got all the land in set-aside?" he asked, talking about the government crop reserve program where farmers were paid a small stipend to keep unworked fields clear and available for future use.

"Come inside, and we'll talk," Mom invited.

Art didn't like the sound of that but he was through the front door before he remembered his trepidation about being home. He glanced up the stairs where had shared a room with Otto. He wondered if Mom planned to put Andy there. Art looked back to where his son stood with his backpack hooked around his thumb and slung across his shoulder, staring with morbid fascination while one of the perpetual cats gnawed on something. Art grinned and went to greet his father.

"Dad." Art's father, Otto, sat in his faded plaid easy chair. Art bent to talk into his left ear, the one not deafened through years of being flooded by loud machinery. "Hi, Dad. I brought Andy." Dad was not quite seventy, but could have passed for eighty-five. Art forced himself not to wipe the slight line of drool. A series of strokes had left his father mostly paralyzed on his left.

"Arthur." Dad's voice remained a harsh whisper, one reason they rarely spoke on the telephone. "Good to have you home."

Home. Home had been many places for Art: Tessa and Phil's, and the places he'd lived with Amy. The only one where family remained intact, apparently, was this one. The home where he'd grown up.

Andy and Lindsay banged into the room bringing a whiff of early summer heat and fresh enthusiasm.

"Come, eat, Arthur," Mom said. He followed her into the kitchen. Tessa and Dana sat at the battered round table where abandoned cups sat on placemats. Instant familiarity flooded Art's senses. The lazy susan with the sugar bowl and spoon, salt and pepper shakers hadn't changed. The red linoleum on the floor looked just the same, and so did the miniature ivy curling around the kitchen window. Even the curtains with blue saucers and teacups were the same from his childhood memories.

Art sat and mechanically forked coffee cake into his mouth while he listened to the conversation his arrival had interrupted.

"They can't really deny our application

384

for a new septic permit, can they?" Tessa asked Dana.

Mom poured herself another cup of coffee. Art noted that her hands trembled a bit. From nerves or strong emotion, or age? He hadn't remembered so much lawn around the house before, even swaths along the driveway out to the road. Who took care of that? Not to mention plowing in the winter. He felt ashamed now that he was here to see it. He hadn't thought about how his folks managed this place on their own. He eyed Tessa. He'd left his sister with a massive burden. And now what was going on?

"What permit?" he asked.

"Your folks repeatedly turned down offers to sell," Dana stated. "Fact is, they haven't worked it in years and the well and septic are failing and the new regulations state they have to put in a mound system. And there are other issues that I can't divulge. But your mom could."

Art looked at his mother. "What other issues?"

"It's our land," she said. "Been in the family since the first Hasmers came to Wisconsin. No one can tell us what we can and can't do on our property. There's plenty of life left in the septic system for two old

385

people."

Art raised his eyebrows at Dana whose lips had pursed. He forced himself to remain calm while his mother continued to vent just under her breath. "That's ridiculous. This is our house."

"In order to live here you have to do so safely, LouAnn," Dana said.

"We can fix the well."

"The septic system?" Art reminded them.

Tessa snorted. "Hiriam Bakersfield and his cronies! You should see what shenanigans they're pulling now. Trying to deny a new septic permit."

"Sounds hokey," Art said. "Is that where you come in Dana?"

"Otto and LouAnn can petition for a variance —"

"You betcha!" Art's mom cried. She stood and raised a fist. "I'll petition that Hiriam —"

"Mom!" Tessa broke in and tossed a glance toward the doorway. "Kids!"

Lindsay, his youngest niece, and Andy had come in. Lindsay elbowed her cousin and snickered. "Kids!"

"Speak for yourself," Andy said and grinned. He elbowed her back.

Lindsay opened the refrigerator and took out a pitcher of something dark. Probably

Mom's grape juice. "One kid. A twenty-four-year-old woman with a master's degree in business is not a kid."

"So, petition?" Art asked. "Why? I didn't know you'd gotten offers to sell. Why don't you just sell and move into town? Wouldn't that be better for Dad? You're —"

"What?" Mom's eyes blazed. "Don't you start in on me, young man. You have no idea."

Dana got up and took her cup to the sink. "I'd better get going. Thanks for the visit, LouAnn. Nice to see you, Tessa. Art." And then she was gone.

Art shook his head. "Somebody tell me what's going on, please."

"I told you!" Mom said. "We're handling it."

"Oh, Art." Tessa shook her head. "Why now? Why'd you have to come home and stick your nose in it after all these years?"

Art stayed for dinner, then headed back to Madison. The garage door rumbled shut behind him and closing the door sent an echoing hollow ring through the first floor. Art set his keys and wallet and phone on the desk before he turned off the coffee maker he'd left on that morning.

His first trip to the farm could have gone better.

The answering machine blinked two short red angry times, on off, on off. Probably work. He hoped the new assistant and Peggy were getting along. All they had to do was set up the forms and data for the new project. Peggy had already received permission from the mall to conduct the random interviews from agreeable patrons.

The first message was a request for more information on his fall class for the scheduling system from the main office. Did he require lab time? Yes. The other question was a simple problem with the database. He left detailed directions for Alana and said he'd be in later the next morning.

He kicked off his shoes and sat in the recliner. Restless, he got up again and decided to go for a run.

An easy lope through the neighborhood and back at almost dark an hour later, the house was as empty as when Art left it. When was the last time he'd been alone in his own house? He couldn't recall. Should he call Andy? Find out if he was okay or had forgotten anything? Art reached for the phone, but let his hand rest on the receiver. He sighed. Probably not a good idea. Andy hadn't said much when he left. The boy had been staring at his grandpa who slowly set up a checker board with one trembling hand. Yeah, thanks for abandoning me, Andy's parting look accused.

A week apart would do them good. Art got ready for bed, surprised that he was already thinking about the return trip. Maybe Dana would be there again. She already told him her class was over for the summer, so she wouldn't be in Madison until August. When he was back at the farm he could call, she'd told him.

Art turned over and scrunched the pillow. At least he had an excuse to talk about the farm problem. An excuse? An excuse for what? He reached out to touch the other pillow on the bed. After a year, he still slept on his side. Was he really ready to move on? Should he wait longer before dating? If anyone would even date him. He couldn't think of anyone at work, except maybe Professor Karen Graham who was two offices down the hall and smoked like a dragon. She'd never been married and had sort of hinted around last winter about two lonely people having dinner sometime. But was that a date?

Art let his thoughts return to the farm.

He couldn't figure out why keeping the place was such a big deal. The folks should move in to Oakville, especially with Dad's condition. Even Lindsay wasn't planning to stay long. What was Tessa thinking, encouraging them to stay? Unless she wanted the place. But what would she do with it, especially if Phil was really gone? If Phil was gone, they could move in with her.

If they could just sell the land to the developer instead of having to go through all the questionably legal problems of getting a septic permit and the huge expense of a mound system and new well, they should just do it. The money would take care of them.

With the place bulldozed and a new crop of cement, maybe all the bad memories would finally be buried and Otto could rest in peace. No one would ever get hurt or killed there again.

In the middle of an interview, Art's phone vibrated. He ignored it until he waved goodbye to the senior couple fifteen minutes later. The phone number showed Oakville's area code, but wasn't familiar. He'd given in and called Mom last night, who assured him that Andy had settled in and even met some of the local boys at the park.

He tapped his code and listened to the message. At the first words, Art's hand went numb and the phone slipped from his grasp. He scooped it up and held it to his ear in time to hear "they're holding him," before he ran for the exit.

CHAPTER FIVE

"Doc! Hey, Doc! Wait up. Where're you going?"

Art slowed long enough for Peggy to get within hearing distance in the echoing East Towne mall. "There's been an accident. I have to leave. Can you take care of things?"

"Sure. But what kind of accident? Who —"

Art kept going. "My son," he called back over his shoulder. "A car accident. I have to —"

"Of course you do. We'll be praying. Just give me a call when you know more. Alana and I have the fort."

The last thing Art saw was Peggy, waving, before he burst into the warmth of the parking lot, heat waves shimmering off the cars. Where had he parked?

Art plugged in his phone and attached the headset before maneuvering out of the lot and heading east on the freeway. After talking with the nurse who'd placed the call from Oakville's tiny med center, a clinic with a small lab, X-ray, emergency area and ten-bed hospital wing, he almost had to pull over again. Andy had suffered multiple lacerations to his face, some requiring stitches. "Don't worry, he can have plastic surgery later if he needs to. Lucky nothing got in his eyes."

Lucky? She couldn't tell him anything about the accident or if anyone else had been involved. Was he bringing his insurance card?

Yes.

Art tried his mother next. "Dial LouAnn Hasmer," he instructed his voice-activated com unit.

"Arthur, where are you? I've been trying to reach you. Andy's hurt, but —"

"The hospital called. I'm on my way."

"Oh, I'm so relieved. When no one answered your office or home numbers —"

"I was at work. You have to use the cell phone number."

"I hate those things. I hardly ever remember to use mine."

Art sighed. "I know Mom, but if there's an emergency, that's how you reach me."

"Well, anyway, thank goodness you're coming, Andy will be happy to see you."

"Tell me what happened."

"Well, as far as I know, someone knocked him off the road. You know that curve on Highway P?"

"What was he driving? Did anyone else get hurt?"

"I don't think so. Your dad's truck was the only casualty. That nice pastor's girl called an ambulance."

"Pastor's girl? I thought you said he had met boys, not girls. And was she with him? Like a date? Is she all right?"

"She wasn't with him, not that I know."

"The truck? That old Ford dad and I remodeled? I didn't know that thing still ran."

"I had to call Roger to tow it." Art heard muffled sounds in the background. "Your father wants to speak to you."

It must be serious. "Okay, put him on." More muffled sounds.

"He says not on the phone, dear. Stop in."

"Shouldn't I go to the hospital?" The thought of going to the med center where they'd taken Otto made him nauseous, even if he knew he had to be strong for his son's sake. His second line buzzed. "Just a minute, Mom. Hang on, will you? I have another call. Yes?"

"Hey, Uncle Art, it's Lindsay. I just

wanted you to know that I'm here at the hospital with Andy."

"Lindsay, thanks for calling. How is he?"

"They're cleaning him up now. They haven't done any X-rays or anything. He had a lot of glass in his face. Be prepared. He might look pretty messed up."

"Okay." Art swallowed. "He's not in pain or anything?"

"I don't know. I only peeked around the curtain."

"Grandma said there was some girl —"

"Ella, yeah. She's cool. She called the squad."

"She just happened to be in the area?"

"I guess. So, anyway, I just wanted to let you know, I think they'll let me take him home later. In case you can't get here in time."

"I'm on my way now, but if it works out, you can do the honors. I'll call when I get to the farm."

"Sure. See you when you get here. 'Bye."

The rest of the family could call him every kind of chicken, but Art knew only relief that he could put off the hospital visit. He preferred to face his demons one at a time and with his first trip to the farm only days past, the rest of memory lane could wait.

When he neared home, Art decided to

detour to the accident scene on Highway P. Black rubber marks clued him in on what his son had been up to. He could practically hear the screech of tires and rev of engines at the starting point, an old field road onto the Weaver farm. Racing. He might have figured. What was the kid thinking? Did he have some kind of death wish?

Art pulled off the road and got out, staring down the stretch of rural highway lined with century oaks. He felt small under the canopy of verdant rustling leaves. He looked up through the arms of the nearest tree to glimpse robin's egg-blue sky. Peace filled him and he sighed. Birch catkins from the messy forest across from the farm lined the shoulders. A brown and gold marker proclaimed this part of P had been designated a "Rustic Road," part of Wisconsin's attempt to identify particularly scenic drives for tourists.

"I applied for that," a woman's voice said quietly, out of nowhere.

Art choked and went light-headed for an instant again. "Dana!"

"Sorry. Thought you heard me drive up. This where it happened, I assume?"

"Everybody knows already, I take it." Art swallowed the sour feeling in his stomach.

"Within a day, my son's already raising Cain."

"At least he wasn't badly hurt."

Art pointed to the newly scraped tree down the road. "I suppose that tree will die now." Acid rose to his throat. He swallowed again.

"Maybe not." She pointed to the old Weaver house. "I live here now, you know." Art followed her gesture to look toward the old brick two-story home. A driveway behind them meandered to a detached single garage. "My grandparents' place."

"I'd forgotten." He reversed his gaze from the house to its owner. Dana might be middle-aged to the rest of society, but to Art, she looked nearly as good as she had at prom. Ah, yes, she'd gotten contact lenses back then, surprising him with the longest lashes around deep, gray eyes. Her mouth was soft today, not smiling, but not frowning. She folded her arms across her sleeveless navy shirt.

He didn't get any further than her firm tanned arms when she asked, "So, do I pass?"

Heat prickled his forehead and cheeks. He looked away, anywhere else, but her sardonic smile. "Um, sorry. Guess I was lost in thought."

"Hadn't you better be getting on to see your boy?"

Art heaved a quick sigh. "Lindsay's taking him home, but I suppose I should check in. I said I'd call when I got here."

Dana nodded once and tucked a wayward curl behind her ear. "I love these trees. We can't seem to stop the kids from using this road as a drag strip. I've been fighting the rest of the board long enough. There are too many accidents and if cutting the trees will save some lives, I should give in."

"Who wants to cut the trees?"

"Hiriam says he's had dozens of calls from residents." Dana put her hands on her hips and looked both ways along the highway. Art could count the mailboxes on one hand. Dana patted the nearest tree which towered over them. It had been severely lopped on the side facing the road and looked more like half a tree. A squirrel perched on the lowest branch and chattered a warning.

"Last storm felled that one," she said, pointing to a stump not far. "Blocked the road, nearly causing an accident. I suppose these trees are so old they're starting to die."

"Trimming them around the power lines didn't help, looks like," Art said. "Shame to cut them, though."

"Yep." Dana nodded, then headed toward

her car. "Everything changes," she said.

"Uh — wait a sec?" Art caught up with her. "Could I, ah, talk to you?"

"What about? We already covered our jobs. Maybe, the good old days? High school hijinks?"

Art hadn't prepared for a cross-examination. Dana had seemed perfectly gracious when they'd had coffee in Madison. And at Mom's. What had happened? And did he want to relive what a jerk he'd been in high school? He looked down the road again. Like father, like son. At least she hadn't left yet. He took the risk. With a racing heart threatening to choke him, he realized that he did want to talk to her again, no matter what had gone on in the past. "Maybe we could clear up the high school thing once and for all, and move on?"

She seemed to relax from her stiff stance. "Maybe."

"Can we get together after I see Andy? Say, at the diner? Buy you a piece of pie?"

"Your son needs you."

A little flare of anger sent his pulse jumping. He squelched it. "Andy is in good hands. I need to see my dad, then think about what to do."

"Sorry. I didn't have any right to comment. I'm not a parent."

Art stood down from challenge mode to pity in a flash. "So, how come you —"

"Don't let me keep you." Dana strode to her car and got in.

"Wait!" Art thought fast. "Would you be willing to stop in by my folks? With me? To see Andy? Then later, before I head back, we could catch up?"

She frowned. Showing his chicken side again wasn't in his best interest, Art decided. "Okay." She sighed. "I'll meet you there in a couple of minutes. I have to check on something at home." She drove off without a glance.

Again with the disappearing act. Art shook his head and got into his own car. A line from one of Amy's favorite movies came to him. "People come and go so quickly here." He laughed at himself and drove to the farm.

Andy and Lindsay weren't there yet, so that left him free to have a talk with Dad. Mom met him at the door, wringing her hands and commenting about her lack of parenting skills in her usual gruff manner until Art grabbed her in a hug and whispered that he didn't blame her and he was sorry for foisting Andy on them. "I had unrealistic expectations," he said. "It was wrong of me to just leave him."

"We love him, Arthur. He's had a rough time is all." Mom stepped back and gestured toward his father. "There, now. Dad has something to say. Might turn out all right yet."

Tessa sat on a chair by the side window, book in hand. She gave him a bleak little "how are you" smile and eyebrow quirk.

He gave her a pressed-lips rueful wordless "good enough, thanks" back.

His mother's acknowledgment of Andy's hurt stung a bit. He'd lost loved ones too — a wife, not to mention his twin bother. Art went to sit at his father's feet.

"Been watching him," Dad wheezed. "Your boy. Like Otto Junior."

Art nodded. The similarity hadn't escaped him.

"Wrecked our truck." Cough. "Reckless. Could have been hurt worse."

"I know. I'm glad. It's been a tough year for both of us. I'm afraid I'm losing him, Dad."

Otto shook his head. "No. Talks of you . . . shows some respect under . . . all the bluster." Cough. "Good for him."

Art shook his head. "I can't leave him here, after what he's done. I'm not sure what yet, but I have to do something. I'll take him home."

"No."

Art waited through another gasping fit. He looked at Mom, who didn't seem particularly worried. Surely this breathlessness wasn't a good sign. He didn't recall it being so bad last — no, the Christmas before. He'd been away too long.

"Work it off," Dad said.

"What?"

"Boy needs to be responsible. Get a job. Pay for damages."

"I'll see that he does, Dad. He can make regular payments to you."

"This summer."

"Well, it's kind of late. Most of the jobs are taken around home. All the students from the colleges pick up summer work, you know."

Mom stepped in and placed her hands on Dad's shoulders. "What your father means is we've already gotten him a job."

Art raised both brows. "But —"

"At church. Pastor Mike needs a janitor while Gene recovers, and agreed to let Andy come and work."

Andy could hardly keep his room clean. A church? "Does he know this?"

"Not yet. We wanted to let you tell him."

Oh boy.

"You'll want to get the rest of his clothes

and things, if he's staying the summer," Mom added. "We don't expect you to stay, but you could come back this weekend."

Art breathed out, strangely relieved. He got up and kissed his mother's cheek and noted that Dana stood next to her. So she'd come, after all. He hadn't been sure she would. "Let's give it a try," he said to Mom, although maybe he hoped Dana would pick up on the sentiment. Art was willing to reclaim his life, starting with baby steps. What was the next one? Guilt. Definitely guilt over all the wrong choices and wallowing in self-pity. "I'll go check in at the hospital now, see if he's ready to come back yet."

CHAPTER SIX

Lindsay answered the number Art called at the hospital. As soon as Andy got on the line, any sympathy for his son vaporized with his son's smart remarks. If the kid had been hurt worse things might have been different. After the snarky call was over, Art realized that he had not even asked how he felt, or told him about the job. This was piling on the guilt, not dealing with it. And Dana had heard. He rubbed his forehead while he paced. He rolled up the sleeves of his dress shirt and loosened the tie.

When Lindsay drove in, Art hung in the background, anger battling with fear and remorse. He let Mom and Tessa greet Andy with tender hugs and murmurs, and when they stepped away, he felt sickened at the sight of his son's face. He closed his eyes at the thought that the worst wound might have blinded him. Art swallowed and watched Andy show remorse to Dad. Good.

He forced himself to put on his neutral interview face to keep from letting Andy know how scared he'd been.

"Andrew." Why couldn't he touch the boy? So much like Otto. He swallowed again. Mom saved the day by asking if they'd like something to drink. "No, thanks, I can't stay." He sought out Dana who had disappeared to a corner during the reunion. "I have some catching up to do." He cleared his throat. "With Dana."

Her name felt like a lifeline, something to look forward to after making himself go through with this painful discussion about a job and the fact that Andy was staying until he worked off the cost of repairs. He winced at the thought of dealing with the insurance.

"Don't worry, Dad. It hurts me a lot worse than it hurts you."

Art straightened. The regret of letting this situation with Andy get so out of control stung. Amy wouldn't have allowed it. But she wasn't here, and Art had no idea how to stop it. He looked at Dana.

"I'm glad you're all right, Andy," Dana said.

"I'll be back with Andy's things this weekend, just like we discussed." Art felt a little silly addressing his family as if they were his students. The immediate stillness made a trickle of sweat dribble between his shoulder blades, as if he'd assigned an impossible task. He rolled down his sleeves anyway and picked up his suit coat. Despite this incident, his mom would be so much better at watching out for Andy. At least Andy showed them some respect. And Tessa would help. "So long." He looked at Andy one last time before following Dana outside. "I'll call you later."

He hoped Andy would pick up when he did.

"So, he looked pretty good," Dana said, as they looked at each other across a table at the diner. "That should relieve some of your worry. He didn't act like he was going to try racing again anytime soon."

Now that he'd left the farm, Art's hands trembled in reaction. He gripped the thick brown coffee mug in an effort to hide the tremor. "Stitches and tape everywhere. Came close to blinding himself." Was that harsh tone his?

At the look of surprised dismay clouding Dana's face, he bit his lip and looked away. Maybe Andy was right — he'd be better off on his own.

He turned back in time to see Dana sit

back in the booth and fold her arms. "I suppose his accident brought back memories."

Art recognized the defensive posture she put up. He guessed he sounded like a monster of a dad. "The memories never left."

Her face paled. Why?

"Look, this was probably a mistake," he said. He slid out of the booth and pulled some bills from his wallet. "I'd better go home and get Andy's things together. I'll be back on the weekend. After that . . ."

He really needed to turn around and leave. If his feet would obey him.

Dana stared at him. Twin spots of color burned on her cheeks. "You're telling me that you've never really dealt with Otto's death? That's your excuse for running when the going gets tough?"

The spark of anger she'd ignited hours earlier on the highway reignited. "He's my son. You have no idea —" Art stopped, confused. That's what his mother had said about the farm.

"Then act like it." Dana sat up, her eyes no longer soft, but steely. "I'm making this my business. Too many kids are lost and out of control these days because there's no one teaching them any different. I care about — about your folks too much to let you ditch your problems on their doorstep."

"How dare you?" Art didn't care that the other two customers at the lunch counter were fully engaged in their discussion.

"That's it! I dare! I dare you to stop walking in the past and live in the present."

Outraged, Art watched her slump back again with a little cat smile playing around those peachy lips. The smile mocked him. Art took a breath and skewered the men on the round stools with a death ray look. He recognized one of them as a grown-up Del Andersen, who'd lived up on the next farm. He ran with a different crowd than Art. Funny how the rowdy one stayed and farmed while Art the FFA groupie, had left. The anger seeped out slowly.

She dared him, did she? "Just what are you suggesting, Miss London?" He'd bet his years of therapy and his PhD that she didn't have anything different to add to anyone else's advice.

"Come back. Just for the summer. You once cared about everything going on around here. Find that person again. Help your parents. Spend time with your son."

"You're joking. I have a job I can't just leave."

She puckered. "Mmhmm." And waited, and smirked some more.

The research project was more Peggy's than his. He wasn't teaching right now. He stared back until Del got up and paid. The lazy grin and wink from Del made him feel seventeen again. Art waited until the cash register and bells over the door went quiet. He felt as though the diner itself waited to hear his reply. A faint whiff of cinnamon and fried burgers conjured boyhood memories.

Art shook his head. "You can't expect a man to drop everything. That's irresponsible."

Dana dropped her gaze. She picked up her glass and ignored him.

Art knew when he was being dismissed. He nodded at Mr. Nelson and left.

He carried on with the argument all the way home. Amy had never spoken to him like that. What was with Dana? She didn't even know what it was like to be married, let alone raise a child. He shouldn't even be giving this whole idea another thought. Oakville had always been sort of ingrown, as if everyone had some kind of brain link. He hadn't really seen that until he'd moved away. Surely that wasn't healthy.

Even though it was late, Art drove right to the office. Funny, he could see lights from the lab. And hear voices. He relaxed when he realized that one of the voices belonged to Peggy. He frowned. She was laughing.

Art stopped in the open door at the sight of a large man sitting in his desk chair. Peggy leaned against a nearby lab table and looked up as if she sensed his presence.

"Doc! Hey, how's your boy?" She pushed herself away and came toward him. "And am I glad to see you! Guess who decided to come to his senses? After less than a week?"

Art gathered himself and turned to shake the hand of the dark-skinned man who stretched at least six-foot four out of his chair. "I'm guessing you're Steve."

A smile lit the other man's smooth features. "That's right. Steven Peterman. Sir, I'm sorry I got so riled up last week. I'd still like a chance to work with you."

Art nodded. "Harrison's project not to your liking, then?"

Steve flushed. "The way he outlined the work, and the actual work, weren't in tune."

Peggy butted in. "Doc, this is a fantastic opportunity you should not pass. I told you, Steve is one great catch."

Art put his hands on his hips as he studied her blush, which matched Steve's. He wagged a brow that told her "caught you!"

Not to be daunted, Peggy gushed on.

"And you should see the way that Alana girl manhandles your database. You'll see, doc. We hardly need you."

Was everything a conspiracy? Art felt like his head had been twisted off and handed to him on a pike. Had Dana called here? He shook his head.

"Of course, it's not like we don't need you at all, you know." Now Peggy sounded a tad worried. "It's just that, well, you work so hard. You hardly took any time off since — well, it's not really my place, but —"

"It sounds like you're trying to kick me out of my own lab, Peggy." Art couldn't resist the tease. His fingers and toes tingled like he'd been asleep for a long time and were just waking up.

"Now, Doc, you know I'm only looking out for you."

Art eyed up Steve, who seemed both confused and in a state of admiration. "Do I need a better mousetrap?" Art asked.

"Huh?" Both Peggy and Steve said. Then Steve laughed and elbowed Peggy. "The cat," he choked out, pointing at Art. Peggy laughed slowly until she caught on. "Oh, yeah . . . hoo-hoo."

"Steve, I'll meet with you on Monday, if I may? I have some thinking to do. You might just be the answer to a prayer."

411

Peggy whistled. "That serious?"

The word prayer sent a warm hug around Art's heart. He shook it off. "Just lock up on the way out, okay?" He looked at Peggy. "And I haven't hired Steve yet."

"I know, Doc."

At home, Art opened and closed the refrigerator, not hungry. He felt as antsy as the night Andy had left. He didn't bother to turn on lights as he wandered into every room of the house. Amy's easel was still set up in the third bedroom. She gave away most of her pastel landscapes she based on Bible verses. She had a good eye for color and enjoyed the hobby.

Art hadn't spent any time in the formal dining room the past year. Hadn't needed to. Amy liked to come in here to study. Some of her books were on the table yet, he could see by the street light through the side window. Art reached for the book on top, but knocked it to the carpet.

He bit his lip at the thought that sprang to mind. Amy wouldn't have been pleased. He flipped the light switch and saw the book lying face down. Amy's Bible. Art picked it up slowly and turned it around. A sentence had been underlined. "For he himself is our peace, who has made us both one and has broken down in his flesh the dividing wall of hostility."

Peace, hostility. Peace Art longed for; hostility was what he had with Andy, and too often had with Amy, and maybe now with Dana. But how could he find peace when all he did was live in the past and mess up the present? He? His flesh? How could flesh ease so much pain?

Art set the book down and sat in Amy's chair. Maybe it was time to do something about his messed-up life and relationship with his son. He liked that feeling of coming back to life. Could Oakville and the farm hold the answers he needed? Dana had challenged him. She couldn't have been serious, but she did point out that his family needed help. If things were really as cozy at work as Peggy indicated, maybe he could take some time — not much, but some — time off to help them out.

Was there broadband Internet in Oakville?

Now he was sounding like Andy who moaned about the loss of cable.

CHAPTER SEVEN

The next week Art set his suitcase down on the front step of Tessa's house. Tessa had agreed that their old home was crowded enough and he could stay at her empty one. The least he could do was help Tessa by taking care of the place for her, keep it from looking abandoned, although all the neighbors knew to look out for her since Phil's decampment.

The department had agreed to a six-week quasi-sabbatical, semi leave of absence. In theory Art was gathering potential information on small town population stats, and he was available on the current research project being conducted by his very capable students. Too easy. Maybe he had needed a break, something he'd been afraid to take since the loss of Amy. And then there was the great organic garden caper his niece Lindsay was cooking up. Salsa. Who would have thought salsa could save a farm? He'd been proud of her telling him that it had been Andy's idea to sell shares. Sure, that was popular around Madison, but would it work in Oakville? They'd have to do some fancy selling.

Tessa had told him the code for the garage door. Art entered the eerily quiet mud room and crossed the kitchen to the front hall. An open staircase spiraled to a narrow second floor balcony over his head. He could pick either of the kids' bedrooms, Tessa said. Art decided the futon in the den would work fine after the creak of the second and eighth treads creeped him out when he'd ventured half-way up.

He opened his case and checked his watch. Changing the battery hadn't been that traumatic. He simply walked into the jewelry store where Amy had bought it and handed it over. Ten minutes later he paid and walked out. Not yet lunch time and many hours to go until he agreed to meet Andy at the church after work to take him back to the farm.

The back seat and trunk of the Corolla was loaded with his and Andy's belongings. Art went back to grab his boxes of work-related files and computer. He grinned as he set up his own work station in Tessa's formal dining room. Her big cherry wood table had plenty of room. He set up his computer and checked in. Praise be! Broadband. His stomach growled. Lunch.

What would Dana think about his picking up the gauntlet? Would she even remember her challenge? Maybe he'd casually walk into the diner and see if she was there.

Silly. Like shooting in the air hoping not to hit something. Better stay here. Art went to check his sister's kitchen cupboards. As he entered the sunny space, he caught a faint whiff of what? Burned toast? Had that been there before?

A glass and bowl and spoon had been left in the sink. He hadn't noticed that earlier. Most unlike his neatnik sibling. Art dialed her cell phone.

She answered on the second ring. "Get in all right? The key still work?"

"Hi, Tessa. Yes, all's well. A little stuffy in here. I turned on the air."

"Good. Don't want any mold." Art heard her sigh. "I guess I should have thought of that. Maybe you'll open the windows upstairs tonight? And flush all the toilets —"

"And wash your dishes."

"What? Excuse me? I would never leave dirty dishes."

"Well, someone did."

Art felt her stillness through the airwaves

416

that connected them. "Art, I'm telling you, I didn't leave any dishes."

Art shivered, feeling very alone. The air conditioner kicked in again, sending the drapes at the patio rippling. He turned a slow one-eighty, trying to figure out if anything was out of place, or if any of the creaks and rustling noises were unusual.

"Art?"

"I'm here. Maybe you'd better come and look at this. Maybe you just forgot." He knew he'd spoken nonsense the instant the words came out of his mouth.

"Maybe you just walk out right now and call the police."

For dirty dishes? "What should I say?"

"Forget it. I'm hanging up and calling Tony right now."

The dial tone in his ear shook Art out of his trepidation. What kind of a man runs away from a dirty spoon?

A creak from the direction of the front hall sent him through the mudroom and out the back door.

A cautious man, that's who.

He circled the yard and waited outside for the man named Tony. Art eyed the garage door, chagrined that he hadn't thought to peek inside. But that's probably where the whatever was hiding, right? He took in a

417

breath. Or the basement. Art was glad he hadn't visited Tessa's downstairs rec room.

A pale blue cruiser painted with the Oakville city logo and police department phone number pulled in about five minutes later. Must not be anything too exciting going on around town. The name Tessa mentioned hadn't registered, but now Art was delighted to see "Tony" meant the same Tony Hephner who'd been one of his former FFA officers, get out of the squad.

"The prodigal doc returns," Tony said, offering his hand. "Tessa called. What's up?"

"Oh, you know Contessa the neat queen," Art said. "Hey, I didn't know criminals grew better than acorns in Oakville. Thought you were working your dad's place."

"I let Grant take over," Tony said. "Wife preferred city."

"Your brother." Art nodded and smiled. "I can appreciate that."

"So, Tessa thought there was some trouble here. Shall I take a look?"

"Sure. Tess said she hadn't left any dishes, but I found some in the sink. I haven't been here in a while, so I don't know if anything else is out of place. I didn't check the garage or basement." He wasn't about to admit that he hadn't gone all the way upstairs. "I only got here an hour ago."

"Okay. Wait here until I call you."

Tony the tiger walked into the house. He reappeared ten minutes later and beckoned. "I can take the dishes in and send them for fingerprinting," he said. "But that could take months, and would only give us an ID if the owner was in the system. You said you couldn't tell if anything else was out of place?"

Art nodded.

"I didn't find anyone in the house, or sign of forced entry on any outside doors. You plan on staying around?"

"Six weeks," Art replied. "My son's staying with the folks."

"I heard." Tony went grim for a moment. "We got a statement from him and the Suchar girl about the accident. Says he was unfamiliar with the road. Glad he wasn't hurt worse."

Art nodded, unsure whether or not to fuel the fire. Racing was only a theory at this point.

Tony smiled. "Also heard your folks got quite a little hotel going."

"Should keep them happy and out of trouble."

"Oh, I don't know about that." Tony got into his squad. "Yer ma can conjure a thunderstorm out of a sunny day when she puts her mind to it. Let me know if you have any trouble here. I'll see you around."

Tessa drove in while Art was still deciding whether or not to go back inside or go out for lunch. "Anything?" she asked when she got out of her Land Rover.

"Tony came and checked the place out. No signs of forced entry and no one was in the house," he said.

"You still want to stay here?"

"Tess, why don't you go in and look around? I have no idea if anything else is out of place."

Art followed her around the house.

"You're going to sleep in here?" she asked when she got to the den.

He shrugged. "Seemed like less trouble."

"All right."

He kept up with her while she checked the four upstairs bedrooms, opening and closing each door. He waited for her just outside of her bedroom. Tessa paused in the middle of the room. Frowning, she folded her arms.

"What's wrong?" Art entered the room.

She shook her head. "I don't know. Just feels funny." She nodded at the bed. "Like a wrinkle, you know." Laughing, she said, "Sort of like Goldilocks. Someone's been sleeping in my bed."

"That was Baby Bear. How about the bathroom?"

He watched her go in and come out, face ashen. "The seat's up."

"Maybe you left it that way when you were cleaning."

"No. You weren't in there, were you?"

Instead of shivery and nervous like before, Art felt drained and in sore need of a week without problems. If he couldn't find it here, he wouldn't get it anywhere. "No, I wasn't. What kind of a burglar uses dishes and a bathroom?"

Tessa stared at him.

"Nothing's missing, right? Or damaged?"

She shook her head. "You think I just forgot, don't you?"

Women. "Tess, I'm always on your side. We've been under a lot of stress — both of us." He put his arm around her shoulder and squeezed. "Even if we had the police back to dust for prints," he continued, "it'll probably be the same person who left the glass in the sink. Whoever it was is probably long gone."

"You're right. I guess." She exhaled loudly and looked around again. "I just feel violated, you know?"

"Take me to lunch and tell me about it."

■ ■ ■ ■

Beatrice looked up from pouring coffee when they entered the diner. "Hey, Art. Glad to see you again. Be right with you."

At Tessa's raised brows, he gave her a lopsided grin. "I came in the week before last." He slid into a booth and surreptitiously glanced around. His heartbeat galloped until he was certain Dana wasn't here. Was he relieved or disappointed?

"Who you looking for?" Tessa had been watching.

Art's cheeks warmed. "Just seeing if there's anyone I know."

Tessa's eyes narrowed, but she smiled. "That's Del Andersen at the counter. He's working his dad's farm now. Messy divorce when his wife left and said she didn't want their kid." She narrowed her eyes. "A boy about Andy's age. Will. In fact, I think they might have met, because I overheard something Andy said on the phone one night." She grimaced. "Walls are pretty thin at Mom and Dad's. The Andersen boy's trouble, Art. I hope they stay clear of each other."

Art righted his coffee cup as Bea came toward them with the pot, a couple of menus stuck under her arm. "Thanks, Bea. What's good today?"

Bea, whom he'd never seen without her signature beehive hairdo, grinned. The casual uniform of jeans and white top with an apron emblazoned "Diner" felt homey.

"Tuna salad," Bea said, her pencil raised.

Tessa groaned under her breath. Art grinned and ordered it on toasted whole wheat. "I'll have the French Dip," Tessa said. "And iced tea. Sweet, thanks."

"Coming right up. How're your folks?"

Art leaned back and listened to his sister chat with the waitress. They weren't in any hurry. He looked around the place again to see the clientele were mostly retired-looking folks. He recognized a couple of Mom and Dad's friends and waved. Seemed like farm folks moved into town once they turned the place over to the next generation. So, why'd they eat out instead of cooking? Were farm wives tired of —

Tessa touched his hand. "Earth to Doc."

Art blinked. "You got me. I guess I'm always in research mode."

"You're worse than a writer who sees a story in every face. So, research about what?"

Art sipped from his mug, then spooned in half a teaspoon of sugar and stirred. "I'm writing a grant to study how older people adapt to life changes in smaller communities. Do you have any idea how many of Mom and Dad's friends have moved into Oakville?"

"We could ask."

Tessa's lips were tight. He turned to see what was so fascinating in her line of sight. A young man in a button-down shirt and rolled sleeves sat reading the paper, an empty soup bowl in front of him. A leather portfolio rested on a nearby chair.

"Behold, thine enemy," Tessa whispered.

"What? Who?"

Tessa nodded and looked down again quickly. Art heard the scrape of a chair as someone — the young man, Art presumed — got up and gathered his things. When the doorbell tinkled, Tessa looked up.

"Brandon Calloway."

"So?"

"He's the guy who's causing all the grief around here. And his father." She tapped the glass of ice tea, as she flushed and pursed her lips. "The developers you know, trying to take the farm."

"Come on, Tessa. Don't you think the folks would be better off in Oakville? They could use the money to buy a nice little house. Dad could be close to the hospital.

Mom wouldn't terrorize anyone on the roads."

"You don't get it, do you? All you think about is yourself, your own problems. Mom and Dad would curl up and die if all they had to look at was their neighbor's houses. They don't want to live anywhere else. It's our heritage, Art. Even if you don't care anymore, I do. I'm a Hasmer and I want to make sure my children have something to be proud of." She pointed her finger at Art's nose. "Otto's buried there."

Art twitched his mouth to the side and forced himself to think about his next words. Bea saved them by silently setting their lunch plates in front of them.

Tessa closed her eyes and prayed out loud without bothering to consult him. Art watched and listened, hoping no one was near enough to hear.

"Father, thank you for your precious gift of eternal life in your son, Jesus, who gave himself up for us on the cross. Thank you for the gift of family, even my brother, whose head is — just, thank you for the family you've given both of us, Lord. Keep Lindsay from making a fool of herself. Keep Robin's family and Andy and Mom and Dad safe and healthy. Bless this food and the hands that prepared it. Amen."

"My head is what?" Art asked when his sister had taken her first bite and couldn't answer right away. He grinned at the flash of irritation in her eyes.

"That is such an old trick, waiting for me to start eating," she said, wiping her mouth. "I love you, little brother. I've missed you." She took a gulp of her tea. "I'm glad to see you're finding your feet again after Amy. I loved her. We all did, but she'd be the first one to tell you to find someone to share your lonely brainiac life. You'll get your head on straight yet. If you stay around long enough."

"Yeah, okay. Lindsay?"

"That man. Can you believe it? She thinks she likes him."

"What man?"

"Brandon Calloway."

"Calloway? Lindsay's grown up. Talk about letting the apron strings go." Art tsk'd.

She sipped her tea and waited until he'd filled his mouth with the delicious tuna. "Letting go, huh? What's with you and Dana London?" She flashed an evil grin. "And how can I help?"

CHAPTER EIGHT

At two-thirty Tessa jumped up, claimed she had an appointment and stuck him with the check. Art left a generous tip for Beatrice, paid and drove slowly out to Community Church. He'd been in the youth group, of course, and always had gone to Sunday services with the folks. Otto's death had soured him on faith, though, when Pastor Gerley kept answering his questions with "It was God's will, son. Your brother is in better hands now. Continue to work out your faith with fear and trembling so you'll be able to join him in heaven."

Art wasn't all that interested in running into Pastor Gerley again and decided to walk around the grounds while he waited for Andy to finish work. Art stood under one of the bigger trees. He stuck his hands in his pockets and thought about taking a walk later along the wooded Ice Age hiking trail. The woods would be cooler than this heat. A bee hovered to check him out before zipping away. He closed his eyes and opened them to see a strawberry blonde angel on the other side of the tree.

Nothing surprised him much today, he mused. Not even an angel in shorts.

"Hi, you must be Andy's dad."

Art shifted his feet, then reached for her outstretched hand. "Yes. Hi. I'm Art Hasmer."

"Ella Suchar." She nodded back at the church. "The pastor's kid."

"Suchar? The pastor's name is Gerley."

"We came when I was little. I think the other pastor was Gerley, but we can ask my dad. You want to meet him? I know he'd like to meet you. Andy's been a great help."

"Sure. Um, now?"

"Yep. This way."

Art followed the young lady, who kept a constant stream of chatter flowing. "Andy's great at lawn-mowing, but I had to teach him which were the weeds to pull, and not flowers. He left the goat's beard and pulled out my impatiens last week. Then he planted only half the new ones and clocked out." She lowered her voice when they entered the cavernous sanctuary. "He's not so great with dusting corners, either, but then, he's a boy."

Art chuckled. The sound echoed into the choir loft. Church looked quite a bit the same, with stained glass windows lining each side of the rectangular, towering room. Fans whirled overhead and the windows had been cranked. The screen was new. Ella went to fetch her father from the office.

Ella? That was the name Lindsay had mentioned. The girl who helped Andy after the accident.

Footsteps made Art swing away from the altar. A man about his own age walked toward him. Dressed in a T-shirt and jeans, with short hair and mustache, he didn't look much like any pastor Art had ever seen.

"Mike Suchar," the man said and stuck out his hand.

Art shook it, puzzled.

Mike laughed. "Ella told me you expected to see Pastor Gerley. He's retired."

"Oh, sure. It's just that you don't look much like a pastor."

"I get that a lot," Mike said. "We've been so thankful for your son. He's doing a great job."

"That's good to hear. I'm afraid he's not much into cleaning. At least, it's hard to get him to do his chores at home."

"I'm that way too. If Ella didn't keep after me, I'd be hopeless."

"Your wife doesn't nag?"

"Passed away when Ella was a tot," Mike said, matter-of-factly.

"Oh, I'm so sorry. No one said anything."

"I understand you lost your wife."

"Just a little over a year ago. Amy — Amy was a nurse. She was killed on a Flight for Life mission."

"I read about that in the papers. My deepest sympathy."

"Thank you."

"So, Andy tells me you're a member at Monona Christian."

Art shouldn't have been surprised. Amy had been the one to push church and he'd attended once in a while to please her, but he'd never joined. "No. His mother was."

Mike didn't act surprised or put out.

"Dad." Andy came upstairs. "I finished the bathrooms, Pastor Mike. That was the last of today's list."

"Good. I was just telling your dad how glad I am to have your help."

Andy flushed under the man's praise. Was it that simple? Art couldn't remember the last time he'd praised Andy. Hardness squeezed Art's thoughts. Of course, Andy hadn't done much praiseworthy lately.

"Nice meeting you," Art said.

"We'll see you Sunday." Ella's voice piped

from behind Andy.

Art just nodded and led Andy outside to the car.

"I brought your things," Art told him. "That girl — Ella? Lindsay mentioned something about a girl called Ella who —"

"Yeah, Dad. There aren't too many girls with that name around."

Art buckled slowly, trying to think of other things to talk about that wouldn't ruffle his son's feathers. He drove toward the farm, only a couple country miles away. "So, everything going okay with Grandma and Grandpa?"

"I haven't trashed anything else of theirs, if that's what you're asking."

Art squirmed and counted to ten. "I'm not asking that. I just want to know how you are. Your face looks better. Healing. Does it hurt much?" He waited, expecting to hear something about it being a little late to ask.

"No." Pause. "It's better." Pause. "The Suchars are nice."

"They both seem to like you."

Andy tapped some kind of beat on his jeans-clad knees. Art just realized that the boy wore pants that fit him and had no noticeable holes. Should he say something?

"Driveway's coming up."

"Oh, yeah, thanks." Art signaled and slowed. Before they got out, he wanted to tell Andy about the possible intruder in Tessa's house. "Andy, Aunt Tessa thinks someone might have been in her house. We had the police look around, but there's nothing missing."

Andy stared at him. "You're still going to stay there?"

"I am."

"Okay." Andy got out and bounded into the house.

Art followed more sedately, taking time to notice that the eaves had been freshly painted and the lawn neatly clipped. No weeds dared touch his mother's flower beds, which overflowed with the great leaves of hollyhocks elbowing patches of pink and white bleeding hearts. Amy's favorite color had been pink.

He studied the rolling hills again and had a sudden longing to visit his childhood secret hideout, a spring-fed pool in the middle of a small glade. Was it still there? He shaded his eyes with his hand and looked across what he now recognized as Lindsay's organic produce beds to the green tangle at the edge of the back eighty. Maybe he'd get out there in the next month.

For the first time Art realized that it didn't

hurt to be home. Step one at getting his life back: going home without freaking out — check. Tackling the second step, getting over the guilt of letting Otto die and making all the wrong choices, was tougher. Maybe he could bypass that one and move on to step three: making things right with Dana London. And he'd wait and see what else if it came to that. He'd never ask Amy to wallow in widowhood. After all, he had his son's permission, right? Andy had told him to move on.

Art didn't want to wait any longer. When he got back to Tessa's that night, he made himself dial before he could talk himself out of it. Four — five rings.

"Hello?"

"Hi. Dana. I'm back."

"Who's calling?"

Art smacked his forehead. Rural Bakersfield didn't have caller ID. "I'm so sorry. Um, Art. This is Art Hasmer."

"I didn't recognize your voice."

Since he'd never called her before, he wasn't surprised. "I'm staying at Tessa's house this summer. Six weeks. Doing some — some research."

"Ah, good to hear."

Her voice had warmed up. Art could only

hope she was happy to hear it. "I'm sorry to just call out of the blue like this. I wondered, that is, I wanted to ask if we could have dinner. Sometime."

"So I can help you with your research?"

A straw! "Sure."

"Good."

Did he read a moment of disappointment in her voice? He grinned.

"How's Tessa?" she asked.

"Fine. We think someone may have come inside the house after she left it to stay with Mom and Dad, so a little shook about that, but I'm here now." So what? Like he was some kind of hero now?

"Well, you'll certainly scare any burglars away. You're not worried?"

"Nah. Maybe I can see you tomorrow?" Slow down, cowboy — too eager. She should run screaming while she could. Art crossed his arm over his chest and tried to squelch the teenaged feelings that choked him.

"You would not believe how much your sister has been badgering me to call you. I'm sorry, though. I can't tomorrow. I have an emergency board meeting."

Tessa? "My sister has been trying to get you to go out with me?"

Dana chuckled. "Don't worry. I can take

434

care of myself."

Despite the glass-blowing heat of embarrassment, a tiny little thought peeped: Art wondered what it would be like to have someone like Dana take care of him. "Phew — I'm so sorry. I'll get Tess to back off. She doesn't have anything better to do than interfere with other people's lives."

"Tessa means well."

"So, you're going to a town board meeting? Could I come?" At least he would see her.

"They can get pretty raucous, especially since the emergency has to do a rezoning at your folks' place."

"I'm not surprised. I'm the bad guy, I'm afraid, since I'd just as soon they sold out."

"You and Phillip Murphy."

"What's good old Phil got to do with this? I thought he left town."

"He did. But nowadays, distance doesn't stop anyone from wreaking havoc. Phil is listed as one of the partners in the Sunrise Senior Living Center project that the developers are proposing in their mixed residential plan for your parents' farm."

Hoo-boy. "Does Tessa know?"

"That's none of my business." Dana closed up again.

"I understand. So, do you want to have

435

dinner with me?"

"Sure. Just not tomorrow."

He mentioned the next day, which was occupied with choir practice and Bible study, which he declined to attend. By the time they'd matched their schedules they were laughing. Art hung up, relishing the delight of feeling happy and the tingle of life spreading up his arms toward his chest. *I'm waking up,* he thought, *from a long, long nap.*

Art removed his watch and set it on the kitchen counter. He rubbed the spot where his wedding ring had encircled his finger.

The creak of the stairs startled him. He fought off the desire to chase settling noises in Tessa's house and unpacked the sack of groceries he'd brought in. He fixed himself a stack of cheese and crackers and wandered back toward the den to check in with Peggy via Internet. A shadow crossing the hallway stopped him cold.

"Who's there! Come out! I'm calling the police." Art raised the plate like a flying disc. No one answered. Art tiptoed toward the hall.

"Who's there?" He crouched near the door and with his free hand he fumbled for his cell phone. It wasn't in his pocket. "I've got a weapon."

436

The rustling sound of shuffling feet broke the silence. "Don't shoot! I'm unarmed!"

Art rose slowly and heaved a sigh of pure exasperation. "What are you doing here?"

CHAPTER NINE

"It's my house," Phillip Murphy said, eyeing the plate of cheese and crackers in Art's hands. "What were you going to do with that? Assault me? Kill me with cholesterol? I thought you had a gun."

"I didn't say that. And what are you doing? How long have you been here?"

Phil had the grace to look ashamed. His wiry hair was disheveled and he was stocking-footed. Art had never seen Phil without shoes on, he realized, or unkempt in any way.

"A week."

"Does Tessa know you're here?"

"It's my house."

"Then why are you trying to hide?"

Art dropped the plate when Phil lunged and grabbed him in a bear hug, sobbing. "Please, please. You can't tell her. You can't."

Two weeks later, Art could do nothing but

admire his brother-in-law's ingenious method of survival. Phillip had hidden in the attic the day Art had moved in, and continued to sleep during the day and work in the basement at night. He'd set a motion sensor alarm to go off if someone entered the driveway, and that's how he'd been avoiding Tessa's visits to do laundry or pack things up. His refusal to deal with Tessa left Art in a major quandary since Tessa's college boyfriend — the senior Calloway, go figure — was hanging around. What a mess! Ann Landers would have said not to butt in, so he wouldn't. Yet.

Sharing the house with a silent partner was wearing on Art and his budding relationship with Dana. So far they'd managed to outmaneuver Tessa's attempts to set them up by making plans of their own — which usually meant showing up at the same place at the same time. Art couldn't invite Dana over to the house because of Phil, and he was beginning to feel like a high-school kid who wasn't allowed to have a girl over without supervision.

On the other hand, maybe it was a good idea, given his growing feelings for her. Dana was a softie, he'd discovered, despite her independence. He grinned. Or "spinsterhood," as she put it. He'd not yet gotten an answer about why she'd never married. He hoped she wasn't determined to remain single the rest of her life.

Phil was more of a cloying nuisance than he'd ever imagined. How had his sister put up with the man? Guy didn't even know how to work the washing machine and seemed proud of it. If they hadn't agreed on how to handle the farm and Art and Tessa's folks, Art would have put his brother-in-law out to pasture long before. Tessa could have him back.

"But why did you leave?" Art asked.

"It was for Tessa's sake. I didn't want her to have to watch the demolition process."

"You knew Tessa would never leave home."

"Buddy, there are things going on you know nothing about."

"Right back at you. Enlighten me."

"Once the development project goes through."

"Well, then, why did you come back? And why don't you talk to your wife?"

Phil had clenched his stomach, moaned about an ulcer and clammed up. He avoided Art, which suited Art fine. But he wasn't washing the guy's underwear, that's for sure. He was not planning on hiding the guy much longer. And since Tessa had completely taken leave of her senses and started fawning all over that development guy's father, Art washed his hands of them both. Any day he expected Mom to toss her out.

If Mom and Dad lost the farm, it would hurt them. Art had Amy's insurance settlement coming. He'd planned to use it for Andy's college expenses, but maybe he'd consider paying off their bills if the money came in time.

The early July evening, a stormy one, was like a sauna when he drove to Dana's house to pick her up for their third real date. They were going into Milwaukee for the Music and Lights show at Mitchell Park's Domes, something Dana said she'd always wanted to see. A folk band was playing at the three-domed conservatory. A restoration project had installed lights among the triangles that made up the huge complex. He wasn't much into folk music, but the light show sounded intriguing. Anything that made Dana happy worked for him.

Art liked Dana's eclectic taste in conversation, reading and entertainment. Amy had seemed stuck in religious mode and frowned at a lot of the suggestions Art had given until he rarely offered to take her anywhere but church. Dana was a Christian, sure, but she also knew how to have fun. He'd even gone to church with her the past two Sundays and agreed to attend Bible study.

Thinking of Amy didn't hurt anymore, either, Art realized. Last week's sermon bubbled in his conscious. Mike had talked about the things Christians should feel guilty about, not just nameless sin in general, but real things like not caring or helping those in need. Christians should feel guilty about breaking the commandments and challenged the congregation to name them. Art could only remember two and Dana kindly offered to help him find the rest. Was a month too soon to fall in love? Was he ready? Maybe he was fooling himself. And marriage — was it too soon to even consider?

Art signaled and slowed to pull into her driveway. Dana stood in silhouette, staring at the sky.

Nope. Art was a lovey-dovey gooey mess of a goner. Big time.

"What do you think about keeping secrets?"

"Secrets?" Art had been lost in Dana's soft gray eyes and the contemplating of pressing his mouth against hers when he watched her lips form the question a second before it registered. They sat in her porch swing after Bible study. The *zzt* of her bug zapper competed with the frog chorus from the wetland to the west. Art took his arm from her shoulders and dry-wiped his face. She knew! "I should have figured that I couldn't keep it from you," he said.

"What are you talking about?"

Art furrowed his brow. "What are you?"

Dana crossed her legs and examined her fingernails under the soft yellow glow of the porch light. "The Bible study, remember?" She gnawed on her bottom lip. "We're still talking about guilt, like telling lies or telling half-truths."

"Oh, right." Art set his elbows on his knees.

"So you have something to tell me?" Dana asked.

"Um, nothing in particular. But I would like to ask you why you never married."

She gave a little twisted smile. "No one asked me."

"That's hard to believe."

"Not that hard, when you've lived in one place all your life." She cocked her head. "I've been watching you these past few weeks."

Art grinned at her. "I hope so. Been watching you too, pretty woman."

Dana snorted softly. "Funny guy. You're learning how to fit in again, and spending more time with your son. It's good." She paused and took a quick breath. "I need to tell you something."

He sobered and sat up straight. Great. His heartbeat hitched and his fingers felt cold. "Okay." He tried to lighten the mood. "Sounds serious."

"It's about Otto."

The heartbeat trotted painfully out of sync. He couldn't speak. "I had such a crush on him. It was so bad. He knew it. I let him — I let him —"

Art reached out, grabbed her hands and squeezed. "All the girls liked him, I was jealous. So you hung out with him." That's all, right? His thoughts screamed but he refused to voice them. Otto would never have done anything worse than that. Not his brother. Art would have known.

"Oh, Art." Dana pulled away and jumped up. She went to stand at the end of the porch and faced the dark yard. "I knew it was wrong but I just wanted someone to — like me."

Art could barely hear. He unstuck himself from the safety of the swing and approached her. "I liked you."

She smacked the rail. "I didn't know!"

"They dared me to ask you to the prom."

"You think that's news to me? Dared you to take your brother's leavings?" Dana hunched and put her hands to her face. "I didn't have anyone to talk to, and I couldn't tell my grandparents about it."

He'd never known why the others had dared him. He hadn't dated in high school, not really; just gone with the gang after youth group or football games to BigMac.

Art closed his eyes to hear Otto's laughing voice and face in the locker room after track practice. The other guys whose names he had trouble recalling blurred in the steam of the showers. Otto had changed. He had a secret that he wouldn't share and Art felt the loss. "Time to grow up, brother," Otto sneered. "You're gonna need a farmwife to go with all the farming you're going to do. Someone who will work hard and not care about looking classy. Like that Dana geek. Lives with her grandparents and wears her grandma's dresses to school."

"She does not wear her grandma's dresses. Leave her alone."

"Art, Art, bro — wake up and smell the coffee. Ask her out. I dare you to take her to prom."

The other guys laughed.

Art opened his eyes. How did he feel abut

keeping secrets? He gingerly touched Dana's shoulder. "It's in the past. I don't . . . blame you."

"You don't understand." Dana sniffled. "He came back later and apologized. I — I believed him. He said he was going to talk to you."

"He never did."

Dana raised her tear-stained face. "He died. I think he felt so terrible about what he did that he got careless. It's my fault your brother died."

CHAPTER TEN

The thought of going back to Tessa's house unnerved Art. Only one place he felt safe anymore: the farm. As he parked in the familiar driveway, exited the car and breathed in the magnified night scents of warm earth and roses and caught the whoosh of a barred owl overhead, he realized how terrible it would be for his parents to be forced from this place they loved. He knew he loved it too and always had.

Art clenched his fists. Otto had betrayed him, and so had Dana. Phil. Even Tessa sneaking around, thinking no one noticed her with that Calloway fellow. The weight of deception and confession parked between his shoulder blades.

The only good thing had been Andy. Dana had challenged him to make things right with his son, and with the help of the Su-chars, things were moving in the right direction. On that field, at least. Mike had become more than someone to swap widower stories when Art waited to pick up Andy. They'd talked about how to make room in a broken heart for someone else. Mike's daughter had such a sweet relationship with her father. The look on Andy's face whenever the boy saw them together convinced Art it wasn't too late to mend their relationship. They'd gotten the truck back, dented but running. Just like the time he and Dad had originally spent on the vintage Ford, he'd invited Andy to tinker with him. Memories of grease and advice came back readily, which he shared with Andy out in the old tool shed as they worked together; Andy touching up the paint while he fiddled with the belts and plugs. The thing they couldn't talk about was Dana and Andy's frowns whenever he saw her. Or Andy's obvious attachment to Ella.

Dana had had no one to talk to, but Art did. Feeling the exhaustion of being blindsided, Art climbed the steps of his parents' house and their unconditional love.

Dad was in the living room, planted in front of the television. He clicked the show off as soon as Art sat heavily on the stool near his feet.

"Wish we still had that truck to work on," his dad rasped out. "Glad you and Andy have it."

"We never needed it. We could always talk."

Dad chuckled and coughed. "Not always. Young farmer whipper-snapper . . . had some pretty fancy ideas." Cough. Sip of water. "Didn't think much of tradition."

Art laughed. "I guess. I understand now."

"When I was a child I thought . . . like a child. When I became a man I gave up childish ways," his dad said. "You lost your way, son. But now you're back? You remember . . . your faith?"

"Yes, Dad. You're right. I didn't have much use for it after Otto. But Mike, he's quite a guy. Good man. Helped me remember a lot of things I'd forgotten."

"You're troubled."

"Yeah. I learned something about Otto and . . . and Dana that I wish I hadn't."

Art's dad shifted in his chair. "Otto had a wild streak. Not like you."

"I thought the accident was my fault, that I hadn't been able to keep him from being so reckless."

Dad shook his head, wiped his mouth.

"No. No blame."

"Dana thinks . . . All these years, Dad, she's had it worse than me. He treated her badly, and she told me tonight she feels like she's guilty of causing his death."

"Bitter envy. Rage. Jealousy. Evil things."

"But how do we stop feeling bad?"

Otto took Art's hand in his gnarled one and closed his eyes. "Peace. Peace I leave with you. Not as the world gives . . ."

When his father's prayer ended, Art knew what he needed to do. Forgiving himself was easy compared to convincing Dana she had to do the same.

A puff of humid air forewarned Art of company. He raised his chin, surprised to see Andy shifting from side to side, wearing a visible cloak of guilt.

Art sighed. His one second of peace was up. "What?"

Andy's voice still tended to squeak when he was nervous. Art shook his head in an attempt to follow his son's flood of mumbled sentences while he automatically checked for blood. "Start over."

"I said," Andy enunciated with the hyper-accent of the very annoyed, "I didn't know it was church property. Besides, Pastor Suchar was impressed and said I had a good eye, and he was fine with it. I don't even have to pay to get it repainted."

"Get what repainted?"

"The church van. Uh — Will said he was going to burn down the Nelson's barn unless I did some tagging with him."

Art heard *Will and Burn* and reached for his phone.

"Dad! What are you doing?"

"After I call the police, I'm calling Will's father and having a conversation."

"Dad, stop. It's my word against his. I have no proof, and you know Will's gonna deny everything. I'm already the biggest annoyance to ever hit farmtown, so don't help me by making it worse, okay? Like I said, it's cool with Pastor Suchar. I told you. And I confessed like he said, and we're all right, so can I go to bed now. Please."

Art studied his only child, trying to recall acting like this in front of his father. He glanced at Dad, who wore a smirk, and sighed again. Yup, one of those "comes around" grins. No help there. "You said Mike knows about this? I'll have to talk to him."

"Yeah, already. We're meeting him in the morning. Six."

"Thanks for telling me," Art said. He rubbed his eyes. "You're grounded, and I'm taking the laptop."

Andy opened his mouth, gulped like a goldfish that had leapt out of the bowl, then closed it and thundered to his room.

Two hours later, Art had calmed down enough to try to sleep. He crawled into the lower bunk under a snoring Andy and closed his eyes.

Art accompanied Andy to see the result of the tagging incident at glowering daybreak the next morning. Mike had put a good spin on the van, and Art had been surprised at the depth of emotion his son tickled from a can of paint. Would Andy ever get it? He'd seemed remorseful and promised never to do it again. Art decided to trust Mike's instincts, and follow his lead. The grounding should make sure the remorse stayed real. Art wasn't sure if he felt sorrier for Mom or Andy.

Art found his mom reading the paper at the kitchen table, ever-ready coffee cup attached to her hand, when he got home. That was Mom, and Art wouldn't have it any other way.

"Morning." She didn't seem surprised at his appearance.

"I bunked with Andy last night." He pulled a mug out of the cupboard. "Early risers have something to crow about," it proclaimed. He filled it with steaming black coffee from the percolator.

"I recognized your snore," she said. "Had a good talk with your dad?"

Art smiled. "Just what I needed."

"It's been good to have you all together," LouAnn replied. "And it'll be just as good when you all skedaddle again." She raised her cup for a refill. "Not that I'm packing your bags, mind you."

"I know." Art stared out of the window toward the back eighty. A confession of his own popped out. "Phil's been back at their house."

"Figured as much. Got a couple of hang-ups last week, but I could hear him breathing through his adenoids. Didn't think he was far."

"He's a pain. How does Tessa put up with him?"

The newspapers rustled behind Art. He turned away from the window.

Mom's lips pinched like she'd added lemon instead of half-and-half to her mug. "Amy thought you were perfect, did she?"

Art let that barb sink deep. He'd rather be grounded than turn that microscope on himself. "I'm sorry." He looked out the window again. "I think I'll go for a walk."

His mom flipped a page. "Sounds good.

Another storm's brewing, so you should take advantage of the nice weather now."

Art trudged across the deeply furrowed fields, wading through gut-high goldenrod and grass. An occasional cornstalk sprouted from old seed. A red-winged blackbird shrilled its single-note cry as a warning.

"I'm not about to hurt you," Art said. Then he parted the curtain of weeping willow and entered the hideout. The big rock throne was exactly how he'd remembered. The soft burble of the spring echoed around the enclosure. Footprints in the soft earth indicated recent visitors.

Would God hear him here? Of course.

The curtain parted for Tessa. "Mom said you spent the night."

If he couldn't be alone, at least he could do something nice for his big sister. Time to stop keeping someone else's secrets. "Yeah. Tess — why'd Phil leave?"

She hopped on the throne rock and curled her legs under her. "He couldn't stand living with me anymore." She shrugged. "It happens."

"What if you found out that wasn't true?"

Her eyes went wide. "Why would you say something like that? Besides, there's someone from my past — it's just complicated."

"Tell me about it." Art's snort echoed.

"You could be a little more discreet, you know."

"I told him I didn't want to see him anymore." She hopped down and made her way toward the willow branches.

"Wait! If you could have Phil back, wouldn't you want him?"

"He was the one who left."

"You chose not to follow."

"I told him when we got married that I'd never leave Oakville. It's my home."

"Your kids are grown up. Robin moved across the country, why can't you? Wouldn't you like to travel?"

"No."

Art plopped a pebble into the spring. "One thing I've learned this summer is that in order to grow, you have to forgive, accept yourself and your inability to be perfect. Sometimes you even have to take risks."

"What if the truth hurts?"

"Ah, Tess." Art embraced his sister. "It often does. But we shouldn't be afraid of it." He patted her back. "I think you need to go home."

She sighed. "You're right. I'm not proving anything by staying with the folks."

Art filled the morning with tasks for his parents, repairing this and that, washing dishes, hauling the laundry basket while he thought about how to approach Dana.

He took flapping towels and sheets from the clothesline while watching thunderheads roll in late in the afternoon. Mom came out the back door and waved at him.

"What's up, Mom?"

"Your Dad —"

The towel Art was unpinning went flying from his numb fingers. "What's the matter? Is he okay?"

"It's happened before. Don't worry, son. Clogged tube. I already called the doctor and they're expecting us."

"What can I do?" Art trotted to the house.

"Help me get him in the car. Then you can make sure the laundry, all of it, gets it the house. Maybe even folded."

"Sure. You don't want me to come along?"

They walked into the kitchen where Dad sat in his chair, leaning forward slightly and gasping quick little breaths. Lindsay hovered, looking like an angel that forgot how to fly. Art knelt close to his dad. "What can I do?"

Mom grabbed the handlebars. "Open the garage door and help me transfer him. We'll be fine. Hate the fuss. Don't worry. We've been through this before."

Art opened and closed doors and berated

himself for years of not being here when they needed him.

"It's all right, Uncle Art," Lindsay said. "It happened once before, and everything turned out all right. How about pizza for supper? Andy ought be home soon."

"Andy would like that. I have to go out." At least with Andy, he could try and make up some of the time they'd lost. As long as he was grounded, maybe they could work on the truck later on. After he'd talked to Dana. Yeah, that sounded like a plan.

Art grabbed the rest of the laundry just before Andy let the screen door bang.

"Um. Dad? Could I talk to you?"

"Sure? What's up?" Art hoped his son wasn't going to start an argument over the unfairness of being grounded. Andy had gotten off pretty lightly as it was. He set the basket on the dining room floor and folded towels, stacking them on the table. "Can you make it quick? I'd like to check on Grampa before I . . . well I have some unfinished business in town."

Andy studied his dirty toes. "I forgot my extra work shirt at church. Could I pick it up after dinner?"

"A work shirt?" Art stared at his son as he snapped and folded the last towel. The boy looked straight at him, but still, should he be trusted? *Trust him.* Art put his arm around Andy's shoulders, pleased to feel the muscle tone that hadn't been there at the beginning of summer.

Andy shrugged.

"Why don't you leave that for tomorrow? You must be exhausted. Kick back and relax. And, uh, do me a favor? Put your socks and shirts away? I'll get the rest when I get back. Maybe we can work on the truck later." Art dropped his arm. "Why don't you go see if Lindsay found that pizza. I have to take off. See you later."

Art drove through the rain, following the dotted center line. When he reached Oakville, he dropped in at the hospital, relieved his dad was fine and getting ready to go home. Pastor Suchar, that nice young man, had come to visit, then gotten a phone call and said he had to go. Art nodded and said he'd meet them later. He decided to drive back out to the church and wait for Mike. Maybe they could grab a burger, talk.

In the church parking lot, Art wasn't surprised to see Tessa's Land Rover. Dana's Cruiser, however, made him pause. He still hadn't worked out what to say to her. Everything he'd practiced to the mirror seemed condescending. The guilt they both carried definitely needed excising. Maybe she thought Pastor Suchar could work a miracle, but he wished they could talk to Mike together.

Art parked and unbuckled slowly, eyes glued to the strange sight of Phil shaking his hand after punching the lights out of Josh Calloway. Tessa and one of her friends stood there along with Dana.

He got out and approached the women. "What's going on?"

Tessa snorted and muttered something that sounded like "testosterone."

Tessa's friend rushed toward Josh, who was holding his cheek and wobbling.

"I just came to see the pastor," Dana said, drawing Art's attention away from the rest of the planet.

"Me, too," Art replied, unable to look away from Dana's pink cheeks and shining eyes.

"Is he here?" Dana said.

"Let's go check." Art and Dana went in the side door. A teenaged boy hurtled past them. Dana jumped out of the way.

"Are you all right?"

Dana nodded.

Art recognized the young man and guessed who else he'd find. "What's the rush, Will?"

"Andy?" Art was prepared to light into his supposed-to-be-grounded son, when the pastor's daughter slid to sit at the floor. One look at the girl, and Art realized what had happened. Dana's hand on his arm was the beginning of a rush of warm pride. His son had been concerned about Ella's safety, not wanting to get in trouble with Will when he made up that flimsy excuse to get back here. Chagrined, he admitted he wouldn't have accepted the real reason from his son. He really needed to work on that trust factor. Dana squeezed his arm and went into the sanctuary. Fascinated, Art listened as Ella pulled herself together and gave the most tear-jerking testimony of forgiveness he'd ever heard. After she wound down, he gathered his son in his arms, sorrier than ever that they'd ever been at odds. The best gift was Andy's grin and declaration of forgiveness. Art looked down the aisle toward Dana. "I have to talk to her."

"I think I do, too." Andy said and tugged Ella along to stand beside Dana.

In a dream, Art listened to Andy say, "I'm sorry I've been acting like a jerk around you this summer." He sighed and blinked his eyes. Art's heart melted for him. "I was the one who said we needed to move on, Dad, I know." Ella took a step closer to him. He looked at her, then at Art, then at Dana. "You're all right."

Dana's face relaxed and she smiled softly. "Thanks. I'm not going to take your dad away from you, or try to act like your mom, you know."

"I know."

Ella circled his arm with her small hand.

Andy's chest rose and fell. He stepped back. "So then. I'll, ah, just leave you two to it." Art watched them walk out of the sanctuary.

Sure only that he loved her and wanted desperately to assure her that she wasn't to blame for Otto's choices, he slid into the pew next to Dana. If he could forgive himself, hopefully she could forgive herself. Ella had been so eloquent. Who could have guessed a teenaged girl would have such a lifeline to the Word?

Dana didn't look at him, but held out her hand. Art grasped it and held it to his cheek. "Dana." He swallowed. "I love you."

She wiped her eyes with her free hand.

"Please, look at me?"

Her tear-streaked face glowed in the soft light of the choir loft.

"Are you okay?"

She nodded and tried to pull away. Art gently tugged her closer. He rubbed the back of his hand over her damp cheek. "I like you, you know."

Dana laughed and cried harder. "Which is it?"

"Both." Art let go of her hand and cupped her face. "It's always been both," he whispered before he kissed her.

When they pulled back and faced each other, she spoke first. "No regrets." It was a promise as much as an affirmation. Art nodded.

"Next month is August," she murmured.

Art smiled. "Yup."

"I was thinking since I'm going to be taking classes again, maybe we could spend time together? In Madison?"

Art took her hands in his and tightened his grip. "I was hoping for a little more."

She flushed. "As long as we're thinking along those lines, this middle-aged lady doesn't want to spend much more of her life alone. I've always dreamt of a Christmas wedding."

Art stared into the depths of her adorable eyes. "Me too." He touched the rim of her ear. "Middle-aged, hmm? Then we'll still have the best half of our lives to be together." He stared at her mouth. "On second thought, do we have to wait until Christmas?"

At her slow smile, a flood of remorse filled him. "I just have this little problem."

"Oh?"

"I don't know. Maybe next year will be different."

"Tell me." She touched his jaw.

"Every anniversary, you know in June, on the second, I take a trip." He grimaced. "More like a screaming meemie getaway."

"Where?"

"Anywhere. No matter what, I have to run. I don't know if I can stop."

She waited until he looked her in the eye despite his shame. "Then I'll go with you."

Art pulled her close, letting her commitment and love fill the empty places. "I think that will be just fine."

ABOUT THE AUTHORS

Lisa J. Lickel is a Wisconsin writer who lives with her husband in a hundred-and-sixty-year-old house built by a Great Lakes ship captain. Surrounded by books and dragons, she writes inspiring fiction. Her novels include mystery and romance, all with a twist of grace. She has penned dozens of feature newspaper stories, short stories, magazine articles and radio theater. She is the Editor in Chief of *Creative Wisconsin Magazine* and loves to encourage new authors. Lisa also is an avid book reviewer, blogger, freelance editor, writing mentor, and contest judge.

www.LisaLickel.com

Shellie Neumeier holds a degree in Secondary Education from the University of Wisconsin, Madison, with a minor in Psychology, Sociology and Social Studies. A devoted mother of four, Shellie previously worked on staff with Northbrook Church as the King's Kids ministry assistant (serving children in grades 2nd through 5th). She is an active member of SCBWI and ACFW as well as a contributing author for various blogs.

www.ShellieNeumeier.com

The employees of Thorndike Press hope you have enjoyed this Large Print book. All our Thorndike, Wheeler, and Kennebec Large Print titles are designed for easy reading, and all our books are made to last. Other Thorndike Press Large Print books are available at your library, through selected bookstores, or directly from us.

For information about titles, please call:
(800) 223-1244

or visit our Web site at:
http://gale.cengage.com/thorndike

To share your comments, please write:
Publisher
Thorndike Press
10 Water St., Suite 310
Waterville, ME 04901